Dr Elizabeth Corley walked over to the window and pulled a cord. The room darkened; Charlie relaxed a little. He sighed again, slightly confused. What was wrong with him? He tried to focus his mind. How *did* he feel? It was a simple enough question.

'Lousy,' he mumbled at last. 'Lethargic. And kind of ... numb.' It was the only way he could think of to put it.

'Have you had any particularly stressful experiences lately?' she asked. Her voice was sympathetic and Charlie didn't know why, but he found himself laughing. Stressful experiences? His whole life was a stressful experience! He laughed and laughed. It was some time before he realised Elizabeth wasn't laughing with him. She seemed uneasy, embarrassed.

She flicked a non-existent crumb off her knee. 'I think that some form of counselling would indeed be appropriate.' She glanced up to see Charlie's reaction. 'Forgive me for being blunt, Charlie. But you need help. As soon as possible.'

She looked at him carefully before she spoke again. 'You do want to avoid a full-blown nervous breakdown?'

Also from Warner Books

CASUALTY: THE EARLY YEARS

CASUALTY

SWINGS AND ROUNDABOUTS

Lynda Del Sasso

*From the television series created by
Jeremy Brock and Paul Unwin*

WARNER BOOKS

Acknowledgements

My gratitude to Sebastian Beaumont, for his assistance in the
preparation of the typescript, and to Eddy and Simon, whose efforts
saved my sanity.

A *Warner* Book

First published in Great Britain in 1993 by Warner Books

ISBN 0 7515 0666 4

Typeset by M Rules
Printed and bound in Great Britain by
Clays Ltd, St. Ives plc

Warner Books
A Division of
Little, Brown and Company (UK) Limited
165 Great Dover Street
London SE1 4YA

1

Charlie didn't notice the breeze ruffling his unkempt hair as he crossed the road to the imposing door. The name plaque simply said Elizabeth Corley – no mention that she was a stress counsellor. Charlie sighed. Better get it over with, even though he knew the whole thing would be a waste of time. At least it would silence Duffy and Paula for a while.

He entered the doorway. A crackly voice on the intercom answered his ring. 'Yes?'

'Er . . . hello,' Charlie shifted nervously. 'I've got an appointment. Fairhead. Charlie Fairhead.'

Charlie pushed the door open as it buzzed loudly. The hallway was dark but homely. No disinfectant odour, no clinical atmosphere. This place smelled like, and looked like, a private house, which it was, he assumed. But in what would have been the sitting-room there were several easy chairs and a desk, with a young girl behind it.

'Please, take a seat,' she smiled. 'Dr Corley won't keep you a moment. She's on the phone.'

Charlie sat in a lumpy armchair, immediately regretting his decision to keep this appointment. It was all Duffy's fault. The tragedy of the fire – of that whole nightmarish evening – it had brought things to a head. Oh, he'd coped all right at the time – everyone in A and E had coped – but Charlie had noticed a change in Duffy's attitude towards him after that. They'd always been fairly close, always worked well together, but she'd started 'advising' him, and though he didn't mind a bit of that, it had become an almost daily habit.

'Take it easy, Charlie,' she'd say, in that sympathetic but no-nonsense tone she usually reserved for the more difficult patients. Then it became, 'Take a few days off, Charlie. Do you want to talk about it, Charlie?'

He hadn't, of course. Why burden Duffy, when it was all coming together for her at last; now that she was starting a new life with Andrew? Anyway, nobody really knew how he felt. How could they? And then she'd kept on and on, nagging at him to see someone. He'd seen her chatting to Paula in the canteen. Paula wasn't a friend of Duffy's, but she was trained in psychiatric care; it was obvious they were talking about him, but he'd let it drift past – things were easier to cope with that way.

So she'd made this appointment for him, and stupidly he'd agreed to come along. What excuse could he use to get out of it? My car is double-parked? I think I may have left the gas on? Or he could simply get to his feet and walk out, couldn't he? He needn't even glance at the girl if he didn't want to . . .

'Mr Fairhead?'

A woman was standing in front of him. Charlie shook himself and forced his eyes to focus on the tall figure: sympathetic open face, dark tied-back hair. Huge dangling earrings. She smiled and extended her hand. 'Elizabeth Corley. How do you do?'

He shook her hand. 'Look, I don't think I should be here. Not really. I mean, I don't want to waste your time.'

'Oh?'

'You see,' Charlie fumbled for the right words. 'Someone else made this appointment, by mistake.' What was wrong with him? Why couldn't he think straight? 'I mean, not mistake . . . they thought I needed to see someone. But I'm fine.' He shrugged and forced a weak smile. 'A bit overworked, that's all.'

Elizabeth Corley studied his face, her expression inscrutable.

'I work at Holby City, A and E,' he tried.

'I know.'

'Well, then,' Charlie shrugged again. 'You know how it is.'

With a sweep of her arm she motioned him towards the open door of her office. 'No, actually, I don't. But I hope you're going to tell me.'

Reluctantly, Charlie got to his feet. He didn't seem to have a choice. The woman followed him into her office and closed the door. 'Look, I don't know what you've been told,' Charlie tried again. 'But it isn't counselling I need. It's rest. Sleep.'

'I haven't been told anything,' she said matter-of-factly, as she produced a blank record card from a drawer. 'Please, sit down. Let's just have a chat, OK? Don't worry about wasting my time for the moment, and I won't worry about wasting yours.'

Two armchairs faced each other in front of a large, executive desk. Behind the desk was a black leather swivel chair and a huge bay window with horizontal slatted blinds, the sort they had in the expensive new boardroom at Holby City. Charlie sank into one of the armchairs. At least there wasn't a couch. Elizabeth Corley, to his surprise, didn't sit behind her desk, but took the other armchair. She sat facing him, her legs crossed at the ankle. The record card lay on the desk.

'Paula Simpson is a friend of mine. She asked me to see you because she thinks you've been suffering a lot of stress lately.' She paused. 'I heard about the fire at the hospital . . .'

Charlie bit his lip. What would she know about it?

'Now, Charlie,' she continued. 'Can I call you Charlie? Please call me Elizabeth . . . that's all I know. Where we go from here, if anywhere, is up to you. Why not start by telling me a little about yourself, and we'll see how it goes.'

Charlie considered. Was there any point in talking to this woman?

'I know you're a charge nurse in the Casualty department,' she prompted. 'Want to tell me something about that?'

'Not really.'

'Because it's a difficult job, or just difficult to talk about?'

'It isn't charge nurse any more,' he corrected her. 'The title's been changed to clinical manager.'

'Just the title? Or the responsibilities, too?'

Charlie shrugged. 'Everything has changed. Responsibilities, titles. I'm expected to budget the department, balance the books, hire, fire and oversee the staff – and that's before we even get the patients in.'

'Sounds like some responsibility.'

Charlie nodded. She would never understand how much. He shifted in his seat, scratched his head. Sighed again.

'OK,' she said, calmly. 'Let me ask you a couple of things. Off the record. No pressure, OK?'

Charlie nodded.

She clasped her hands in front of her and studied Charlie's face thoughtfully. 'You said you're tired—'

'Overworked.'

'—and all you need is sleep.'

'Yeah.'

'So you're exhausted. You work long shifts, day and night. But when you get home and try to sleep, what happens?'

Charlie frowned. Was his insomnia that obvious? He knew he looked a bit rough – he'd stopped shaving regularly weeks ago, just didn't see the point any more. He ran his fingers over the stubble on his cheek. So what? He

4

could manage emergencies and run the department perfectly well whether he had shaved or not.

It was three-thirty and he'd just come off the early shift at Holby City. His body felt leaden and drained after his heavy work-load – they'd had three RTAs and a respiratory arrest to cope with before lunch. Two porters had been off sick, but the nursing staff had managed, as usual. He felt totally exhausted, but he knew he wouldn't be able to sleep when he got home. He hadn't slept for more than an hour at a time for weeks. He couldn't even remember when the insomnia had started – it had just crept up on him somehow.

As Charlie sat staring into space, Elizabeth waited patiently for his reply. This was a woman who didn't give up easy, Charlie thought, as his eyes focused again. In spite of himself, he found himself liking her. She was a professional, as he was, and her attitude was professional. Trained to put people at ease. 'All right,' he said, 'I've been going through a difficult patch. I'm under a lot of pressure.'

'Have you seen your GP?'

'I went once, but . . .' Charlie trailed off. 'He put me on a course of anti-depressants.'

'Oh? Which ones?'

'A tricyclic. Imipramine. But I never bothered taking them.'

Elizabeth sat back. 'OK,' she said. 'Let's try something. Tell me how you feel. Right now.'

Charlie shifted uneasily. He glanced at the window. The bright, glaring sunlight hurt his eyes as it poured in through the bay window, piercing the slatted beams of the venetian blinds, striping the carpet and stabbing at his tired, sensitive eyes. Funny. Outside he hadn't even noticed the weather – he'd just assumed it was another grey day.

'Could we have those blinds closed a bit?' he asked.

Elizabeth walked over to the window and pulled a cord. The room darkened; Charlie relaxed a little. He sighed again, slightly confused. What was wrong with him? He tried to focus his mind. How *did* he feel? It was a simple enough question. 'Lousy,' he mumbled at last. 'Lethargic. And kind of . . . numb.' It was the only way he could think of to put it.

'Have you had any particularly stressful experiences lately?' she asked. Her voice was sympathetic and Charlie didn't know why, but he found himself laughing. Stressful experiences? His whole life was a stressful experience! He laughed and laughed. It was some time before he realised Elizabeth wasn't laughing with him. She seemed uneasy, embarrassed.

She flicked a non-existent crumb off her knee. 'I think that some form of counselling would indeed be appropriate.' She glanced up to see Charlie's reaction. 'Forgive me for being blunt, Charlie. But you need help. As soon as possible.'

She looked at him carefully before she spoke again. 'You do want to avoid a full-blown nervous breakdown?'

2

Charlie felt dazed as he walked out on to the street. He'd known he was tired, that the pressure was getting to him, but surely Elizabeth Corley had been exaggerating when she'd said he was in need of urgent counselling? He'd seen that need in others, but found it difficult to imagine in himself. But then, the woman was trained to recognise the symptoms and she didn't seem the type to use scare tactics.

So, she was warning him of an impending nervous breakdown. He shook his head, trying to clear the muddled thoughts. He was aware of an odd sensation of distance, as though he wasn't really there, almost as if he was inhabiting the body of someone else, a tired-looking stranger. How shocked and bewildered that stranger looked.

He needed to get home. He needed to be alone, to think about what had been said, to read the pamphlet Elizabeth Corley had given him: 'Nervous Breakdown: An Everyday Occurrence'. Averting his eyes from passers-by, Charlie headed for the bus station. The woman had to be mistaken.

As he passed the Job Centre, he thought he heard someone call out his name, but he kept going. A few moments later, a tall, good-looking man grabbed his arm. Charlie tried to walk on but the man blocked his path. There was something about his likeable face, his dark hair, Roman nose and broad smile, that seemed familiar. The hair wasn't right, but . . .

'Charlie? It is you!' the man grinned.

Charlie stared at the face for some time before it dawned on him. 'Stuart?'

Stuart Stonehouse, a friend from years ago. They'd worked together for eighteen months when they'd first trained.

'Must be nearly twenty years,' Stuart beamed. 'Twenty years!'

Charlie was overwhelmed. What should he do? He wasn't even sure what he thought about meeting Stuart again after so long. They'd got on well, back then, but Charlie didn't know if he could cope with an old friend right now. Especially not one as enthusiastic and outgoing as Stuart. Almost the opposite of Charlie, Stuart had always been popular; never short of girlfriends, never lost for words, he'd been the ward charmer, a favourite with the patients and staff alike, especially the females.

'Let's go for a drink or something,' Stuart grinned. 'You can tell me what you're up to.'

A few minutes later they were sitting in a little coffee shop on the High Street. Stuart was still energetic and lively. 'In charge of a casualty ward?' Stuart's eyes widened. 'Not bad, Charlie boy. You always were a hard worker.' He laughed. 'That explains the bags under the eyes and the burnt-out look. You look as tired as I feel. Only I've got an excuse. Jet lag.'

Charlie frowned. 'Thanks, Stu.' He couldn't bring himself to ask where Stu had been to get jet lag, not yet – he was too preoccupied with his own problems.

'Come on, only a joke. Casualty always was a killer. The majority can't take the pace. Some of the things you lot have to cope with – well, you've done well to take it in your stride.'

'Maybe I haven't.'

Charlie didn't know what made him say it. Maybe it was the cheerful, friendly face, the sympathetic tone of voice. Maybe just the relief of talking to someone who was, at that moment, almost a stranger, but who under-stood about the pressures of nursing. Whatever it was, Charlie found himself telling Stuart about Holby City opting out, becoming a Trust hospital. About all the management changes, about accountants adding up the cost of every last swab and dressing, about the fire in A and E, Rob's injuries, everything. It all came pouring out.

'Sounds like you've been to hell and back, Charlie.' Stuart was quiet for once. He studied Charlie's face, put a comforting hand on his shoulder.

Charlie managed a weak smile. 'It's good to see you, Stu. Good to talk. But what about you?'

'Just back from the Middle East. Been travelling. Round Asia, Australasia.'

'Wow.' Charlie was impressed. All those years ago Stuart had dreamed of travelling, but most people never do more than dream. Obviously, Stu had actually managed it.

'Yeah,' Stuart nodded. 'Been away for a year. Flew into Heathrow this morning. Got to Paddington and hopped on a train heading west. Thought I'd see how old Holby was doing.'

For the first time, Charlie noticed the sports bag by Stuart's feet. 'So, where're you staying?'

'Don't know yet. My other bag is checked in at Holby Central station.' He gave a little laugh. 'Travelling is an expensive business, you know. I kept going until the money was nearly out.'

'Yeah?'

'I've had a look in the Job Centre. Things have changed since I've been away. There's even less work about.'

Charlie knew it. 'It's the same everywhere,' he sympathised. 'In A and E whenever someone leaves, they're simply not replaced. Cost-cutting, it's called. Business efficiency. The patients wait twice as long, the staff are twice as busy, but that's all right because the Trust must make a profit.'

9

'You sound bitter, Charlie.'

'Not bitter. Just . . . frustrated.'

Strangely, just getting this off his chest in Stuart's company had cheered Charlie, made him feel less overwhelmed by everything. Even so, when the time came to say goodbye, and Stuart confessed he had nowhere to stay that night, Charlie hesitated before extending an invitation. 'You're welcome to stay at my place for a couple of nights,' he said. 'I'm at work most of the time, anyway.'

It was difficult for Charlie to make this offer. He wasn't in the mood for entertaining, for being polite. But Stuart was an old friend, and besides, perhaps it would do him good to have someone around for a few days.

As they travelled home on the bus, Charlie explained that he'd given up using his car. A collision with a lamppost a few weeks previously had badly dented the bumper and smashed the front light panel. His fire, theft and third party insurance hadn't covered it, and Charlie didn't have the estimated £700 it'd take to get it back on the road. Now he was thinking of selling the car, even though it was useful. It was too expensive to run. Although his responsibilities had increased at work, his salary had, in real terms, decreased.

It wasn't funny but somehow, by the time they got home, Charlie had managed a brief smile about his situation. It was quite a novelty having someone to talk to, someone who remembered the good times. It helped him realise that there was a life outside Holby City and its Accident and Emergency department.

'Maybe we could help each other out,' Stuart said casually, as he and Charlie relaxed with an Indian take-away and a couple of beers. 'I'm looking for somewhere to stay, and you could do with a bit of cash to get your car back on the road.'

'So?'

'So, what about that spare room of yours?'

10

Charlie frowned. 'You're welcome to it, Stuart, but I couldn't charge rent to a friend.'

'No, but what if I wasn't your friend. What if I was your flat-mate?'

Charlie took a swig of beer from his can. 'I don't know, Stuart, I quite like living on my own.'

'I wouldn't interfere with your private life—'

'I haven't got a private life,' Charlie cut in. The beer was beginning to get to him. 'I've got nothing but my work, Stu. It may be sad, but it's the truth.'

'Dedication to your work isn't sad, it should be a source of pride, Charlie. So don't say you've got nothing. Besides, you've got a friend – me. And I'd pay you the going rate.'

'But you don't have any money.'

'I'll get a job. Don't worry. I've got connections.'

'What connections?'

Stuart shrugged. 'Just a manner of speaking.'

'And I suppose there's always the DSS until then?'

'Yes,' Stuart said, carefully. 'Well . . .'

'You've no idea what you'd be letting yourself in for, you know.'

'We shared digs before, remember? We got on all right, didn't we?'

Charlie nodded thoughtfully. It was tempting. What did he have to lose?

'OK, it's a deal,' he said, offering his hand.

They shook on it.

'So when do you want to move in?' Charlie asked.

'Half an hour ago?'

Charlie laughed and opened another can of beer while Stuart went off to the railway station to collect his other bag.

Later, they talked some more and the beer, the company and the reminiscences helped Charlie blot out his problems for longer than he had in a long time. But as the evening drew to a close, he found himself mulling over his

11

meeting with Elizabeth Corley. 'Stuart, there's something I've got to tell you,' he said, as they were about to go to bed.

'Tell me in the morning.' Stuart staggered towards the spare room, exhausted.

'I probably won't want to talk about it in the morning,' Charlie admitted. 'I usually don't.'

Stuart returned and dropped on to the sofa. 'What?'

'It's . . . well, about the problems I've been having lately.'

'Money-wise, you mean? Or something more serious?'

'Yeah. It's not just my financial situation and all that. My colleagues at work have been on at me. They recognised there was something . . . I've been keeping it all inside me, you see. That's where I go wrong.'

'You always were a loner, Charlie boy.'

'Look. I don't want you to have to deal with this, so I'll tell you now, before we go any further. If you decide to live somewhere else once I've told you, that's OK.'

Stuart was suddenly sober, concerned. He looked at Charlie and his usual bright grin disappeared.

'The fact is . . .' Charlie took a long, deep breath. 'Today, when we met, I'd just come from a doctor – Dr Corley. She's not a GP – she specialises in stress counselling. She reckons I'm having some kind of breakdown.' Charlie turned to face Stuart. 'A nervous breakdown.'

Stuart didn't speak for a moment. Then he breathed a sigh of relief. 'A nervous breakdown, eh? And here was me beginning to think it might be something incurable.'

'You don't mind?'

'Come on, Charlie. Everyone goes through tough times, we both know that. From what I've heard today, what you've been telling me of Holby City, you've been working too hard. For years, not months. Anyone would crack under that sort of strain.'

'You think so?'

'No worries. You let this doc sort out your work problems, and I'll liven up your social life. Stick with Stu and you'll be all right! But seriously, Charlie,' Stuart nodded with mock sternness, 'all you need is to take it a bit easier at work and make more time for yourself. Simple.'

Charlie looked at Stuart's smiling face and felt hopeful for the first time in months. Could it really be that simple? If so, why hadn't he realised it himself? People always said it took an outsider to see the obvious, and Charlie wanted to believe what Stuart said was true, but something in him remained unconvinced.

That night in bed, Charlie slept fitfully, as usual, but found his attitude slightly changed. He wasn't worrying quite as much. Worrying, he knew well enough, only aggravated problems. The thing to do was to act.

First thing in the morning he would ring Elizabeth Corley and book an appointment to begin therapy.

3

As Charlie pushed through the doors of the hospital A and E department the following morning, he felt better than he had in weeks. It wasn't even quarter to seven, yet he'd already eaten breakfast – a slice of toast and honey – almost unheard of for him. He'd left Stuart busily scanning the Situations Vacant column of the newspaper.

There seemed to be more builders and workmen in Reception than patients. The fire had left quite a mess, the place still stank of smoke, but at least the department was being renovated now, and properly, at the insurance company's expense. If the board had had to have found the money, it would have been a different story altogether.

'Morning, Norma.'

'Good morning. You're looking chirpy.'

And he was feeling chirpy, Charlie thought, as he entered his office and began to glance through the night's reports. The shave had made all the difference. He'd enjoyed it, scraping all that itchy stubble from his chin. This morning he felt fresher, cleaner and ready for anything.

As he hung up his jacket and put on his white coat, Janice Hope entered. A large, motherly woman, Janice was the sister who had been in charge of the night shift. 'Not a bad night.' She handed him the keys and pointed out a couple of urgent observation cases. 'I hear you had some nasty road traffic accidents in yesterday morning.'

'Two DOA's. Pretty mangled.' Charlie checked the

remainder of the night's paperwork. 'All up to date.'

'Not bad, eh?' Janice smiled. 'Lucky we had time. Didn't want to take any chances with that new general manager coming in.'

'What? Not today?'

'Don't tell me you haven't seen the memo. Forbes, his name is, Gavin Forbes. And the word is he's keen. He'll be checking the medical store inventory by eight-thirty, I bet you.'

Charlie held a chest x-ray up to the light. 'I get the feeling you know something I don't, Janice.'

'Let's just say that Gavin Forbes' reputation precedes him. One of our temps worked with him before, and says she'll never forget it. Pedantic. Bureaucratic. You name it.'

'Great. Just what we need in this department.'

As Janice prepared to go home, Charlie wandered up the corridor to Admin. Mike Barratt, the tall, approachable consultant, was reading through some notes. Duffy was on the telephone. 'Morning,' Charlie smiled.

Mike looked up. 'Hi. You're looking well today.'

'So I've been told.'

Duffy raised her hand in greeting. She was advising a patient on the proper procedure for washing out an eye – not the simplest of tasks by telephone.

Charlie did a quick survey of the cubicles: only three occupied, and no serious cases at that. Maybe it was going to be a quiet day after all. Everything was organised and, by the looks of it, there were only three or four patients waiting to be seen. He'd clear this lot up in no time.

In Reception he looked up the details of a couple of regular patients who were due in that morning. He did a detour to the coffee machine, smiling at two builders who were crouching on either side of it, taking measurements. He was carefully lifting the plastic cup out of the machine when a sharp voice behind him nearly made him drop it.

'Just what are you doing?'

Charlie straightened up. Was this bloke talking to him? He turned to look. The man was thin, balding, with angular features and a prominent nose. Thickly overcoated although it was the middle of summer, the man had the hungry look of a hawk.

'I'm getting a cup of coffee,' Charlie replied calmly. Today was the first good day he'd had in a long time, and he wanted to keep it that way.

'This machine is for patients' use only. Staff, I believe, may purchase beverages from the canteen.'

Charlie frowned. He and all the other staff in the department had been getting drinks from this machine for years. Besides, who would even think of objecting?

'Gavin Forbes,' the man introduced himself. 'General manager, Surgical Directorate.'

'Charlie Fairhead, clinical manager.'

'Are you on duty, Mr Fairhead?'

Charlie checked his watch. He was one minute into the shift, although he'd been in for almost twenty. 'Just,' he said.

'Please come to my office later this morning, Mr Fairhead, say at eleven-fifteen? I have some items I wish to discuss regarding your department's budget. Also, you might like to explain to me then why you are not wearing your name badge as prescribed in the Patients' Charter.'

Gavin Forbes turned on his heel and walked up the stairs towards his office, on what was fast becoming the managerial floor. Pompous git, thought Charlie.

Duffy came along, glancing left and right at the various workmen. 'This place is going to be pandemonium once the builders start the restructuring work,' she said. Pulling a coin from her pocket, she stretched her arm towards the drinks machine.

'Just been told by the new general manager that we are not supposed to buy drinks from this machine.' Charlie rolled his eyes towards the stairs. 'You think Simon Eastman was bad. Wait till you meet this one.'

Duffy groaned and shook her head sadly. 'Where do they get them from? Most of these administrators don't know a thing about medicine.' She dropped her coin into the machine anyway. 'By the way,' she asked, as they watched the cup filling with muddy liquid. 'Did you go to see Dr Corley yesterday?'

'I did,' said Charlie.

'And?'

'You were right. It might do me good to see her for a while.'

'Charlie, that's great news!'

For a moment he thought she was going to hug him, but she smiled instead and patted his arm enthusiastically. 'Just you get yourself back to being as cheerful as you are this morning,' she laughed. 'Then you'll do us all some good.'

It was a busy morning. At one point, a man was brought in on a stretcher, his feet jammed into a stainless steel toilet from a public facility. His ankles were stuck fast in the U-bend. The fire officer accompanying him explained that the man had been trying to stash some drugs in the overhead cistern. He'd slipped, fallen in and his feet, now swelling fast, were getting more and more tightly stuck. The fire brigade had unbolted the whole toilet from the floor and brought it to the hospital along with the by now extremely embarrassed patient. Charlie couldn't help but smile as they carried him past. It was incredible what some people got up to. And, unless they could somehow pull him free, it would be a lengthy process getting that contraption off him. It would probably require some pretty sophisticated metal-cutting equipment.

At eleven-fifteen Charlie knocked on the door of what

had, until very recently, been Simon Eastman's office. Simon had been general manager for a few months, but hadn't been successful enough for the Trust's liking. Within forty-eight hours of their interim report, he'd been removed. Charlie entered, confident he was ready for anything. But nothing could have prepared him for the shock that was Gavin Forbes' new regime.

'General tightening of the belt . . . A and E budget to be cut immediately by five per cent . . . no agency staff to be employed . . . no regular staff to be paid overtime . . .'

'Hold on, hold on,' Charlie interrupted as the new manager paced his carpeted office, reading from a beautifully printed list. 'Look Mr Forbes. I'd like to help you with your efficiency drive and your shrinking budgets, but everything has already been cut to the minimum. If there are no agency staff and no nursing staff allowed to do overtime, I'd like to know who's going to look after patients if one of my regulars is off sick, or away on holiday?'

'With all respect, Mr Fairhead, it is your responsibility to see that problems don't arise. I said "no *paid* overtime", not "no overtime". The nursing staff will be expected to help one another out at difficult times, such as during absences or illnesses. Flexibility is to be encouraged. The board has every confidence that you'll be able to maintain Holby City's high standards.'

Charlie stared at Forbes in disbelief. This couldn't be happening. It suddenly seemed as if Forbes was at the end of a long, long tunnel. Charlie experienced that odd, detached feeling again. He got to his feet. 'Well,' he said slowly, 'I'm telling you it won't work. People can only be flexible if they've got the time to be flexible. And how about you? Have you even considered giving instead of taking away?' Striding over to the door, Charlie let himself out without waiting to hear Forbes' response.

In the corridor he took several deep breaths, but he was

too angry to calm down immediately. Forbes was the limit. Charlie knew he'd be in trouble with the hospital trustees for his angry outburst – after all, Forbes was technically above him – but as far as he was concerned, the man was one bureaucrat too many.

By the time Charlie had finished the shift and left Holby City late that afternoon, his exhaustion had returned. After a good start, things had got progressively worse. Forbes had immediately submitted an official complaint about him, of course. He could see real trouble looming ahead on that score. As he let himself into the flat, he found that he'd completely forgotten about Stuart and their mood of optimism the previous evening.

Stuart was in the kitchen preparing dinner, humming happily to himself and sipping from a glass of wine. He hadn't had any luck job-hunting but he'd been out shopping and, better still, he must have been to the bank, because he presented Charlie with two weeks' rent, in cash.

Charlie waved the banknotes in his hand for a moment, bemused. 'I thought you had no money?'

'Don't worry about it, Charlie boy,' Stuart grinned. 'I've always got enough to tide me over. Trust me. Now pour yourself a glass of wine and go and put your feet up.'

Charlie carried his wine through to the living-room. Makes a change from beer, he thought, savouring the crisp tang on his tongue. He slumped back against the cushions of the sofa and sighed. 'Hell!' he said to himself suddenly, 'I forgot to ring Elizabeth Corley.'

4

Charlie wandered through to the kitchen. He was sure he'd written Elizabeth Corley's number down somewhere. Perhaps he'd pinned it to the cork noticeboard . . .

'For heaven's sake, Charlie.' Stuart waved the clutch of red reminders at him over the steam emerging from a large saucepan. 'You should've said.'

'What?'

Stuart transferred each red bill from his left to his right hand. 'Gas, electricity, water, telephone, council tax. You can't just ignore these. In a couple of days you'll be . . . ' he passed the bills back from right to left, '. . . cold, dark, thirsty, incommunicado – and in prison!' His mock angry, incredulous tone broke then, and he laughed. 'And they put you in charge of Accident and Emergency?'

'I'm bloody good at my job.'

'I know you are, Charlie. I was just winding you up. But seriously, I hadn't realised you were so short of cash.'

'Cash?'

'Yes, cash. To pay these bills.' Stuart pronounced the words slowly, as if to a child. Charlie heard them, but it took a while for their significance to sink in. The bills needed to be paid.

'Hell!' Charlie ran his fingers through his hair. 'The bills.' He moved across the kitchen to the blue and white Chinese jar and lifted the lid. It was stuffed with banknotes.

'Huh?' Stuart frowned.

Charlie always put money aside for the regular bills. It was an automatic thing he did, putting a couple of tenners into the blue jar each week, so that when the bills came in, they were covered. But he'd forgotten to pay them. How had that happened? 'I don't know what's wrong with me,' Charlie shook his head. 'I thought I'd paid them. I always pay them.'

With a wry grin, Stuart patted Charlie on the shoulder. 'You're right, Charlie boy. You are overworked. The walls are papered with red reminders and you don't see them. So who opened the envelopes then? Goldilocks?'

'I . . . '

'Food's nearly ready. You go through and sit down, take it easy.'

'Are you sure?'

'No worries.'

Charlie was almost overwhelmed by a surge of gratitude. It was all he could do to stop the tears welling as he turned and padded back to the living-room. He had a vague intention of watching the early evening news, but instead he sat on the edge of the sofa and pondered these strange emotional highs and lows he had been experiencing lately. When had they started? He had no idea. He became aware of them only when other people were around, or when he had to fight to control a reaction, as had happened just now, with Stuart. Or that day a few weeks ago when he'd exploded in front of poor little Max, just because she hadn't emptied a bedpan.

Get yourself under control, he repeated to himself, glancing round the room at the pile of newspapers by the door, the discarded shoes, the general mess. I guess everyone goes through bad patches, but things are going to be different now, he told himself. Right. Tomorrow morning, nine o'clock – no matter how lousy or preoccupying his day turned out to be, he would make an appointment to see Elizabeth Corley.

It wasn't until he and Stuart sat down to eat that Charlie realised how long it had been since he'd had anyone round to the flat. He stared at the tablecloth, the cutlery, the place-mats that Stuart had carefully arranged to take the big, steaming bowl of spaghetti. It all seemed so alien, as though it had materialised in his flat from a different world. A world where families and friends sat down together to share their food and their day's experiences, good and bad.

'You first.' Stuart slid the serving spoon and giant fork across the table to him. Charlie dug in.

'You're a lot quieter than you used to be, you know, Charlie,' Stuart remarked as he ladled pasta on to his own plate. 'Do you remember when we used to double-date sometimes? Even though you were shy, once you'd had a couple of pints you usually turned on the charm. The jokes. If Karaoke had been around then, you'd probably have been up there like a shot, singing away and showing off.'

Charlie smiled. 'Well, that's what living alone does for you, I suppose.'

'So where's the night-life around Holby these days?'

'Search me.'

'Come on, Charlie. Where do you usually go in the evenings?'

'If I'm not working?'

'Yeah.'

'Bed.'

Stuart's laugh trailed off when he looked at Charlie's face. It hadn't been a joke. His eyes narrowed. 'What, no girlfriends?'

'No time. Anyway, I'm not much in the mood these days. My libido has been at rock bottom for months.'

'That's not right for a man of your age, Charlie. You should be enjoying yourself. Going out at least. We'll do something about that, though, don't worry. There must be a pub around here. A local.'

'Take your pick.'

Stuart sat back in his chair. 'You know, I always thought of you as the relationship type, Charlie. I reckoned, back then, that you would settle down as soon as you got the chance. You know, married with two kids by the time you were thirty.'

A shadow passed over Charlie's face. He pushed his spaghetti around his plate for a while. 'Some things don't work out,' he said simply. 'There was someone. Trish. Not that long ago, I suppose, but Trish . . . I don't know, we just . . .' Charlie shrugged. His relationships never lasted. A trail of failures, that was his love-life.

Stuart was right. Charlie had been the settling-down kind. Perhaps if he'd had a loving wife and a couple of kids to come home to, he'd be a different man today. Way back, when he'd first known Stuart, he used to look at families in the park, enjoying their picnics, walking their dogs, laughing with their children, and think, one day that'll be me. He'd even made a mental list of favourite names, special names like Ellen and Alex, or Harriet, after one of his close friends when he was training; names he'd choose from when he had children of his own.

Now it seemed that Charlie would always be the outsider, looking in. He'd congratulated one friend after another as they got engaged, then married. Later, some got divorced and married again, while all the time Charlie remained alone.

'So, you're young, free and eligible,' Stuart gave a cheerful wink. 'It's the only way to be, believe me.'

'I seem to have a problem with long-term relationships.' Charlie felt apologetic, though he forced a smile as he said it.

'Problem? What problem? You've got it exactly right. Enjoy your life while you can. Responsibilities only drag you down, take it from me. I'd still be paying for mine if she could find me.'

Charlie had heard that Stuart had got married – it must be ten years ago now. He'd also heard about the divorce. 'Did you have any kids?' he asked.

'One. He'd be about ten, eleven now, I suppose.' Stuart shrugged off the memory of his son, and helped himself to more pasta. 'You, Charlie boy, need to do something with your time when you're not at work. Have you ever tried any of those computer dating agencies?'

Charlie pulled a face.

'I know, a lot of people scoff, but there's plenty of talent hidden away in those computer databanks. As many blind dates as you want for a hundred quid a year.'

'Yeah?' Charlie felt slightly embarrassed. And surprised. Stuart didn't seem the dating agency type. He was good-looking, charming – he'd never had any trouble getting girlfriends.

'It's a short-cut, that's all,' Stuart explained. 'Cheaper than going to clubs. A good night out guaranteed for the price of a meal.'

'I wouldn't know.'

'No, well maybe you should. There's application forms in all the papers.' Stuart signalled towards the evening newspaper, lying on the sofa, with his eyes. 'I'm game if you are.'

'No, thanks.'

'You value your freedom too much, eh?' Stuart grinned. 'I don't blame you. But a lot of these girls are just looking for a good time. And there's nothing wrong with that, is there?'

'Thanks for the meal,' Charlie pushed his half-full plate away. 'It was great. I'm just not that hungry these days.'

'We could go out on a double-date, like we used to.' Stuart's eyes were open wide. 'How about it? You need to get out more. Come on. What have you got to lose?'

'How about a hundred quid?'

Stuart rose from the table and went over to the newspaper. He found the right page, and read aloud in a teasing voice, like someone advertising a rich chocolate cake: 'Preferred age group: eighteen to twenty-five. Twenty-one to twenty-eight. Twenty-eight to thirty-five. Thirty to forty . . . Height – tick a box. Other requirements – tick a box.' He placed the paper, open at the full-page advertisement, in front of Charlie. 'Where else can you tick a box for your precise requirements, eh?' he laughed. 'Do you want someone warm-hearted, considerate, adventurous? You name it, they've got it.'

'Look, Stuart. Sorry. I'm not good company at the moment.'

'That's exactly why this'd be perfect for you.' Stuart picked up the newspaper and carried it over to the coffee table. Spreading it out in front of him, he started reading out the categories with relish. 'So,' he asked, 'how would you describe yourself?'

Charlie couldn't help smiling. Stuart was a real character.

'Is it the cost you're worried about?' Stuart called after Charlie as he carried the plates through to the kitchen. 'Because this'll be my treat. I owe you one. You know what they say: nothing ventured!'

Charlie frowned. Hadn't Stuart told him he was nearly out of money? He hadn't got himself a job, so how could he afford a hundred pounds? The DSS weren't interested – Stuart had said he'd been down, but they'd told him he wasn't eligible for benefit after being away abroad for so long.

'Thanks, but I can pay my own way,' Charlie said when Stuart returned to the living-room.

'Does that mean you'll join up with me?'

'No. It doesn't.'

'Don't be so miserable.'

After some more haranguing, Charlie eventually agreed to a trial membership, to silence Stuart more than

25

anything else. Three introductions for twenty-five pounds, guaranteed refundable by Stuart if not delighted.

'I'll read out the categories, so we can decide what we want, if you like, then I'll fill them in for both of us,' he said.

Charlie had to decide whether he wanted someone petite, slight, medium or corpulent; someone interested in the outdoors, sport, music, art, literature and so on. It was fun in a way, but Charlie found it embarrassing trying to pick words from the list to describe himself. Was he tolerant, sensitive, moody, affectionate? Did it make him uncomfortable to openly disagree with someone in public? Did he think that worrying too much about money spoiled happiness?

Still, he thought as he lay in bed that night, it just might work out. The right woman might exist, and she might be looking for a world-weary charge nurse who was overworked, oversensitive, overdrawn and now, secretly, over-optimistic.

5

A few days later, Charlie sat facing Elizabeth Corley. This time she was sitting behind her desk, in the traditional doctor's position of power. Her quiet, professional manner and reassuring smile didn't help him. He still felt uneasy about being there; embarrassed, on edge. OK, he acknowledged that he needed to rearrange his life and his priorities, but he couldn't shake off the feeling that he ought to be able to do all that for himself without recourse to professional help.

'Take your time. Try to relax,' she told him. 'It'll be easier once we get to know each other a little. Now, what I want you to do, when you are ready, is to tell me something about yourself.'

The sentence echoed in Charlie's head. What was that really for? What did she really want to know? Would she listen to what he said, or look for some hidden meaning behind it? Charlie stared at the ceiling, considering what to say, how to begin.

Who was he? A clinical manager. They kept changing the job title – and every time they added a little more responsibility. Clever. Insidious. More work for the same money.

'Charlie?' She smiled again.

Charlie Fairhead. That's who he was. Forty-three years old, single, blue eyes, fair hair, average build, average intelligence, average life, he supposed. So why was he here?

'Listen,' he said at last. 'I'm sorry. I can't seem to . . . I don't know what you want to hear.' He felt like a small boy who was being targeted for punishment by the teacher.

'Anything you want to tell me. We could start with your job.' She tapped her pencil on the side of her hand. 'You've just finished a shift. What was it like?'

'Hectic.' Charlie gave a nervous laugh and cleared his throat. 'Always is. Especially at the moment, with all this renovation going on. We're understaffed as well. Officially the posts have been cut because they were superfluous, but we're busy.'

A silence. Elizabeth waited, but Charlie didn't speak. 'Do you have trouble switching off after work?' she asked.

'Sometimes. Well, I'm not sure what you mean.'

'Unwinding. After the stresses of the day. Some of the patients you deal with must be upset.'

'They all are.'

'And it's only natural that this has an effect on you.'

'You get used to it.'

Charlie cursed inwardly. Why was he so defensive? Why was he finding it so difficult to talk to this woman? He knew that he wanted to tell her that it was bloody awful sometimes, a lot of the time, in fact. But he'd learned early on that if you let it show how things were getting to you, then that was the beginning of the end. OK, at first, there would be sympathy. But being seen continually not coping ruined your professional standing. Your reputation. People who couldn't cope didn't last long in the business. That was a fact.

'It's difficult sometimes to *talk* to people,' he said.

'Go on?'

Charlie felt flustered. Where had that come from? 'I mean . . .' he paused, thought for a moment. 'I mean, you get used to chatting to patients, reassuring them, all that kind of thing. And then there's the staff – you can talk to them a bit more, but it's all so superficial most of the time.'

'This is often a problem,' Elizabeth said. 'It's very easy to become cut off from other people. Have you thought about why this is?'

Charlie sat there, trying to, but his mind had gone blank.

'I know this isn't easy for you,' she said eventually. 'Bringing feelings out into the open never is, especially when they've been hidden away – often deeply. It takes practice. And courage, and trust. You've done well today.'

'I have?'

'I want you to understand, Charlie, there is no easy, short-term solution for your kind of stress problem. I can't emphasise enough how important talking is. Like most of us, you have bottled up many of your emotions. Strong feelings of anger, rage, guilt, horror, sorrow. We push these feelings deep down inside us when a strong reaction is deemed inappropriate, or when we simply can't deal with the emotion at the time. We often intend to examine our feelings later, but for one reason or another we don't. Or can't. And this is where the problems begin. Starting to get all of that into the open is quite an undertaking. It's slow at first, and it takes strength. And all the time you have to put up with the debilitating effects of the stress and exhaustion that are symptoms of your condition.'

Charlie nodded. What this woman said made sense. But then of course it would. He'd learned much the same thing while doing his medical training. And how many times had he delivered the same sort of speech to patients himself? The odd thing was that although he'd known this himself, it hadn't prevented him from bottling up his own anger and frustration. As the pressures of his work had grown he'd buried his dissatisfaction deeper and deeper, until his social life had begun to evaporate.

Elizabeth Corley hadn't mentioned the dangers of shutting oneself off from friends and social activities, but Charlie knew that it was another of his major problems.

Still, the fact that she'd actually explained some of the theory behind her counselling methods meant that she knew Charlie was capable of taking it in. He couldn't be too far gone after all.

'How about trying those anti-depressants your GP prescribed?' Elizabeth said suddenly.

'No.'

'I'm not surprised at your reluctance. But I'm asking you to trust me on this. Imipramine won't affect your work. In fact I'd be very surprised if you noticed any side-effects at all on the low dosage you mentioned. But you will feel the benefits, believe me.'

He shook his head.

'Please, Charlie,' she said. 'Won't you just try?'

Charlie wasn't sure about trust any more. So many people had let him down over such a long period. It was difficult to put his faith in someone he hardly knew, even if he did judge her professionally capable. Maybe he'd been let down too many times. Maybe he was no longer capable of trusting anyone. 'Sorry,' he said. 'No drugs.'

At the end of the session, although he was aware that he hadn't progressed very far, Charlie did sense the possibility that further headway could be made. The sensation was a pleasant one. Elizabeth Corley was reassuring as she agreed to see him on a regular basis, at least for the time being.

It was a good job it wasn't going to be too expensive. Elizabeth had dealt with a number of people who worked at Holby City, and offered a good discount for nursing staff there, whom she recognised as having severely limited funds. 'This won't be a protracted business, Charlie,' she said. 'It's just a question of regaining your perspective.'

Perspective. She was right, he decided as he took the bus home. It wasn't what you thought, or what you did, that mattered – it was how you let it affect you.

*

Back at the flat, Stu had a surprise in store. Smiling, he handed Charlie a couple of letters. The first computer introductions had arrived. Stu was itching to fix up their first double-date.

'That was quick!' Charlie exclaimed as he scanned the typewritten letter with dismay.

Dear Mr Fairhead,
Congratulations on joining Wyvern Compu-Date Introductions. We have pleasure in enclosing the name, address and brief details of your first selected introduction, together with our guideline booklet and brochure for subscribers to our services. Remember! We offer a serious and 100 per cent discreet partner search . . .

At the bottom of the page was printed a name, an address in Holby, and a telephone number. Janine Burford, interested in discos, travel, amateur dramatics, windsurfing.

'Windsurfing?' Charlie read aloud. Had this computer read his form before matching him up? He and Stuart exchanged letters. Stuart's potential partner was called Lois Wetherall, and she too lived in Holby. Her interests were listed as watching TV, beauty and landscape gardening. Charlie turned over the cheap quality letter. 'I'd expected a flash computer print-out at least,' he mumbled.

'Let's call them straight away,' Stuart suggested. 'Females always go for a double-date, given the choice – makes them feel safer.'

'Slow down. Let's think this through. Where are we going to take them? And when? I'll have to check my shifts.'

'You worry too much,' Stuart grinned, leaning across to pick up the phone. Charlie watched him sigh with pleasure as he lay back, sinking luxuriously against the cushions of the sofa. 'I'll phone mine first,' he said, 'and then you can phone yours.'

'No way!' Charlie almost shouted. 'I can't do things just like that. I'd need to prepare. Get myself in the mood to talk to someone. I'd have to think of something to say.'

'I forgot you were so shy,' Stuart laughed. 'All right. If it's a problem, I'll phone her for you. What's her name?'

He picked up Charlie's letter. 'OK, Janine,' he said as he dialled. 'This is your lucky day!'

Charlie went through to the kitchen to get his rota from the noticeboard. He scanned it. Next week was pretty difficult. Maybe the week after would be OK, if he had plenty of advance warning. He sauntered back into the living-room, rota in hand.

'Tonight?' Stuart was saying. 'Yes, I think tonight is OK. Let me just check.'

'No!' Charlie mouthed frantically, shaking his head. 'Not tonight.'

'Yup,' Stuart said. 'Tonight's fine.'

Charlie felt his shoulders sag, but he couldn't bring himself to say anything. I suppose I asked for it, he thought, by agreeing to put my name on the list in the first place.

'You know how it is,' Stuart was telling Janine. 'He's a bit shy. Won't come to the phone. Don't worry, though, he's pretty lively once you've broken the ice. Pretty good-looking too, if you must know. What? About five-nine, I'd say, fairish hair, with a bit of grey in it – a distinguished, youthful kind of grey. You like that, do you? Good. Just as well you're not my date for the night, then. I haven't got a grey hair on my head . . .'

Charlie cringed as Stuart flirted. Wasn't he the one who was supposed to be flirting with Janine? He knew it would be impossible for him to be as light and chatty as Stuart. Janine would be disappointed, he was sure.

6

Charlie still wasn't convinced. It was thirty minutes after the phone call to Janine and he still felt that he'd been stupid, agreeing to go along with Stuart's crazy scheme to meet the girls that evening. But now it was all arranged – Stuart had called Lois and charmed her, and now he wouldn't discuss it. He was busy getting ready for the date.

Charlie scanned the contents of his wardrobe. When had he last gone out and bought himself some new clothes? What did the trendy young man-about-town wear for meals out these days? Probably not old jeans and a leather bomber. Still, perhaps they had come back into fashion again. He'd seen people wearing flares in the street recently, and platform shoes, but he hadn't owned a pair himself for longer than he cared to remember.

He squeezed himself into his ordinary straight-legged jeans. He was sure that they were tighter than they used to be. With a green summer shirt and his bomber jacket, he reckoned he didn't look too bad. A quick comb of the hair, a splash of aftershave, and he felt quite presentable.

He walked back through to the living-room as Stuart came out of the bathroom.

'Oh no, Charlie!' he cried when he saw him. 'You're not going like that are you?'

'Why?' said Charlie, looking down at himself. 'What's the matter with it?'

'How about this?' Stu pulled at the elbow of the jacket, where the leather was badly scuffed. 'Or this?' He tugged at the zip, which was coming away. 'You're not a student any more. Far from it. What do you want these girls to think you are? A slob? Come on, they've got to be impressed with you. They've got to think you're a successful professional. You need to put on a jacket and tie at least, to give the right image.'

'All right, all right,' Charlie grumbled. 'I'll see what I can do.'

'Be quick about it,' Stuart told him. 'We're meeting them in forty minutes.'

Charlie rooted around for a minute or two before he found a pale pair of trousers hanging with a blue jacket. He'd bought them for a christening a couple of years ago and had forgotten he had them. He pulled them out of the wardrobe and looked at them, wondering if he could be bothered with all this.

Image? He'd never thought in those terms. He'd never been image-conscious. He had always relied on personality when he was in his student days with Stu, all those years ago. But people never worried if you were scruffy then. As he put on the jacket, he wondered what Duffy would think, or Ash, if they saw him now. Would it fit their idea of the kind of person he was? He wondered briefly what they really thought of him, deep down. He'd been so hassled lately, and so touchy, he didn't like to make a guess.

'Why the railway station?' Charlie asked Stuart as they set off. 'It's hardly the most romantic setting. We could have met in the lounge of the Gloucester, say. It's classy in there.'

'Because there's a lot of people coming and going,' Stuart explained. 'We can have a good look at them there, and if we're not keen, we can walk past. Pretend to be travellers.'

Charlie laughed. 'You've got it all worked out, haven't you?'

'Haven't I always, Charlie boy?'

It was warm as they walked, breezeless. Charlie felt uncomfortable, dressed as he was. Too formal. One of them was supposed to have a copy of *Q Magazine* under their arm as identification. Charlie smirked at the thought: it was so tacky, really. Of course they didn't have a copy of *Q Magazine* at the flat, but they'd be able to buy one at the news-stand on the station concourse.

As they arrived, Charlie felt uneasy; a jitteriness in his stomach that he hadn't felt for so long that it took him a moment to recognise it. He was nervous! He was so used to dealing with people at the hospital that he thought he'd got over having nerves at the prospect of a new face. But it was not just any new face. It was a new face that he was hoping to impress. A new face that he had to talk to; to open up to, perhaps, if it was the right face. What a scary prospect.

They arrived five minutes late, and Stuart insisted on walking through the buffet-bar before they went to buy the magazine. 'Let's see if they're here,' he whispered.

There were two women at one of the tables, but surely they couldn't be Janine and Lois? One was young, fashionable and extremely beautiful. The other must have been, what? Her mother? No, they'd both given their ages as late twenties, so it couldn't possibly be them.

Charlie and Stuart bought their magazine, then went back to get a pint each at the bar. 'Let's face it,' Charlie said as they sat down with their drinks and placed the magazine on the table beside them, 'they're not going to turn up, are they? Look. It's a quarter past. We were supposed to meet at eight.'

'About par for the course, then,' nodded Stuart. 'These girls obviously know what they're doing.'

As he spoke two women walked briskly into the bar. 'So it *was* you,' the first one said, producing a copy of *Elle* from her bag. 'Janine and I saw you come through a few minutes ago and then go out again.'

'Smart,' Stuart whispered to Charlie. 'They know the tricks of the trade, all right.'

'I'm Lois.' The woman held out her hand and smiled brashly. 'And you are . . .?'

'Stu,' said Stuart. 'And this is Charlie, a good friend of mine. Sit down, ladies, please. Let me get you both a drink.'

'No.' Charlie stood up quickly, shaking Janine's hand as she sat down. 'Let me get them.' The last thing he wanted was to be left on his own with these two extremely worldly looking women.

They both chose Martinis and Charlie went to the bar. From his vantage-point he could have a good look at them without appearing nosy. Lois was tall, dark, athletic, almost skinny, with a deep tan. Janine was lighter-skinned, healthy looking, and wearing less make-up. Though they were both well turned out, she somehow looked more carefully groomed than Lois. There was no doubt about it. They were an attractive pair. He carried the drinks over, still wondering what to say.

'Janine and I have known each other for ages,' Lois was saying. 'We've double-dated before. Not just with Compu-Date. Other agencies too. I run a photocopy shop, and she sells double-glazing. Thanks,' she added as she took her drink from Charlie. 'So tell us more about what you do.'

'I'm an international traveller,' Stuart said. 'Business mostly. It takes me all over. Asia, Australia, America. I only just got back from Africa last week.'

'I thought you said it was the Middle East,' Charlie said.

Stuart frowned at him briefly, then looked down at the table. 'Yeah,' he said, then paused. 'Egypt, wasn't it? That's in the Middle East *and* Africa.' He shot a look at Charlie as if to say, don't contradict me again, whatever I say. 'Anyway,' he went on, 'Charlie here's a big-wig in the NHS, aren't you, Charlie?'

'I wouldn't go so far as to say that,' Charlie said.

'Consultants are all the same,' Stuart laughed. 'So modest.'

He flashed another look at Charlie and kicked him under the table.

'You're a consultant?' Janine asked him, interested.

'Well,' said Charlie, 'my job title is clinical manager. I work in the casualty department at Holby City.'

'Sounds impressive,' said Lois. 'My sister used to go to a consultant.'

'I'm not *really* a consultant.' Charlie hesitated. He didn't want to lie, but neither did he want to show Stuart up.

'Let's not get into talking shop,' Stuart said quickly.

'But you *are* a medical man?' Janine asked.

'Yes.'

'That's lucky,' she chirped. 'Because I've got this terrible pain, right up here at the back of my shoulder, see?' She leaned forward and indicated a spot just above her shoulder-blade. 'It's been agony on and off for days. I don't suppose you'd know what it was?'

'That's not really my field,' said Charlie. 'I'm more involved in accident and emergency.'

'But this is an emergency, kind of, isn't it?' she said. 'I nearly didn't come out this evening, I was in that much pain.'

'Don't listen to her,' Lois advised. 'She's always got something wrong with her. It's never as bad as she says.'

'Lois!' Janine huffed. She remained leaning forward, shoulder turned to Charlie. It was a fine shoulder, he thought; the skin of her upper back was bare except for thin blue shoulder straps and he found himself staring at the slightly raised ridge of her backbone.

'Well?' she said.

Gingerly, he looked more closely. 'OK,' he said with a sigh, standing up. He stood behind and slightly to the side of her, placing one hand on her shoulder-blade and one at the top of her arm. He noticed she had a pear-shaped birthmark by her elbow. 'I'm going to manipulate your shoulder in a circular motion. Tell me if it hurts.'

He began moving her upper arm, pulling it back and around. Stuart was grinning, and gave him a wink as their eyes met.

'Ooh,' groaned Janine, 'that's lovely. That's really nice!' Charlie kept it up for a couple of minutes and then, letting go gently, sat down to his pint. 'It's nothing serious,' he said. 'I expect that'll help.'

'Mmm,' she said, 'that's wonderful.'

'Right,' said Stuart, finishing his pint. 'Dinner. Where do you ladies want to go?'

There was a brief discussion before they decided on Langston's seafood restaurant. It was one of the more expensive places in town – which figures, Charlie thought, seeing as we're paying. And he'd thought that women always paid their way these days.

He was already reckoning that the evening was a non-starter. Janine, although attractive, was not his type at all. Lois was more interesting, but that was neither here nor there since she'd come to see Stuart.

'It's not just my shoulder,' Janine told him as they walked to the restaurant. 'It's my entire back, really. My whole family has a history of back trouble. It's the family trait. Well, that and asthma . . .'

Trust me to end up with a hypochondriac, Charlie groaned inwardly. The one thing he'd wanted was to get away from people with physical problems. 'This just isn't my day,' he whispered to Stuart as they entered the restaurant. Stuart laughed and they crossed to the table indicated by the waiter. In spite of himself, Charlie couldn't help but smile back.

'Oh Charlie,' Janine whispered as they sat down. 'I don't suppose you've got any tips about sinus trouble?'

7

Charlie was sitting at his desk, trying to catch up with his paperwork. It was so easy to let things slip, and daily paperwork could build up until it reached awesome proportions. As he checked through some figures, Duffy popped her head into the office. 'Sorry, Charlie. Could you give me a hand for a few minutes? Ash is still dealing with that chemical burns case, and everyone else is busy.'

'What's up?'

'Tibia. A compound fracture, nasty one. Ten-year-old female, just came back from x-ray. Mike says OK to go ahead and set it, but I'll need some help with the initial positioning of the limb.'

'What happened?' Charlie asked as they swept along to the plaster room.

'Fell off her skateboard, poor little thing. She was on a steep concrete ramp and wasn't wearing any protective gear. The mother is with her. Says she has all the pads but never wears them.'

Charlie sighed. It was a familiar story. 'Why do most accidents happen at the end of the week?' he groaned. It was a well-known phenomenon in hospital casualty departments. It was almost as though people got tired or careless as the weekend approached. Bank holidays were disaster areas.

Duffy shrugged. 'Who knows?'

In the plaster room the little girl, Lee, was perched on a trolley. Her mother was wiping her smudged face as

Charlie and Duffy entered. 'Are you another doctor?' Lee asked Charlie.

'No, I'm a nurse, and I've come to help with your leg.' Charlie picked up the clipboard and read the case notes. No complications. No allergies. 'Have you seen this photo of the inside of your leg?' he said, as he studied the x-ray on the light box.

Lee smiled through the pain. 'Can I take it home with me?'

'I don't think that's possible,' he said. 'We're going to need it to make sure we can make your leg better.'

The girl nodded dumbly and then closed her eyes as the pain stabbed her once more for a few moments. Then it seemed to ease. Duffy went over to the sink and started preparing the plaster bandages.

'Now, Lee, I'm just going to take a look.' Charlie removed the temporary dressing from the child's leg. 'Does it hurt very much?'

'Not much right now.'

'Good girl.'

The leg was scuffed and swollen at the ankle, with a small, badly contused area halfway up towards the patella, where the major impact had been. The general area had been cleaned and swabbed with antiseptic. Charlie replaced the dressing so that the sight of the wound wouldn't upset the child or her mother.

About ten minutes later, as Duffy put the finishing touches to the cast, Gavin Forbes called Charlie out into the corridor. 'I've called an emergency meeting in my office. Eleven o'clock.'

'What's the emergency?'

'You'll find out when you get there.'

'Does it have to be this morning?' Charlie had hoped to make a dent in his paperwork. Besides, he hated meetings.

'Your attendance is required,' Forbes said haughtily

40

and strode off, leaving Charlie feeling powerless, as he always did when he dealt with any of the administrators. What particularly annoyed him was the fact that staff were so often called in for discussions when they could be doing better things with their time. How often had he gone along to a meeting only to find that it could have been conducted quite happily without him?

'There's something about that guy,' Charlie said, shaking his head as he joined Duffy at the sink, where she was pouring away the water they'd used for the plaster. 'I can't put my finger on it, but he gives me the creeps.'

'Don't let him get to you. He's got a job to do like everyone else.'

Duffy was right, of course. But still. Charlie remembered the day before, in Admin, when he'd casually told Duffy about the red reminders Stuart had found. They'd had a laugh about how he'd nearly had his electricity disconnected. Duffy had made a joke about the job triggering symptoms of pre-senile dementia. The light-hearted banter was normal, yet a moment later, as Charlie turned to go to cubicle six, he'd almost collided with Gavin Forbes. The man had been standing there – no, lurking – just out of sight. Forbes offered no explanation as to why he'd been eavesdropping. He had merely walked away, down the back corridor towards the stairs.

As he'd tried to get on with his work, Charlie couldn't shake off the feeling that he'd been spied upon; that Forbes had been deliberately listening in to their conversation. Paranoia. That's all I need, thought Charlie.

Even though he posted a yellow sticker on the wall to remind him of the meeting, Charlie still managed to lose track of time and arrived five minutes late. Around the office sat Gavin Forbes, two surgical consultants, Mike, Joyce (the new SHO drafted into A and E to replace Rob on a temporary basis), and – the big surprise – Mr

Dalgleish and Mr Royston, two members of the Trustee Management Board.

Charlie pulled up a chair, mumbling an apology. The meeting had started without him. He hoped it wouldn't last long. Things were hotting up in Casualty downstairs. Already the patient waiting time had increased to three hours and it looked like it was going to be another long day.

Forbes glared at Charlie with annoyance and shuffled some papers. 'Very well,' he said. 'As I was about to say before Mr Fairhead joined us, we have a crisis situation on our hands. Since taking over as general manager, I have discovered certain inconsistencies in the surgical division regarding stock and equipment. I have undertaken, therefore, a complete inventory. I have discovered that expensive equipment supplies are missing.'

There were exclamations of surprise from around the table.

'Not only that, but basic items of stock, such as disposable gloves, Tubigrips and even stationery, have been depleted. It is quite clear to me that this has come about as a result of theft by members of staff.'

'Wait a minute,' Charlie objected. 'It's not possible to keep track of every glove and sheet of paper. We'd be eye-deep in paperwork if we had to record every last item that we used. There's always going to be a certain amount of inconsistency in the records.'

'I can appreciate that, Mr Fairhead,' Forbes said, reshuffling his papers. 'But some of the missing items are more serious than that. Far more serious.'

'That's no reason to start accusing the staff,' said Mike. 'Anything and everything walks. Members of the public have often been caught red-handed trying to walk off with supplies – medicines, boxes of syringes. The level of security at the hospital needs re-evaluating. We have a retired policeman to cover each department, and they're always

42

at the other end of the hospital when you need them.'

'You only have to think back to the night of the fire,' Charlie told Forbes. 'Security was bleeped three times, but didn't turn up. Why? Because they didn't have enough bleeper battery units to go round! I mean, what kind of security is that?'

'He's right,' said Mike. 'Security is appalling.'

'I suggest that you tackle these basic problems before pointing the finger at the nursing staff,' Charlie said. 'Morale is pretty near rock bottom as it is. We have already seen increases in absence due to illness. Accusations like this will only exacerbate the situation.'

'I would expect you to see it like that,' Forbes replied with what amounted to a sneer. 'Are you sure this isn't just self-interest talking?'

'What exactly do you mean by that?' Charlie bristled with anger.

'You know what I'm talking about. There's cardiac equipment missing from the resuscitation area. Twenty thousand pounds' worth, to be precise.'

Shocked mutters went round the table. Charlie was dumbfounded. He opened his mouth to speak, but for a moment he couldn't think of anything to say.

'Is this true?' asked Mr Dalgleish.

'It's true all right. The equipment is supposed to be kept under lock and key. But it has disappeared. And who in the department has ready access to the equipment? You, Charlie. Cardiac equipment is portable, and easily saleable, if you know where to go with it.'

Furious, Charlie jumped to his feet. 'If you're saying what I think you are . . .'

Forbes raised his hand. 'Hold on, hold on,' he interrupted with a slight smile. 'I'm not accusing you personally. I'm saying that you should know where the stuff is at all times. You have the key, after all.'

'You know as well as I do that the equipment has to be

accessible. Any delay in an emergency could cost lives. If I locked it up twenty-four hours a day there might be a disaster!'

'Aren't you in financial difficulty yourself, at the moment?' Forbes asked Charlie. 'I overheard you tell sister Duffin that you were about to have your electricity cut off.'

'My finances are none of your business,' Charlie hissed.

'Keep calm. I only mention it as proof of how other people's minds will work.'

'There's going to have to be an inquiry,' said Mr Dalgleish. 'We can't afford to lose this kind of equipment. If this goes on, replacement costs would place Holby City in serious jeopardy. That, as you all know, could result in closure of the hospital.'

'Theft of sophisticated equipment is a serious matter,' Charlie muttered. 'I'm not saying it isn't, but it doesn't help having people sitting around in meetings like this, pointing fingers.' He glared at Forbes.

'But no one's saying you did it, Mr Fairhead,' Mr Dalgleish told him. 'We must thank Mr Forbes for his efficiency in bringing this to our attention.'

Charlie seethed quietly as the meeting was concluded and it was announced that an official inquiry was to be set up. It was one thing to talk of petty theft, but quite another to be suspected of stealing twenty thousand pounds' worth of equipment. I knew Forbes had it in for me, he thought as he left the room.

As he walked down the corridor, Charlie felt weak. He needed a breather before facing the others, and went along to the Gents. He locked himself in a cubicle and sat down, taking deep breaths. Even after several minutes, he found that he was still shaking.

8

The following evening, Charlie started on night shift. He had to do two nights because there was no one else to cover for Janice, who needed two days off to visit her family.

When he got home at nine-thirty on Thursday morning he was shattered. It had been busy as usual, but that wasn't why he felt so exhausted: he was always exhausted these days. There were a couple of letters on the doormat, and no sign of Stuart. The first letter reconfirmed his annual five-star British Gas Servicecare contract. The second was addressed to a Matthew Frazer. Charlie scribbled 'Not Known At This Address' on the envelope and put it to one side to be reposted later.

As the kettle boiled, Stuart came in, looking bright, almost mischievous, his dark hair falling into his eyes. He noticed the letter at once and picked it up. 'This is for me,' he told Charlie. 'I forgot to tell you, Matthew Frazer is a name I use sometimes.'

'Why?'

'Oh . . .' Stuart looked round the kitchen, then picked up a mug to make himself some tea. 'Sometimes if I apply for a job – if I've already been turned down, you know. Using another name helps occasionally.'

Charlie was sceptical, but didn't want to appear mistrustful. As Stuart chatted over tea, he forgot his suspicions and cheered up a bit. Stuart always had that effect on him.

'Thank goodness that shift's over,' Charlie sighed as he

poured himself a third cup of tea. 'I spent the last hour trying to avoid Gavin Forbes.'

'Gavin Forbes?'

Charlie explained the trouble he'd been having, his
anger bubbling up as he thought about it. 'He really does
have it in for me, though I don't know why.'

'Don't take it personally. He wants you to be another
yes-man, that's all,' Stuart suggested.

'Maybe,' Charlie sighed. But it was still worrying, all
that equipment going missing. He shook his head to clear
it of thoughts of work. 'Right,' he said, standing up, 'I'm
shattered. I'm going for a few hours' peaceful kip.'

Stuart smiled and pointed at the Wyvern Compu-Date
letter pinned to the cork noticeboard. 'So long as you're up
and about by six o'clock,' he said. 'Sue and Isabel are waiting for our calls.'

Charlie groaned. 'I'm not sure about all this, especially
after last time.' He thought back to the meal with Lois and
Janine at Langston's. It had been excruciating to say the
least. He hadn't been able to establish any common
ground with Janine, and she'd become suspicious of his
credentials after a while. At the end of the evening they
hadn't arranged another date, though it seemed to Charlie
that Stuart was holding back for his sake. If he'd been on
his own, he might have got on better with Lois.

'Don't give up at the first hurdle,' Stuart told him. 'You
can't expect success every time. You've paid for your three
introductions – you might as well take them up.'

'Whatever you say,' said Charlie, too tired to argue.

He woke up at around five-thirty, feeling rough. He had a
stale taste in his mouth. Sleeping during the day always
disorientated him. He went straight to the bathroom and
cleaned his teeth.

Stuart smiled at him when he entered the living-room.
'We're all fixed for this evening,' he said. 'Same thing as

last time, only we're meeting in the Gloucester, not at the station.'

'I was going to phone my date this time.'

'Too late,' Stuart smiled. 'I couldn't resist doing you the favour. Tell you what, you can buy me dinner to pay me back.'

Charlie laughed. 'So long as it's cheap.'

They were sitting in the café at the bottom of the road. Stuart was telling Charlie about his job-hunting. 'It's terrible, Charlie. I thought things were bad before I left the country, but now . . . And I'm not going back into nursing. The pay and conditions are so poor. I couldn't face it. No, I was thinking more in terms of going into business for myself. If no one else will employ me, then maybe I can employ myself.'

'Sounds good, but don't you need capital to set up in business?'

'Not necessarily. I could try one of these government schemes – the Enterprise Allowance or something.'

'You're hardly better off than the dole if you do that,' Charlie pointed out.

'Or there's always the possibility of taking over a franchise. You know, selling time-share apartments or cheap flights abroad.'

'I can tell you've been away,' Charlie laughed. 'There's no confidence in those businesses any more. Too many swindlers have fled the country, or found themselves behind bars.'

'There's a lot of money to be made in that kind of business.'

'Only if you're prepared to be unscrupulous.'

Stuart seemed about to say something, but changed his mind. 'Charlie, I've been meaning to ask you. Would you give me a reference?'

'A job reference?'

'Yes.'

'But it's years since we worked together, Stu.'

'All you have to do is say that I'm a decent, honest, hard-working chap. You don't have to mention how long it's been since we worked together.'

'Well...'

'Great! Thanks, Charlie.'

Charlie wasn't sure he'd even agreed, but Stuart obviously thought so. When they got back to the flat, Stuart handed him a letter of recommendation that he'd drafted himself. Charlie scanned it. 'Stuart Stonehouse has always been thoroughly reliable and dependable ... a trustworthy colleague and good friend ... a useful member of any team ... I would have no hesitation in recommending...'

'See, I've saved you the effort,' Stuart grinned. 'All you have to do is copy it and sign it.'

'OK, OK,' Charlie put the letter on the sideboard. 'I'll do it later.'

'Thanks, Charlie. You always were a real friend.'

Charlie walked through to the kitchen to check his appointment schedule with Elizabeth Corley. He found himself looking forward to their next meeting.

Charlie was filled with a sinking feeling as they walked into the bar of the Gloucester later that evening. The prospect of an evening of small talk seemed an insurmountable effort to him now. They sat down with their pints and Stuart placed the *Q Magazine* on the table beside them.

When the women arrived, separately this time, at least, they seemed nervous, less experienced than the previous couple. They obviously hadn't met each other before, and there were introductions all round. Stuart went to get drinks.

Isabel, Stuart's date, was broad-shouldered and

confident. She had short, light brown hair and a toothy grin. She was perhaps in her early thirties. Sue was smaller, younger, with a slight build and a nervous smile. Charlie liked the look of her because she seemed as nervous as he felt.

'I've never been on a date with a consultant before,' she began, shyly.

'But I'm not . . .' Charlie began. He sighed. What was the use? ' . . . very experienced at the dating business,' he said instead.

'You must be too busy most of the time.'

'That's definitely true,' he agreed, with feeling.

'Actually,' Sue admitted, 'this is my first time with Compu-Date. I've never done it before. It seems a little – odd, meeting like this. But if you're on your own like me, you've got to try something. Or else nothing will ever happen.'

Charlie noticed that her eyes were darting here and there as she spoke. He couldn't work out whether she was doing it because she was nervous, or if she was always that way.

Stuart came back with the drinks. Charlie gulped his beer as Stuart started joking and laughing with Isabel.

'It says on your details that you're a PA,' Charlie said, turning back to Sue.

'My boss is the administrator of Highgate and Jones.'

'Oh?'

'They're a chemicals manufacturer out at Hewley Down.'

'Right.' Charlie searched frantically for something to say. 'That sounds interesting,' he added lamely.

'Not really.'

'Oh.'

Sue picked up her vodka and orange and downed two-thirds of it in one.

'Sorry, but I'm that nervous,' she confided.

'Did you have far to come?' Charlie asked. Stuart was already chatting away to Isabel about his travels. He envied him his ability to fall into conversation so easily. Here he was, desperately searching for something to say – and Sue was obviously in the same boat.

They managed to get by for a few more minutes until they'd finished their drinks. 'Same all round?' asked Charlie, standing up.

'Our turn,' said Isabel. 'Come on Sue, we'll get the next round.'

'What exactly did you put on my form?' Charlie whispered as soon as he and Stuart were alone. 'She thinks I'm a consultant.'

'That's what I said you were. A medical consultant.'

'But—'

'Impressed, wasn't she? What's wrong with a bit of exaggeration if it gets results?'

'You should've told me. I'd have been more prepared. What about you? What did you say you did?'

'Me? I'm an executive in a PR company.'

Charlie shook his head in disbelief.

'Don't worry about things that aren't important,' Stuart said.

Charlie sighed and glanced over his shoulder to the bar, where Sue and Isabel were obviously discussing them. 'You seem to be getting on brilliantly with Isabel.'

Stuart shook his head. 'She's nice enough, but she's a single mother. Three kids. The whole point of meeting people like this is to get away from the whole business of kids.' He smiled ruefully. 'How about you?'

'We've got about as much in common as a porcupine has with a jellyfish,' Charlie told him. 'She seems desperate, too, which is off-putting.'

'Oh well,' Stuart sighed. 'Third time lucky perhaps.'

As Charlie and Stuart walked back to the flat, alone,

Charlie pondered the fact that Stuart had lied so blatantly on their forms. It made him uneasy that Stuart could be so dishonest. Had he done the right thing when he'd written out that glowing reference earlier in the evening? Don't worry about it, he told himself. Stu's a good friend. It's only exaggeration with these women. He would never lie to me.

9

'I need to learn how to talk to people more easily,' Charlie told Elizabeth. 'I clam up all the time. In social situations, I mean.'

'That's because of the cycle of preoccupation you have with your job, Charlie. You think about work all the time. You feel that people won't be interested in you if you talk about what you do for a living. You say to yourself if I can't talk about work, what does that leave? Nothing.'

'It's not exactly encouraging, putting it like that.'

'There is a way out of it. What you need is some interests and activities away from work. Not that there's anything wrong with work – in fact, it's fine as a subject, within reason – but confine it to a small part of your conversation. The problem is that most people, when they talk about their jobs, just grumble. If you can't make work sound interesting, don't say anything.' She tapped her knuckles with her pencil and looked at Charlie. 'It's important that you do things outside work. Get out more. Take up some sport or hobby.'

'Easier said than done.'

'I'm going to set you a task,' Elizabeth said. 'It's very simple, though you can make it as difficult or as easy as you like. I want you to tell someone how you feel, and I want you to do it every day. It doesn't matter how small it is, so long as you make a statement about your emotional state. Any subject. Tell a friend or a stranger. It doesn't matter. It might simply be that you feel cheerful because of the weather, or it could be something more serious. Whatever it is, I want you to set out each day with the specific task of telling at least one person about your feelings.'

'I'll try,' Charlie agreed. If he was ever going to have a hope of maintaining any kind of relationship, he'd have to pull himself together. He hadn't told Elizabeth about Compu-Date. He was a bit embarrassed to mention it. But what she said was relevant, whether she knew it or not. He decided to meet Elizabeth halfway.

'I'm so pleased,' she said, when he told her he'd eventually decided to give the imipramine a try after all. 'You'll find it helps you achieve an equilibrium that will eventually maintain itself without the need for drugs of any kind.'

'I hope you're right,' he muttered.

As he walked home from Dr Corley's, he pondered on their session. So she'd persuaded him to take imipramine. He wasn't completely happy about the idea, but she seemed so sure it was the right thing to do that he felt it wouldn't do any harm to give it a go. He could always stop taking it if it didn't help.

He sighed as walked beneath the plane trees that lined the street. He was filled with a satisfying sense of gradual unwinding. The session with Elizabeth had begun it, but the most significant reason for his relaxation was the fact that he had the day off tomorrow. It was Friday evening, and he wasn't on duty again until Sunday afternoon.

As he passed an ornate Victorian infants school, he mulled over the last night's shift. One thing of particular interest had happened: he'd bumped into Gavin Forbes in the corridor, and he'd actually stopped to say hello. It was extraordinary. For one thing, Forbes shouldn't have been in the building. Not in the middle of the night. Duffy reckoned it was because he was ultra-keen. But the main surprise was that he'd smiled at Charlie and mumbled something about the building work coming along well. And then he'd wandered off towards Reception. He appeared to have forgotten about their argument over the missing equipment. His smile had been somewhat strained, and decidedly insincere, but it had been a smile nevertheless.

'I bet he's been told off for the way he treated you,' Duffy had told him. 'Mike said he virtually accused you of being a thief. Honestly! It's enough to make you sick.'

It was enough to make him livid, but if the whole thing could blow over, he was prepared to let the personal slur pass. Better that than face endless ructions. They still had to sort out the question of missing equipment, but one thing was certain – if it had been stolen, a member of his staff hadn't done it.

Still, Charlie wasn't going to worry about it right now. He'd go home, perhaps enjoy a beer with Stuart, then watch a movie before bed. And then, luxury – he had what amounted to two-thirds of a whole weekend free!

Charlie opened the curtains in his bedroom the following morning, screwing up his eyes against the bright early sunshine. He yawned sleepily and peered outside. A whole Saturday stretched in front of him – what a rare pleasure. And the weather looked extremely promising.

Still groggy, he padded through to the kitchen, already looking forward to his first cup of coffee. Before Stuart had moved in, Charlie had got into the habit of spending most of his infrequent days off in bed, catching up on sleep. But this morning he thought he'd make an effort. Having company around gave him a reason to get out of bed.

As he rinsed a coffee mug under the tap and thought vaguely about a trip to the supermarket to stock up on some basics like bread, milk and baked beans, Charlie was faintly troubled by the feeling that he'd forgotten some-thing. It was a familiar feeling: he always had so much on his mind that he never quite seemed to get all his thoughts organised the way he once had. Old age, he thought to himself, spooning two large heaps of instant coffee into his mug. He liked his coffee extra strong.

Twenty minutes later, Stuart joined him at the kitchen table. 'Morning, Charlie boy!'

'Morning. Do you always have to be so hellishly cheer-ful in the mornings?' Charlie chuckled. 'I was just about to make some toast. Want some?'

'Stay where you are. I'll get it.' Stuart sprang to his feet and crossed to the breadbin. 'You save your energy for later.'

'Meaning?' Charlie felt his eyebrows knit.

'Today's the big day.' Stuart popped their last two slices of bread into the toaster. 'Westbourne Cove.'

Charlie groaned. That's what he'd forgotten. They'd arranged to spend the day at Westbourne Cove, a coastal resort about forty-five minutes' drive from Holby. In itself Westbourne wasn't a bad place, and Charlie hadn't been there for years, but . . .' Oh hell,' he groaned. 'Do we have to?'

They were supposed to be meeting two more women from Compu-Date there, for lunch.

'You always look on the dark side, don't you?' Stuart stared at Charlie as though he was a hopeless case. 'Don't think of the last two dates, think of what *might* happen.'

'That's what I'm afraid of.'

'It's worth a try, surely, now that everything's set up?'

'Sorry Stu. I don't think I can face it. You go.'

'And what are you going to do all day?'

'Catch up on sleep. A bit of shopping, maybe.'

Stuart shook his head and made a tutting sound. 'What an exciting life you lead, Charlie.' He brought the toast over to the table and sat down. 'I'll make a deal with you,

OK? We'll suss 'em out from a safe distance. If you don't like the look of them, we'll walk away.'

Charlie gave a wry grin. 'We tried that before, remember, at the station? It didn't work then.'

Stuart shrugged for a moment, then smiled. 'OK, then. We're meeting them at twelve. We'll have a quick drink, maybe a pub lunch, then we'll say we've got an appointment to keep.'

'An appointment? In Westbourne Cove?'

'I could get toothache, perhaps. Painful, agonising toothache. As soon as we meet them, I'll say I've been having trouble, been treated by a special dentist or something. If you don't feel comfortable, we can dash off.'

'It's a bit weak, Stu.'

'But it'll be enough. If you're not a hundred per cent happy with these girls, just tap me on the shoulder . . .' Stuart demonstrated.

'Ow.'

'. . . and before you know it, I'll be in agony and you'll have to take me for emergency treatment.'

Charlie grinned in spite of himself. He bit into his toast. How had he got himself into this? 'I don't know, Stu. Let's face it. This computer dating is a disaster. I don't know how they do the matching up, but the women I've met haven't been anything like what I asked for. I expect I'm just as much of a disappointment to them.'

'Come on, Charlie, that's no way to look at it. One last try. Just for me.'

'It's turning us into schoolboys, all this. I don't enjoy playing silly buggers. And as for the women—'

'Please.'

'Stuart.'

'You've got to be an optimist in this life, Charlie, or you might as well give up.'

Charlie sighed, feeling that he was being pushed into a situation that he'd only regret. But maybe I need to be pushed, he thought. 'All right,' he said. 'But it's the last time.'

'Agreed.'

'Positively the last time.'

'Positively.'

'After this, if we want to meet girls – and I'm not even sure I've got the time for a social life at the moment – we'll do it in the usual way.'

'And what's that?'

'I don't know. Pubs, clubs. Whatever people do nowadays.'

'Whatever you say, Charlie. We can always join the Darby and Joan club if you like.'

'Don't laugh. It may even come to that.'

10

Charlie and Stuart drove down to the coast via the scenic route. Thanks to Stuart's rent Charlie had got his light panel replaced. The bumper was still dented, but he was pleased to be back on the road. The Saturday traffic was lighter than expected, and both were cheered when they rounded a bend and caught their first glimpse of the sea, silver and rippling in the morning sunshine. Westbourne Cove, with its white-painted houses, seemed welcoming, as did the dark, traditional oak-beamed pub where they'd arranged to meet the women.

The pub smelled of good beer and freshly baked bread. A few well-dressed people chatted quietly at Tudor-style oak tables as Charlie and Stuart strolled through to the dining area, pints in hand. One of the women, Joy, had told Stuart on the telephone that she'd be wearing a red dress with a white collar. Only one woman fitted that description. A small, almost waif-like blonde, sitting in the far corner with a dark-haired woman who had her back to Charlie.

They hadn't been spotted yet, so Stuart ducked into an alcove and signalled Charlie to follow. 'Well? What do you think?'

Charlie shrugged. 'They look OK.'

'OK?' Stuart's eyes popped. 'That blonde is something special.'

'Just your type.'

Stuart had always had a soft spot for attractive women.

And they liked him, too. Funny how good-looking people always seemed to gravitate towards each other. 'So. Give it a try then, shall we?'

Almost before Charlie had nodded, Stuart was leading the way to the women's table.

The blonde looked up as they approached. 'Hello,' Stuart flashed his best smile. 'Are you Joy?'

She said she was. Up close she was quite beautiful, in an ethereal kind of way. She was very slender with white, almost translucent skin and large green eyes.

Stuart beamed. 'Can we join you?'

Joy smiled shyly and slid along the bench seat. Stuart immediately sat next to her, almost throwing himself down, leaving Charlie to take the chair next to the second woman, who now turned to face him.

'I'm Angela,' she said.

Charlie smiled and sat down, hoping his palpitating nervousness wasn't as obvious as he thought it must be. 'Hello,' he croaked to the table.

'I'm Stuart, and this is Charlie.'

'Pleased to meet you,' said Angela.

Angela was obviously the bolder of the two. She had an open, friendly face. Not as conventionally attractive as Joy, she radiated confidence and robust good health. Charlie was briefly disappointed that Joy wasn't the one he was supposed to meet. Her shyness was very appealing, given his own state of mind. But Angela was his date, so he might as well make the most of it.

'So you found it all right,' Joy said quickly, then immediately blushed a deep shade of pink. 'Sorry,' she bit her lip, flustered. 'That was a stupid thing to say. Of course you found it.' She stared at her hands, twisting the glass of wine on the table in front of her.

'It wasn't stupid at all,' Stuart soothed. 'We've had a good drive down, actually. How about you?'

'We came by train,' Angela smiled. 'Only half an hour

from Holby. We met each other in here and introduced ourselves. It was a good idea of yours to meet here,' she told Stuart. 'Neutral ground. And it's wonderful to get out of the city.'

There was brief silence as everyone smiled nervously. Charlie gulped his beer.

'Can I get anyone another drink?' Stuart asked.

Angela and Joy said they'd love a glass of wine. Charlie instinctively put his hand over his beer – stupid thing to do – and said he was fine for now, thanks. As soon as Stuart got to his feet, Charlie cursed himself for refusing a drink. Stuart was leaving him here at the table alone with these strange women. He half-rose. 'Shall I help you?'

'I'm all right.' Stuart sauntered off happily towards the bar.

Charlie smiled at Angela, then Joy, wondering if the panic showed in his eyes. He took another gulp of beer.

'So, Charlie, what do you do?' Angela drained her glass.

'I work in a hospital. Accident and Emergency department.' He nodded pointlessly. 'Charge nurse. Except they call it something else now.' Now he was here he wasn't going to make things even more difficult for himself with all that consultant business.

Angela didn't seem to notice that there was a discrepancy between what he'd said and what was on his Compu-Date form. 'Must be hard work.'

Charlie nodded again. 'How about you?'

'I look after children,' she said. 'At a nursery.'

'Oh. That must be hard work, too.'

Angela laughed. She had a pleasant, easy laugh. 'Hard work and noisy. You need a dozen pairs of hands, I can tell you. It has its gory side, too. Nappy changing. But I enjoy it.'

'It takes dedication to do messy jobs,' he said.

'It sure does.' Angela laughed again.

Charlie liked her. She was down-to-earth, unpretentious.

Joy smiled, twisting her empty glass nervously. Charlie wished he could help her – she looked so vulnerable – but before he could think of anything to say, Stuart was back with the drinks. 'Here we are, and I brought the menu too. You girls haven't had lunch yet, have you?'

They hadn't. The four of them studied the menu. By the time the food arrived, the initial tension had drifted away.

'I'm between jobs at the moment,' Joy explained. 'I usually do temporary work. Reception, switchboard operation, exhibitions. If I could find a job I loved I'd stay with it.'

'Wouldn't we all?' Stuart laughed.

The conversation continued, but Charlie's eyebrows raised when Stuart described himself as a medical professional 'like Charlie here'. He supposed it was true – Stuart was a trained nurse. He just didn't want to go back into the profession, that was all.

After the meal, Charlie found himself trying to think of something the four of them might do together when the pub closed. Something Joy and Angela would enjoy. A walk along the beach seemed pretty tame, but he wasn't sure what else there was to do in Westbourne. Stuart might have an idea, Charlie thought, but as time was called, and Stu cast a meaningful glance in his direction, Charlie realised that he hadn't come up with anything either.

It was a tricky moment, because all four knew that their date had only been for a drink, at most a pub lunch. Also, Charlie couldn't work out how the girls felt, whether they were keen to extend the date or not. At least they had time for one more drink. Charlie went over to the bar, still trying to think up something. Perhaps if he made it clear to the women that he'd had a good time, they'd get the hint, and might suggest something themselves.

As he placed the drinks on the table, Charlie took a deep breath, patted Stuart, and spoke cheerfully, and loudly: 'This has been brilliant, hasn't it Stu? Best time I've had for ages. Pity it has to end so soon.'

'Yeah.' Stu cast him an uncertain glance, then cried out in pain. 'Aagh!' Stuart grabbed his jaw and rocked from side to side. 'Bloody hell, Charlie! My toothache's started up again!'

Too late, Charlie realised that patting Stuart on the shoulder was the 'escape' signal they'd agreed on.

'Quick,' he said, 'let's get you to the Gents. So I can take a look at what's wrong.' He hustled Stuart out of his chair.

'Sorry, Stu. That wasn't supposed to be a signal,' he explained, when they were alone. 'It was accidental. I wanted us to stay with them.'

'You berk!' Stuart sighed. 'It was going so well, too. What are we going to do now?'

Charlie thought of Angela and Joy waiting in the almost empty pub, thinking that he was performing some sort of emergency treatment on Stuart's mystery toothache. 'We'll have to tell them the truth,' he said.

'Are you crazy?' Stuart couldn't believe it. 'We can't do something like that. We'll say the pain's gone.'

'Stuart, these women are not idiots.'

'But they'll think we're complete pratts.'

'Who cares?' Charlie said. 'You like Joy, don't you? They're both great. If we've got any hope of salvaging anything from this, it won't be through lying.'

'You tell them.'

'Me? I can't.'

'I'm certainly not going to.'

Charlie stood staring at Stuart. If they stayed in the Gents much longer Joy and Angela would give up and go home anyway. What was it Elizabeth had asked him to do? Tell someone what he was feeling every day. Now, it would appear, was as good a time as any to start. It helped that he'd had a couple of drinks. 'All right,' he said. 'Let's go. And leave this to me.'

'You see,' Charlie explained. 'We really do like you. Both of you. It was a stupid and childish thing to do.'

'I agree.' Angela looked a bit miffed. 'Grown men.'

'So do you always make these escape plans when you meet people?' Joy wanted to know.

Charlie felt like a naughty boy. Stuart shuffled his feet around. 'This is only my third meeting through Compu-Date,' Charlie said. 'The first two were complete disasters.'

Suddenly Angela threw her head back and started to laugh. Joy began to giggle.

'Are we forgiven, then?' Stuart brightened. 'Do you want to go somewhere? The beach? The pier?'

'At least you had the guts to tell us the truth,' Angela told Charlie. 'Even though it made you look a real idiot.'

A conspiratorial glance passed between the women. 'We knew it was an act,' Joy grinned. 'Sudden toothache like that. And you weren't very convincing anyway.' They gathered their bags and stood up. 'So, where are we going?'

As they strolled along the seafront down to the little banjo pier, Charlie marvelled at how good it felt to be with someone, to feel attracted to another person. He'd almost forgotten what it was like. He thought of the surge of relief he'd felt when Angela had laughed, that warm flood of emotion – and pride – when she'd said that at least he'd had the courage to be honest. And the thrill and excitement of being with someone new, finding out about them and not knowing how the relationship would develop, but *hoping*. All these sensations he hadn't realised he'd missed.

'It's lovely down here, isn't it?' Angela shouted through the salt wind on the pier.

'Yes.' Oh, what the hell, Charlie thought, you've done it once, you might as well do it again. 'The sea,' he shouted back, 'it makes me think of freedom. And the power of nature, and the insignificance of humankind. Does that make any sense? Do I sound crazy?'

'Not in the least. I know exactly how you feel.'

Charlie gasped with pleasure. Elizabeth Corley had been right. He had to learn to talk more. Not to bottle things up, but to trust people, to take risks. Looking at Angela, he had no doubt that it was time to start building some kind of life outside the small world of Holby City A and E department.

11

When he woke the next morning, Charlie was still filled with that odd, pleasurable sensation from the day before at Westbourne Cove. It felt strange, but yes, he was actually happy. His outlook had changed, overnight, it seemed. He roamed restlessly around the flat, wondering how to spend the four hours till he had to be at Holby City.

Twenty-four hours ago he'd been so down, so negative. Now, simply because he'd got out of the flat and met a couple of interesting women, everything around him had been lifted from dullness. The great thing was that he'd talked to both Angela and Joy, really communicated, in the way that Elizabeth had meant. And she was right – it did help. It made him feel good, opening up to the right kind of people. Telling them how he felt.

Stu wasn't around, again. He was certainly taking this job-hunting business seriously. He was always out trying to see people, trying to make connections. Even on a Sunday morning he was off early to meet 'a man about a possible job', which was all Stuart would say whenever Charlie asked him for more details.

Charlie stood in the middle of the living-room and looked around. The flat could do with a clean. Stuart had tidied up recently, because the wastepaper bins weren't overflowing and the old newspapers had been piled up outside the back door, but when was the last time the flat had been properly cleaned? He tried to think, but found he couldn't remember. Still, now was as good a time as any. He put on the radio – Jazz FM – rummaged around under the sink for the cleaning materials, and got on with it.

As he worked, he found the physical exercise therapeutic. He thought of the day before, when he and Stuart had gone into that little tea-room on the seafront with Joy and Angela. Those chewy old-fashioned toasted teacakes were the best he'd tasted. It was as though, while he was sitting there, eating and chatting and laughing, his senses had come alive again, were awakening after a long period of hibernation.

It wasn't as if they'd done anything special, only wandered along the esplanade and talked. It just went to show how unimportant it was whether you did something exciting or not – the important thing was who you did it with. That's what happened when you were preoccupied all the time. You lost sight of what was important in life, and what wasn't.

He'd ring Angela later, before he went to work, he decided. He'd said he'd ring her that evening, but there was no need to wait that long. She'd mentioned at one point that she liked jazz. He wondered if that little jazz pub in the city centre, The Derwent, was still going. He'd have a look in the entertainments listings. It'd be good to be able to suggest somewhere they both liked. He could find out who was playing, then ring her up casually. 'By the way, so-and-so's playing at The Derwent on Thursday night. Do you fancy going?'

In the bathroom he scoured the smooth white surface of the bath in time to the music on the radio. Usually he detested cleaning. Usually he put if off and put it off, then tried to do a little bit – the bare minimum – each day until the flat was acceptable. But to get it done like this, all in one go, was quite fun. He might use this system in future, he thought. Let everything get into a state, then take a whole day to clean it all from top to bottom.

'Excuse the mess,' he imagined himself telling people who came in. 'But it isn't my cleaning day for another six weeks.' That was a good sign, thinking of people coming round to the flat. No one but Stuart had been there in ages.

He stood back, arms akimbo. The gleaming surfaces in the bathroom cheered him. They smelled of pine and gritty bathroom cleanser. Certainly a change from before.

Twelve noon. Still plenty of time. Charlie got the hoover out and started working his way from room to room, leaving clean pattern trails on the carpet behind him as he went. He hoovered his room – he'd sort out all those crumpled clothes next – and decided to go the whole hog and do Stuart's too. Stuart's room was almost as untidy as Charlie's. Luckily neither of them was pernickety about things like that. Although Stuart's room didn't have many clothes strewn about, there were papers everywhere. There were copies of Stuart's CV – he'd had it typed up professionally at one of those agencies. Charlie picked it up idly.

'Most recent job,' he read, turning off the hoover. 'Medical consultant.' Hell! When Stu decided to exaggerate, he didn't do it by half. How could he get away with saying he was a consultant? Surely qualifications and references would be checked out?

'Just completed one year's voluntary work with the Red Cross in Somalia.' Charlie nearly laughed aloud at that one. What was wrong with Stu, anyway? OK, he wanted to get a good job, but a fantasy-based CV was a waste of time. He'd be sacked as soon as the references were checked.

I gave him a reference, he remembered. But that had been a character reference and hadn't mentioned specific jobs. Charlie had written that Stuart was scrupulously honest, though, which made him shift uncomfortably as he read the extraordinary CV in his hand. Even with a CV like this one, Stuart still hadn't managed to find any work. Charlie felt sorry for his friend. He'd been making a great effort, getting the newspaper each morning, seeing these 'men' – probably just blokes he met in pubs – but work wasn't easy to come by at the moment and you had to try everything, no matter how tenuous.

Charlie shrugged. He supposed it was none of his business. He started cleaning again, manoeuvring the hoover through the narrow gap between the bedside table and the wardrobe. He caught the edge of the table though, and a pile of papers which had been balanced precariously on the edge cascaded to the floor. They scattered everywhere, fanning out across the freshly vacuumed carpet.

Turning off the hoover, Charlie bent and scooped them up, a handful at a time. Stuart's driving licence was among them. He held it up and read Stuart's name, and an address up north. Must have been where he lived with his ex-wife. His passport, too, was among the papers, in a special leather cover, and Charlie couldn't resist peeping in to have a laugh at the photograph. Passport photos were always gruesome. They never failed to make the person look monstrous – Charlie had yet to see a good passport photo of anyone. It was as if they put a special chemical in those photo booths which stopped people ever looking normal. Probably the customs officials did it to brighten up their dreary days.

Stuart's likeness was as bad as any Charlie had ever seen. He wore that empty, startled expression, so familiar in photographs taken in booths. Flicking quickly through the pages, Charlie was surprised to find them blank. No exotic stamps or entries, not even a visa. Strange. He checked the date. It wasn't a new passport. It was nearly six years old. Stuart couldn't have travelled without it. How had he got into those African and Asian countries he'd mentioned without a single visa?

There were a couple of folded sheets of paper tucked inside the leather cover of the passport. Charlie had assumed they were vaccination certificates, but was intrigued now, even though he knew he was being nosy. Stuart exaggerated so much – wouldn't it be funny if it turned out that he'd only been travelling through France or one of the other EC countries? He unfolded the first paper. It was a page from a small notepad. Some numbers were written in what might have been Stuart's handwriting, though he couldn't be sure. They looked like bank account or credit card numbers. The other sheet of paper was larger, more official-looking.

Charlie unfolded it and read the words: 'HM Prison, Wormwood, London W12'. It was some sort of property receipt, with a list of personal effects: 'One watch, gold-coloured, white dial: one Parker ballpoint pen, blue enamel; one wallet containing one library card, one £5 note, two £10 notes . . .'

The prisoner, on his release, had signed for the return of his property, which presumably had been confiscated when he was locked up. Charlie sat on the bed and reread the paper. It had to be a mistake. The newly released prisoner was Stuart Arthur Holden Stonehouse.

Charlie stared at the sheet of paper. He read it through again several times before he could accept that it was true. The date of release was printed under the prison's address. It was the same day he'd met Stuart in the street. The day that Stuart had said he'd flown into Heathrow. Charlie remembered their meeting. How impressed he'd been with Stuart, and how envious too, in a way. But everything Stuart had told him was a lie.

All thoughts of cleaning the flat left Charlie as a sensation of numbness and distance crept over him. It was as if he no longer saw the flat as being either clean or dirty. It was irrelevant how the flat looked. Elizabeth had warned of emotional extremes. Charlie almost laughed aloud. Only minutes before, he'd been light-hearted and content. And now – where was he?

12

Charlie stared at himself in the bathroom mirror. He had to be at work in half an hour. There was no question of not going in. People depended on him, patients and staff alike. But how could he cope with it all after this?

Stuart in prison! What had he done to get himself sent to prison, for heaven's sake? Why hadn't he told Charlie? Surely he could have confided in him – after all, they went way back. What in God's name was Stu doing?

Charlie splashed his face and went through the motions of getting ready, but his mind was fixed on Stuart. There was no way to contact him, to ask him about this. He still couldn't believe it. Prison. As he dragged the razor across his cheek, it occurred to him that Stuart might be mixed up in something illegal right now. It had been odd, the way he'd produced money to pay rent in advance. Were people given money when they came out of prison? What was Stuart up to when he went off out, apparently looking for work? He had no idea, but one thing was for sure, he intended to find out.

Charlie felt a sharp sting as the razor cut into his upper lip. He cursed briefly before splashing his face with cold water. That's what came of not paying attention. He opened the bathroom cabinet to get some cotton wool and saw the bottle of imipramine. He took it out and held it in his hand. He'd promised Elizabeth that he'd take the course. He tipped the bottle and emptied a handful of the little so-called miracle-workers into the palm of his hand.

Would they do any good? Nothing could work miracles.

Taking anti-depressants wouldn't change the fact that Stuart had lied to him, and was probably using him. If he couldn't trust an old friend, who could he trust? Why was it that everyone seemed out for themselves? No one really cared. They just pretended. Charlie strode over to the toilet bowl and tipped the anti-depressants that he had in his hand into the freshly disinfected water. He took a deep breath then, feeling suddenly angry and bitter, and, yes, sorry for himself.

His jaw was set as he unscrewed the cap and emptied the contents of the bottle down the toilet. He flushed it several times, relieved that he'd taken the decision to discard them all; relieved that they were no longer there to tempt him. Didn't he feel bad enough without drugs pickling his brain?

He checked the time. He had to go, no matter how lousy he felt; he had to face the RTAs, the respiratory arrests, the battered wives, the abused children. Because they all needed him, and he could help. The only one he couldn't help, he thought bitterly, was himself.

The Casualty waiting area was chock-a-block when he arrived. Patients were pacing; one with a furiously pouring nosebleed, one with a half-closed eye. Telephones were ringing, an ambulance crew was passing through; a pair of policemen waited at the desk, probably for the result of an inquiry. Norma, who was on the phone, smiled a frazzled hello to him as he turned down the Admin corridor to his office. It was as though he was in some strange hyper-reality. It was a different world here, full of imperatives. No wonder it was so easy to let it take over. He hadn't even had time to button his coat before Ash entered.

'Hi. Good day off?'

Charlie frowned. 'Yeah.' He'd forgotten it already. How could that happen?

'Hey,' Ash grinned. 'Don't be too enthusiastic.'

'Sorry. I did have a good day. It's just that I've got things on my mind.'

'Haven't we all.'

Charlie felt a pang of guilt. Ash was a good bloke. He'd been through a lot lately, what with his girlfriend Nikki's abortion, and the break-up of their relationship. Charlie had no right to take it out on him. He made an effort to sound cheerful. 'So, what's happening?'

'A lot. Josh and Jane are on their way in with a head injury. Suspected fractured skull with possible spinal complications.'

Wilma, the sister from the previous shift, bustled in and handed over the keys to Charlie with a sigh of relief. 'You are welcome to it, my love,' she said, as she went through the briefing. 'It's chaos out there.'

Charlie blinked and rubbed his eyes. He was overwhelmed by it all before it had even started.

It was four and a half hours before he had a moment to himself. He opened the curtains of cubicle four and sighed. Jim, the porter, had just wheeled the patient off to x-ray. Duffy approached. 'Let's grab five minutes, shall we?' she smiled. 'Mike and Ash have got things under control.'

Charlie glanced down towards Admin, where Mike nodded to him, signalling he was OK. He and Duffy walked through to the little coffee bar. Duffy was cheerful these days, her life had improved a lot recently. Charlie was happy for her. 'How's little Peter?' he asked.

'Great, and so is Andrew. But what about you, Charlie?'

Charlie shrugged. Duffy was kind, but he wasn't sure if he could face telling her. 'All right.'

'You're not. But if that's the way you want it.' She shrugged. 'How was your day off?'

He told her about his trip to Westbourne Cove. Without mentioning the dating agency, he said he and Stu had met two women.

'About time!' Duffy laughed. 'So when are you coming round for a meal? You can bring someone, you know,' she added pointedly.

As Duffy chatted on about her holiday plans, Charlie spotted Gavin Forbes approaching. He stalked the department like a predatory beast in search of a kill. The word was that everyone was under suspicion; there were even rumours that Forbes had brought in plain-clothes security men to keep an eye on everyone. Charlie knew this wasn't true. There wasn't enough in the budget to cover something like that, even though the scale of the theft might warrant such drastic action. The rumour alone was enough to make people edgy and on guard.

'Sorry if I'm boring you,' Duffy's stern tone broke into his thoughts.

'What?'

'You weren't listening to a word I was saying.'

'I was.'

'Really. So where did Andrew and I decide to go in the end, then?'

'Erm . . . '

Duffy stood up. 'It wasn't the most exciting event in the world, but it'd be nice if you'd at least pretend to be interested.'

'Look. Duffy, I'm sorry, I—'

'You don't have to say it, Charlie, I know.'

Duffy walked back towards the ward. Charlie knew she wasn't cross, just a bit hurt. He always got it wrong these days. As he was about to rise and follow her out, Forbes joined him at the table. 'Hello, Mr Fairhead. How's the stress counselling?'

Charlie's jaw dropped. How had he found out about that? This was all he needed. There was no sign of the good cheer of the previous week. Forbes looked well and truly pissed off.

'You have informed your superiors, I presume?' Forbes

continued in the slimy voice that Charlie was beginning to hate. 'Let's face it, you are in charge of a department and psychiatric problems do have a habit of escalating, and then, who knows—'

'Rubbish,' Charlie interrupted. 'It isn't a psychiatric problem for a start, and even if it was, I'm not aware that you've had medical training. On what do you base this theory of yours?'

Forbes bristled. 'When staff become incompetent through illness or anything else, Mr Fairhead, patients can suffer.'

'Incompetent!' Charlie could hardly contain his fury.

'Easy now, Mr Fairhead. A hypothetical situation, that's all I meant. My, my, you are touchy.'

Charlie stood up and pushed his chair back. He couldn't trust himself to speak.

'I'm simply wondering,' Forbes continued as Charlie left the table, 'how someone can run a busy hospital department efficiently when they can't get their own life in order.'

So now Charlie knew for sure. This guy was vicious. He only wished he knew what he'd done to make the man hate him. He wasn't that disagreeable, surely?

Half an hour later, in Admin, Charlie dialled his own home number. He needed to get an explanation from Stu. The whole thing was preoccupying him, distracting him from his work. No reply. Charlie rested his head in his hands. He had to get this sorted out.

'Charlie?' It was Ash. He and Duffy stood over him, hang-dog, concerned expressions on their faces. 'Are you all right?' he whined. At least it sounded like a whine to Charlie.

'I'd be a lot better if you two Mother Theresas would leave me alone,' Charlie snapped. 'Mind your own business, will you?'

As soon as he'd said it he was sorry. Ash gave a hurt,

defensive look, then moved away. Duffy opened her mouth to speak, but then thought better of it and followed Ash to Reception. Charlie was so tired of everybody feeling sorry for him. Sympathy didn't help. He wanted answers. Why had Stu lied to him? What did Forbes have against him?

That evening Charlie walked home. The dark streets soothed him. The only solution he could think of was to ask Stu to move out. It'd been good having him around, but there was no other way.

13

Charlie was half-surprised to find Stu at home, and still up. He'd tried ringing him half a dozen times from work, but there had never been an answer. 'So you came back.' Charlie walked into the living-room. Stu was watching TV, as though he'd been there all along.

Stu caught the tone of his voice. 'What's wrong? Bad day at work?'

'That. And more.'

'Oh?'

'When I was hoovering your room this morning I knocked some of your papers on to the floor. Your passport was among them.'

'Oh.' Stuart looked carefully at Charlie.

'I saw your prison release papers.' Charlie's voice sounded louder, angrier than he'd intended.

Stu sighed. 'What's the point in denying it? I was going to tell you. I was just waiting for the right moment.'

'You expect me to believe that?'

'I'll get us both a beer,' Stu got up and headed for the kitchen. A moment later he was back with a couple of cans.

'Look at it from my point of view,' he said, handing one to Charlie. 'It's not the kind of thing you can tell people. Not without them disowning you.'

'So how long were you in for?'

'Twelve months.'

'Twelve months?' Charlie took a gulp of beer. 'Twelve months! What the hell did you do?'

'Does it matter?'

'Of course it bloody matters. I'd like to know whether I'm living with a rapist, a thief or an armed robber.'

'OK, OK,' he sighed. 'It's none of those.'

'That's something, I suppose. So what did you do?'

Stu looked uncomfortable. 'Before I tell you, let me explain what led up to it—'

'Tell me!'

'OK. It was fraud.'

'Fraud?' Charlie shook his head. Fraud was the last thing he'd expected. But then none of this made sense.

'Please, Charlie. Give me a chance. Let me put it in context.'

Charlie glared at Stu. What kind of a friend would keep something like this from him?

'I know you're angry,' Stu said quietly. 'You have a right to be. But hear me out.' He took a long drink of his beer. 'I was going through a bad time with Carol. She wanted it all: a divorce, the house, maintenance, everything. On top of that, I was made redundant.'

'From St Matthew's? You never told me.'

'I never told anyone. I kept quiet about it. I couldn't stay at home all day – not the way Carol was acting – so I went out every morning, as though I was going to work, only I didn't go to work. I wandered the streets. At first it wasn't too bad. I had the redundancy money. I could sit in cafés, or go to the cinema. I didn't think of trying to save the money, because I thought I'd get another job before it ran out.'

Stuart leaned his head in his hands. 'The end of the month was always the worst. The regular bills had to be paid, and Carol wrote all these cheques, stupid cheques for stupid things because she knew she was going to leave me. I had to cover them all.'

'So you stole.'

'No. I went to my bank manager for extra funds. Of

course, that was before he knew I'd lost my job. I'd previously borrowed from the bank, so there was no reason for him to believe I couldn't pay it back. I kept thinking I'd find another job and everything would be all right.

'A couple of months passed. Then a couple more. I didn't find another job and the bank discovered I was unemployed. No more money from them. So I went to a building society. I had an old account I'd opened years ago and never used. The balance was forty pounds or something. I applied for a loan, and this time I lied. I made up details, said I was a company director, gave the address of a friend's house for financial references. My friend passed the letters on to me and I forged replies. What else could I do? It was the only way to keep going.'

Charlie began to feel sorry for Stu as he continued.

'It was time-consuming, but easy enough to fool them. Eventually they offered me a loan. A big one, because of the salary I'd pretended I was earning. I thought it over for a while. It was more than I needed, but I reckoned in for a penny, in for a pound. Besides, I still intended to pay it back. All I needed was time to get the right job.

'It wasn't long before the strain began to tell. The pressure of what to do with myself all day, even though I had plenty of money in my pocket by this time, was terrible. I kept waiting for Carol to move out. By the time she did, taking most of our furniture with her, I'd sort of cracked up. I didn't realise what was happening at the time, but later, in prison, they made me see their clinical psychologist. He made me face the truth: I'd had a nervous breakdown.'

Charlie, who'd been brooding over the top of his beer can, looked up in surprise.

'I know, I know,' Stu continued. 'With my training I should have recognised the symptoms, but . . .' He shrugged. 'One day, I remember, I just went to pieces. It was ridiculous really. I was sitting talking to a friend –

well, not even a friend, really, more of an acquaintance from the pub. He'd come round to watch a match on the telly. Afterwards, we were chatting about football, and I burst into tears. The poor guy was so embarrassed. He thought I was crying about my team losing or something. I couldn't control myself. Within a few minutes I was yelling, shouting, confessing, saying I couldn't go on.'

Charlie recognised the anguish in Stuart's face. He knew Stu wasn't lying. There was no way that such pain could be faked. The scary thing was that he himself had felt perilously close to what Stuart was describing. He understood how easily it could creep up on you.

'I started throwing things about,' Stu went on. 'Whatever I could lay my hands on. Books, glasses, anything that Carol had left behind. She'd left so little, only what she didn't want. If she'd rejected it, then I didn't want it either. I just chucked all this stuff around the room, chucked her half-broken typewriter through the front window. This guy tried to restrain me and so I turned on him. Lashing out, kicking.'

'What happened?'

'The police came round. One of the neighbours, Carol's friend, phoned them. I ended up in a psychiatric unit for seven days. By the time I got out, the building society had twigged about the fraud and had decided to prosecute.'

By now Stu's voice was low. 'The police dug up some other loan forms and a so-called falsified mortgage application.'

'You've really been through it. You should have told me, Stu.'

'My brief didn't think they'd put me away. But the judge was probably having a bad day. I did my time, Charlie, I paid for it the hard way. Now I want to put it all behind me.'

'What hurts the most is that you felt you couldn't tell me.' Charlie said. 'What did you think I would do? Turf you out?' As he spoke he remembered with discomfort that this had been his precise intention half an hour earlier.

'Would you have offered to put me up in the first place if you'd known?'

Charlie frowned. Maybe Stu had a point.

'Once you've been inside, even your friends don't trust you any more.' Stu got to his feet. 'I'm sorry, Charlie. I should have told you. I just wanted to forget about it, get on with living a new life without having to think of all that mess. You'll want me to move out, then?'

'It's OK. Sit down. You're right, you should have told me. So what about this money you've got? Where's it been coming from?'

Stu gave a wry grin. He seemed a little reluctant, but then explained. 'It's from a bank account. One that I set up before I went inside. We split the money fifty-fifty, you see. Me and this friend I mentioned, the one whose address I used.'

'So you've been living off stolen money, basically?'

Stu nodded. 'There isn't much left. Only about fifty pounds now.'

'But that's criminal.'

'Oh, yes? And what about what they did to me? I had a breakdown, Charlie. I lost my wife, my home – everything. And when I came out of jail, they gave me a measly couple of quid and waved bye-bye at the gates. What kind of treatment is that? I'd be on the streets by now if I hadn't had that bit set by. Either that or I'd be in one of those hostels for homeless men. Cold, dirty and smelling of piss.'

Stu watched as Charlie got to his feet. 'So what are you going to do?' he asked.

'I don't know. Nothing I suppose. Right now I'm going to get us both another beer.'

'You're a real friend, Charlie,' Stu said with relief as he followed Charlie into the kitchen. 'You know, maybe I unconsciously left the passport around deliberately so you could find it. So that I'd have to tell you.'

'Maybe.'

They returned to the living-room and drank their second beer in silence. Charlie knew he couldn't blame Stu for one mistake. Everybody makes mistakes. And, after all, he'd paid for it.

'Charlie,' Stuart said after a while.

'Yes?'

'Thanks. You really are a brilliant friend.'

14

Charlie and Stuart walked along the street of neat terraced houses. It was a good area, without being pretentious. Just the sort of place Charlie would have expected someone like Angela to live.

'Which number is it?' Stu asked, readjusting his grip on the box of groceries he was carrying.

Charlie dug in his pocket for the scrap of paper with the scribbled address. 'Forty-two.'

Angela had been understanding about him not ringing, but she'd suggested they meet at her place rather than go to The Derwent.

'Pubs are OK,' she'd said, 'but not for talking. Not when there's music blaring.' Charlie hadn't thought that far ahead. Angela was the sensible type, no doubt about it.

Stuart counted as he walked. 'Thirty-eight, forty, forty-two. This is the one.'

Angela's house was no different from the others. Tidy little garden, window box on the sill. They walked down the short path and rang the doorbell.

Charlie had mentioned to Stuart that Angela had offered to cook a meal for him, and that he and Joy were invited. Stuart had rung and persuaded her to let him be the cook for the evening. He'd told her it was by way of apology, as it was his fault that Charlie hadn't phoned when arranged.

Charlie and Stuart had talked it through and had decided not to tell Angela and Joy about Stuart having been in prison. He was right when he said people would treat him differently if they knew.

Angela greeted them warmly.

She was dressed in beige and looked slightly plumper than Charlie had remembered her. Not that he had anything against that. It was good to see her.

'Come on through.' She stood to one side and ushered them in. 'Joy is already here.'

Stuart found the kitchen and started unpacking the food. 'Hope you're all hungry,' he shouted. 'Because this is going to be some meal!'

Charlie, in the sitting-room, flashed a joky look of apprehension at the women. 'I must warn you,' he told them, 'that Stuart fancies himself as another Marco Pierre White. You'll have to remember to massage his ego when the food turns up, or he might just have a super-chef tantrum.'

They laughed.

Joy looked paler and more vulnerable than ever in a light cotton floral frock. Charlie wondered how old she was. Twenty-four, twenty-five? She seemed a lot younger than Angela.

While Angela went to fetch a bottle of wine from the kitchen, Charlie asked Joy if she was living in a flat or a house.

'A bedsit, actually,' Joy smiled apologetically. 'It's a bit rough and ready, but I don't mind.'

'Have you lived in Holby long?'

'Three years. I came up from London for a live-in job – I was the assistant manageress in a small hotel – but it only lasted six months. I took the bedsit, thinking I'd find a flat as soon as I got a decent job, but it's been temporary work on and off since then.' She paused. 'I don't mind temping, though, so it's not too bad.'

Charlie wished he knew of a job he could suggest for her. He would have liked to have helped her, but there wasn't much work about in Holby at the moment, as Stu had discovered.

Angela returned with a bottle of wine, a corkscrew and Twiglets. 'How are things at the hospital?' she asked.

'Fine. Busy.'

'Is it a large casualty department?'

'Maybe not in comparison to some of the big London hospitals, but it's big enough.'

'And are there a lot of staff under you?'

'Depends,' Charlie said. 'There's supposed to be six qualified nurses minimum, but that rarely happens. Then there's the HCAs – health care assistants – and porters, of course.'

Angela twisted the corkscrew into the bottle. 'Do you find it rewarding, nursing?'

'Yes, I do, mostly. There's something very satisfying about helping people.'

'It's a vocation, isn't it?' Joy smiled. 'You need a caring nature to start with.'

'It helps,' Charlie agreed, reaching for the Twiglets.

'What about long-term career prospects?' Angela wanted to know.

'Non-existent, to be honest. I've gone about as far as I can go – without training to be a doctor.'

'And you don't mind that?'

'Not really. I'm fairly happy doing what I do at the moment. I'd be happier if it wasn't so hectic.'

'How about private sector nursing?' Angela sniffed the cork like a connoisseur, then poured the wine.

'There's no comparative job in the private sector.'

'But there must be plenty of scope for a highly experienced nurse. Not in casualty, but some other area of nursing. The pay's a lot better, surely?' She passed a glass of wine each to Joy and Charlie.

'Thanks. There's the principle involved, for a start,' Charlie told her. 'Plus I like being at the sharp end of the hospital system – working where my skill helps save lives. That's a great feeling, you know.'

'So you're happy to be a nurse all your life?'

Charlie took a sip of the dark red liquid. It was good. 'Why not?'

Angela looked aghast. 'How about some branch of hospital management? Have you considered that?'

'That wouldn't be . . . that isn't the sort of thing I'm interested in,' Charlie said. 'It's bad enough trying to prepare the budget statements each month. It isn't what I trained to do.'

'Some people might welcome the new challenge.'

Charlie sipped his wine. Angela's tone was friendly enough, but he got the feeling she disapproved of his lack of ambition. 'What about you? he asked. 'Got your career moves all mapped out?'

It was meant half-jokingly, but Angela took it seriously. She explained that she'd been attending evening school part-time to get a proper qualification as a nursery school teacher, rather than remain a helper. She was hoping to open her own pre-school nursery, and after that, maybe a whole chain of them.

'Wow,' Joy was impressed.

'You've got to use your life, do something productive, make the best you can of it,' Angela said. 'At least, that's how I look at it. If you don't plan for the future, you might end up drifting.'

'Like me,' Joy laughed. 'I've been drifting for the last ten years, since I left school. You've got to know what you want before you can go for it.'

Stu joined them from the kitchen. 'All OK and under control,' he grinned, sitting down very close to Joy. 'It's a disaster area in there already, I'm afraid, but the best cooks make the most mess, eh?' He patted Joy's knee. 'You can clear it up for me if you like. Cook's assistant.'

Angela moved to refill the glasses. 'That's a bit sexist, isn't it, Stuart?'

'Why? I'm doing the cooking. Isn't it only fair that someone else does the washing up?' Stu laughed in the light-hearted, charming way he had, but Charlie was struck by his tone, a tone he hadn't noticed before.

He and Stu were friends, maybe closer now that Charlie knew what Stu had been through. But in unguarded moments that evening Charlie pondered on how little he actually knew about Stu; about the man he had become rather than the person he'd worked with years before. Stuart had always been popular because he was fun to be with, but there was a flip side to that, too. He never seemed to take anything seriously, and his superficial attitude to life could become irritating.

Charlie began to remember how infuriating Stuart had been in the old days. When they'd worked together at St Matthew's, Stuart had always been last to arrive for the shift. He often skived off early to meet some girl or other, Charlie recalled, even when it made extra work for his colleagues. Charlie had personally covered for him a number of times while Stu was out cultivating his reputation as a bit of a Casanova. Charlie had envied him at the time, but now it all seemed a bit silly.

Looking at Joy, and the way she hung on Stuart's every word, Charlie hoped that he'd changed his ways where women were concerned. He didn't want to see Joy hurt.

'So,' Angela clapped her hands, interrupting Charlie's train of thought. 'After we've had this delicious gourmet meal, does anyone fancy going out for a night on the town?'

Charlie tried to hide his dismay. It was all right for them, but he had an early shift in the morning. He couldn't do it. But then, he thought, he'd just met Angela, and he liked her. These first few meetings were so important.

He remembered what Elizabeth Corley had said about letting people know about his feelings. Surely if he couldn't be honest now, then no meaningful relationship could ever develop? 'Sorry,' he said. 'I have to be up incredibly early tomorrow. I can't be out too late.'

'Shift work is always a drag,' Joy sympathised. 'I found that all the time in the hotel business.'

'Yeah. But don't let me stop you three going out.'

Stuart beamed a happy smile. 'How about it, ladies?'

Angela glanced at Charlie. He couldn't tell if she was happy about it or not. 'OK,' she said, slowly. 'Thanks, Stu, I'd love to come.'

15

Charlie dashed past the sluice room, then back-tracked. He looked through the door. Duffy was in there, tearing open a huge carton of papier maché bedpans. 'Duffy, have you got a minute?'

'What is it? Her tone was cold, abrupt. There had been a distance between them all shift.

Charlie stepped into the room. 'I wanted to apologise. For the other day. You and Ash meant well when you came to ask me how I was doing, and I appreciate it. I do, but . . . I've got so much on my mind. Sometimes I lash out, at the wrong time. Even worse, at the wrong people.'

Duffy softened. 'It's OK, Charlie. We've all been through a lot lately.'

Charlie hovered, not sure what else to say. 'OK. Thanks. I just wanted to apologise.'

'By the way,' Duffy told him as he turned to go. 'I heard that Rob's doing OK. His burns are healing up well.'

'Great. He's a good doctor, I learned a lot from him. D'you think he might want to come back to Holby City?'

'No way. His future's all mapped out for him,' Duffy smiled. 'A private consultant. Just like his father.'

Charlie missed Rob. The fire had been tragic for him, and it could have been any one of them. That was the frightening thing.

'It may not be the right time to bring this up, Charlie, but *is* there anything I can do to help?'

'I'm OK.'

'I know. That is, you've been so much more together lately. But you seemed so upset the other day. I couldn't help worrying.'

'I have ups and downs,' Charlie admitted. 'More ups than downs, I hope. That's the idea, anyway. Elizabeth is helping, too.'

'I'm glad,' she said as she stacked the papier mâché shapes in rows on the shelf. 'Funny, isn't it, how telling people about your troubles seems to help? I remember how bad I felt after I'd had Peter. Living on my own, trying to bring up a baby single-handed as well as trying to keep my job. I was terrified of telling people how depressed I felt, because I wanted to be seen to be coping with it all. I thought if I told anyone I couldn't manage, they'd think I was failing as a mother.

'One day Mum came round and there I was, acting all stoical as usual, not letting her do anything. She said, "I suppose you don't want any help?" I said, "I can manage." She said, "I'll take it that you mean the opposite of what you say. You used to do that as a child when you felt under pressure." She just got stuck in,' Duffy smiled. 'She was brilliant after that. She'd known I was too proud to ask for help.'

'Yeah, I know what that's like. Thanks, Duffy.'

Ash came in then. He grinned hello, and deposited a soiled bedpan in the papier mâché grinder. 'This working all right now?' he pointed to the machine.

'As far as I know,' Duffy replied. 'Why?'

Ash flicked the switch and the machine started to hum, first softly, then increasing in volume until it rattled and vibrated like an overloaded spin-dryer.

'That's why!' Ash shouted over the din.

Charlie reached over to switch the machine off. The clatter began to diminish. 'It's been playing up,' he told Duffy. 'I read it in the night sister's report. Apparently it overflowed last night.'

'Ugh!'

'But they called the technician out, and it was supposed to be all right now.'

'Nothing worse than a mucky sluice room. I'll ask Norma to bleep the engineer,' Ash strode out of the room.

'So,' Duffy turned back to Charlie. 'What's happening with this woman you met over at Westbourne Cove?'

Charlie shrugged. 'So far so good, I suppose. I've been out with her a few times. It's been good, but it's the same old story in a way. I work shifts, she works Monday to Friday, nine to five. That makes things difficult. When she wants to go to a nightclub or something, I have to say no. I don't think she realises how crippling it is to come in to work after only three hours' sleep.'

'There was a time when three hours' sleep would have been a luxury for you, Charlie.'

He knew what she meant. She was one of the few people he'd confided in about his insomnia.

'So you're sleeping all right now, are you?'

'Not all right. But better.'

Duffy stepped on the empty cardboard carton to crush it. 'Glad to hear it. Interests outside work make all the difference,' she said bluntly. 'This Angela sounds good for you. And having your friend staying with you, too.'

'Yeah. But the shift work—'

'Plays havoc with your social life. Tell me about it – I've been there. When you're on lates, Angela will complain that you're at your most lively at seven-thirty in the morning.'

He laughed and helped her fold the huge carton into a portable size. 'Angela's not really the complaining type,' he said. 'But sometimes . . . Most of the time it's great. I mean, she's good to talk to. She's lively, funny. But she sees things so differently from me. She thinks nursing is a dead-end job.'

'She may be right.'

Ash came through the door just then. 'Uh-oh. What's this about dead-end jobs, Charlie?' He pointed a warning finger at Charlie. 'Beware of women who want to change you.'

Duffy pushed past him with the empty carton, a wry grin on her face.

'Don't look at me like that. It isn't sexist,' Ash insisted. 'I'm speaking from experience, that's all.'

'Sure. And men never try to change women?' Duffy started along the corridor, but couldn't resist a glance back over her shoulder. She grinned. Ash and Charlie were both frowning. They knew she had a point.

Charlie turned to Ash as they walked along the corridor to Admin. 'Thanks for the advice anyway. And sorry I was so curt with you the other day.'

'Don't worry. I'd forgotten it already.' Ash smiled briefly and then became serious. 'Has Forbes told you what he's planning for us?'

'Planning?'

'As union rep, I was warned that he wants to ban all paid overtime. He says if everyone does their jobs properly there'll be no need for it.'

Charlie shook his head. 'Yeah. I knew he wanted to stop overtime. I didn't think he'd get away with it.'

'Looks like he might. The man's a creep.'

'Agreed. Not only that,' Charlie added. 'I think he's got it in for me.'

'You may be right, old mate. He goes blue in the face when anyone even mentions your name. So what have you done to him?'

'I wish I knew.'

'You haven't crossed him in the past, have you?' Ash wanted to know.

They both stopped to wash their hands at the little basin near the Admin area. It was an habitual thing they did. The sluice room had that effect on people. 'I'm certain I haven't.' Charlie lathered the medical liquid detergent into his hands. 'Or at least, as certain as I can be in a job where you see so many faces all the time.'

'Mysterious, huh?' Ash murmured as he grabbed a paper towel. 'I've got to go. Mike will wonder where I am. He's got a patient waiting in cubicle three.'

'Mike's looking for you-oo,' Duffy yodelled to Ash as she returned from the paper bank. She sat down at the computer VDU and clicked in the details of a patient record as Ash disappeared along the cubicle corridor.

'Maybe Forbes is trying to get in with Mike,' Charlie thought aloud. 'Trying to turn him against me.'

'Mike is too clever for that,' Duffy replied from behind the VDU. 'Forbes has caused too much bad feeling already for Mike not to be on his guard. He'd tell you if he got wind of Forbes trying to do your reputation any harm.'

'Let's hope you're right,' Charlie said with feeling.

'And Forbes knows that we're all on your side.'

As he walked along to his office, Charlie felt touched by the concern that Ash and Duffy had shown him over the Gavin Forbes matter. He'd forgotten just how supportive his staff could be, how concerned and loyal. It was strange how, when he'd been so down himself, he'd chosen to hold them at a distance, so that when they tried to help him – which they had, repeatedly – he hadn't allowed himself to respond.

Ash and Mike came up behind him. 'Have you got a minute?' Mike asked. They all entered Charlie's office. 'Just a few words,' Mike said. 'I can't stop.'

'It's about your favourite man,' Ash grinned.

'Not Forbes?'

' 'Fraid so,' said Mike. 'Ash here mentioned that you think Forbes has got it in for you. I don't know about that – not for sure. But I want you to be careful. He overstepped the mark the other day, virtually accusing you of theft. Now, no one will take that seriously. But he's been hinting that A and E isn't running as efficiently as it might, and that it's your fault.'

'Great!' Charlie groaned.

'I've already crossed swords with him,' Mike admitted. 'A and E is my department, too, and I won't have people slagging it off. Or making accusations.'

'It's pure intimidation,' Ash said.

'That's right,' Mike agreed. 'Forbes is a petty dictator, nothing more.'

'Play it cool, Charlie,' Ash advised. 'He's just waiting for you to lose your rag.'

'Anyway,' Mike stood with his hand on the door handle. 'Forewarned is forearmed, eh? Don't worry too much. When Forbes' persecution tactics prove unsuccessful, he'll probably amuse himself with someone else.'

It was all very well for Mike to say that, Charlie thought, when Ash and Mike had gone on their way, but he was worried. Forbes wanted him out. Why seemed almost irrelevant. The man was clearly unethically power-hungry. And dangerous.

Charlie's thoughts were interrupted by the loud beep-beep-beep of the crash alarm. And Forbes calls us inefficient, Charlie thought, as he joined the mêlée of staff scrambling along the corridor towards resusc.

16

'It's normal to worry,' Elizabeth told Charlie when he next visited her consulting room. 'Everyone worries. The trick is not to let it take over your life.'

'Not easy when you've discovered that someone has got it in for you,' Charlie pointed out. He looked across at Elizabeth. She seemed unusually stern, as though she'd had a bad day herself.

'I'm not saying you don't have reason to be concerned, Charlie,' she told him. 'What I'm saying is that you have to find ways of making sure it doesn't take over. Stress control, among other things, is about getting things into perspective.'

'Tell that to Forbes.'

'You don't know why he bears you a grudge. But let's look at what you do know. You are good at your job. You are a respected, long-standing member of staff at Holby City. You are surrounded by loyal colleagues and friends. And, most important, you haven't done anything wrong. You have all this going for you, whereas this Forbes is nothing more than a new broom, already unpopular by all accounts. So how much worry is this individual worth?'

Charlie brightened. 'When you put it like that . . .'

'I've merely stated the facts. What I'm concerned about is that you might be expecting too much, too soon. You're not going to get back to your old self overnight.'

Charlie stared over her shoulder at the slatted blind. He hardly remembered who his old self was.

'Let's look at it in terms of your own work, and you'll see what I mean. If someone comes into Casualty with a broken arm, you don't treat it and say, "That's it. Completely better." You say, "The healing process has started. Now it needs time." Emotional upheaval takes longer to heal than physical troubles. You know that.'

'Yes,' Charlie nodded. 'But it doesn't stop me feeling frustrated at times.'

'You are on the mend, Charlie. You know that yourself. Remember how you were that first day you came to see me? You're so much more positive now. Why, even your appearance has changed dramatically since then.'

Charlie flushed, realising she was referring to his personal grooming. 'You mean because I got my hair cut and started shaving regularly?'

'Small things, maybe. But to me they are sure signs of recovery. They denote an increase in self-awareness and self-respect.'

'My real problem,' Charlie confided, 'is that I feel great one moment, when there's no pressure at work, or whatever, then all it takes is for one thing to go wrong and I'm suddenly plunged into the depths of despair. It comes on just like that, instantaneously. All of a sudden everything becomes insurmountable. Either that, or it all becomes completely meaningless and pointless.'

'When that happens next time, I want you to sit down for a moment. Go somewhere where you can be alone,' Elizabeth told him. 'If it's frenzied at work, the lavatory might be a good place. Sit down and go through a list of good things about yourself. Think of your good attributes, about how well you do your job when you're not being forced into impossibly tight corners. Tell yourself how brilliantly you're doing in the face of the mania around you. Think of yourself as a genuinely valuable person. I promise you it will help.'

Charlie looked dubious. 'I'll give it a go.'

'Good, and now that you've started on the imipramine, you'll find these things getting easier anyway.'

'The imipramine.' Charlie coughed. 'I threw them away.'

'Why, Charlie?'

'Maybe I've seen too many patients in A and E addicted to anti-depressants or tranquillisers, even minor ones. I used to work with a wonderful woman – Megan – who got addicted to diazepam. It almost ruined her life. I know that a course of any anxiety-decreasing drug can be dangerous. Drug addiction is all too easy, no matter how useful they may be in the first instance. Imipramine might be an anti-depressant, but I've seen people when they come off it. Now that's what I call *depressed*.'

'Those highly publicised cases are rare. There are a number of contributory factors – including the personality of the patient.'

'Nevertheless,' said Charlie, 'I'm not going to take them. With all respect. I'm in the profession. I know what I'm taking about. Also, a few years ago – after the death of a very dear friend – I found out how easy it is to fall into a habit. In that case it was alcohol. But it cured me of ever wanting to be dependent on a drug again.'

Charlie's adamant look was clear. 'OK,' Elizabeth raised her hand. 'Fair enough. Let's try it your way.' She paused, then smiled. 'Actually, I'm pleased that you feel so strongly about this. Apathy is the most obvious sign of continuing depression, as I'm sure you know. Perhaps, now that you're feeling stronger, you could try opening up with people even further.'

'I'm doing all right with that,' said Charlie. 'I'm on a better footing already with people at work. Duffy and Ash . . .'

'Last time you came, you mentioned a woman. Angela? How are you getting on with her, communication-wise?'

'Could be better,' he admitted. 'I mean, I know Duffy

well. It wasn't so daunting opening up to her a bit more. But Angela? I'm being nice to her all the time, which is maybe overdoing it a bit. But I don't want to scare her off. What would she say if I told her that I was up to my eyes in problems?'

'She might want to help.'

'Yeah,' he drawled sarcastically. 'Women want men who'll support them, not weaklings who offload their problems. That's my experience, anyway. Maybe that's why I've always had trouble holding down relationships.'

'That's very negative, Charlie,' she told him. 'Negative thoughts like that are cyclical. If you believe that you'll fail, then the chances are that you *will* fail. What you need to do is break that cycle. Do something positive. Buy her some flowers, go and see her, explain how you feel about your relationship. Ask her if she thinks you're doing OK.'

'And if she rejects me?'

'Negative again! She won't reject you. But if she does, at least she'll respect your honesty.'

'I can't talk to people like that,' Charlie gasped. 'I simply couldn't do it.'

'That's interesting,' Elizabeth murmured. 'Why not?'

'I just couldn't.'

'Think about why not when you go home,' Elizabeth told him. 'And see if you can bring up the subject of your relationship with Angela, next time you see her. Don't worry too much if you find that you can't. Don't pressure yourself into doing anything before you feel ready.'

'I'll see.'

'You might find it exhilarating. Being absolutely honest with someone that you care for. The difficult thing is to take the plunge, to say the first few words.'

'Right.'

'Time's up. I'm afraid. We'll have to talk some more about this next session.'

Charlie got up to leave. Elizabeth was always setting

him tasks. Every time he thought he'd achieved what she wanted him to achieve, she came up with something else. Just thinking about talking so openly with Angela made him blush with embarrassment. He wondered why it made him feel so uncomfortable. After all, what Elizabeth had suggested was sensible enough, and buying flowers was no big deal. The scary thing was the thought of asking Angela: 'What do you honestly think of me?'

'Remember, Charlie,' Elizabeth said as he opened the door. 'Expect ups and downs. Be prepared. That way they won't be so debilitating.'

17

Charlie's evening got off to a bad start. The charge nurse on the next shift turned up late today of all days. He cursed his bad luck as he hurried along to the cinema. He'd arranged to meet Angela at six-thirty so they'd make the early screening. He glanced at his watch: ten to seven. As he neared the Odeon he spotted her waiting outside. She was facing him, but looking down at the pavement. The annoyance on her face was clear.

'Hiya,' he called out as he approached. 'Sorry. Usually I can get away on time, but my replacement was late and there were one or two tricky patients who couldn't be left on their own.'

'I should be learning by now that you're more likely to be late than early. Perhaps I should be pleased that you turn up at all. Is it always like this with nurses?'

Angela didn't seem particularly angry, just resigned and slightly bored.

'You might say it comes with the job,' Charlie smiled, trying to lighten things up.

Angela nodded. 'We've only missed the very beginning of the film. Do you want to try creeping in now?'

'Listen, why don't we go for something to eat, then come back for the later showing? My treat.'

'OK.'

'Pizza?'

'Fine.'

When they got to the restaurant, Charlie tried to pluck

up the courage to tell Angela how he felt about her, and to ask her how she felt about him. It seemed the perfect place to do it. But each time he was about to start, there would be an interruption. The waiter came to check their order, or their drinks arrived.

'So,' Angela asked him, as they started on their pizza. 'What have you been up to?'

'Actually,' he said, 'I went to see my counsellor yesterday.' At last, he thought, I've mentioned it.

'Counsellor?'

'Her name's Elizabeth Corley. She's a stress counsellor.'

'But why do you need to go to a stress counsellor?' Angela didn't make any attempt to lower her voice.

Charlie winced and glanced around to see if anyone was listening. There was no sign of interest, although people at adjoining tables could clearly hear what Angela was saying. 'There's been a lot of hassle at work recently,' he told her, quietly. 'It's only a temporary thing.'

'Why don't you talk to your family and friends?' she asked, as though he'd said something unbelievably stupid. 'That's the best stress therapy you can get, as far as I'm concerned. It's outrageous that there are people charging money for something that could be done equally well over a cup of coffee at home. It's become fashionable to go to therapists. It's the thing to do. It makes us feel that we're complicated and important.'

Charlie wanted to sink low into his chair, forget the whole thing. But he resisted. 'I'm sure it's great to be able to get things off your chest to your family, but not everyone has family. And then not always locally.'

'What about friends?' asked Angela stolidly, refusing to be deflected from her point.

'It's difficult to talk to my friends at work, because they're going through enough as it is without me burdening them.'

'Counsellors aren't necessary,' she insisted.

Charlie realised she wasn't going to be sympathetic. 'It's not a big deal. I get set little exercises to do.'

'Like what?'

'Oh. You know. Talking to people. That kind of thing.'

'You need a counsellor to tell you to do that? I can't believe that anyone would have trouble simply talking. You're doing OK with me, aren't you?'

'I hope so.'

She frowned thoughtfully. 'Have you got some kind of problem?'

Charlie wished he hadn't mentioned it now. But in for a penny. 'Not really. Just work. It can be incredibly stressful.' He speared an olive on his pizza. 'You know. Life-and-death situations, on a daily basis. Some of it . . . well, some of it is pretty gruesome. There's no point talking about it. Not while we're eating.'

'It's OK,' said Angela. 'Don't stop. I'm not squeamish. I'm interested.'

If only she'd seen some of the things I have, Charlie thought. 'Some of the injuries I see are appalling,' he began. 'Some of them stay with me for days, keep flashing into my mind. Some I'll never forget. And that's only a part of it.' He glanced up. Angela seemed riveted. She carried on eating, but her eyes never left his face.

'Then there's the friends and relatives of the patients – we deal with them, too. That can get hairy. Especially when they're traumatised or can't take in what has happened. They go into shock themselves and need treatment. Also there's the whole business of breaking the news to relatives when someone dies. Sometimes I'm so busy I only have a minute or so to get it over with. It seems so impersonal, sometimes.' Charlie's pizza was getting cold. He cut himself another slice.

'I hadn't realised you had to do all that,' Angela said, chewing. 'Which do you find the most difficult?'

'I don't know. There isn't a *most* difficult . . . except maybe the time you have on your own, later. When you mull it over. You wonder if things wouldn't have been better if you'd done something different with a particular patient. I had a patient the other day who'd been mugged. He was out for a walk down by the river and he was mugged for the couple of quid he had in his pocket. I knew he was seriously traumatised, but we've only got the time to treat the physical symptoms. I didn't have time to stop and talk it through with him and I felt bad about that.'

Angela was silent for a few moments as Charlie ate. She took a sip of wine and then looked at him kindly. 'It must be upsetting,' she said. 'But surely you get used to it? Isn't that why you chose to work in Casualty? If you can't cope with these things, then maybe you should transfer to another area of nursing.'

'That's what I was trying to explain earlier, only I expressed it badly. I love my job. Ninety-nine times out of a hundred it's fine. I can cope. Only one per cent of the time it gets too much.'

Charlie could see she wasn't convinced. Why should she be? She'd never experienced the chaos of a busy casualty department. He began to realise how far apart their lives were. Not always a bad thing, of course. But he sensed that they were on different wavelengths, too. He found it as difficult to understand her point of view as she did his. Fine, it was a great idea to become a nursery school teacher. But Angela viewed it almost as a business arrangement, as though the kids she'd be teaching were simply a commodity from which she could make money. He didn't understand that way of thinking at all. It worked much better, he thought, when they went out as a foursome with Stuart and Joy.

'Enough of me,' he shrugged, smiling, trying to change the tone. 'There's this bloke at work, Gavin Forbes. He really is a little Hitler type. The other day he came up to me and—'

He stopped abruptly. Angela was deep in thought. It was clear she hadn't heard a word of it. 'Sorry, Charlie,' she said, noticing he'd stopped speaking. 'I just remembered something I must do tomorrow. Go on.'

'It's OK,' he muttered. 'Shall we get the bill?'

Charlie paid and they left the restaurant. He felt subdued by Angela's preoccupation, but decided to have another go at conversation. 'I wondered,' he said as they walked, 'would you like to come out to a concert some time? There's a jazz club at The Derwent, and they're doing Monteverdi's Vespers down at St Bartholomew's Church next week. I don't know that much about classical music myself, but we could give it a go if you like.'

'Thanks, Charlie, but you don't have to make so much of an effort. Going to the cinema is fine. I've been looking forward to seeing this film for ages. I love Jeremy Irons.'

'Oh, is he in it?' Charlie asked. 'He's pretty good, isn't he?'

'I always go and see his films.'

Charlie heaved a sigh of relief that they had at last found something that they could both agree on.

They got to their seats as the advertisements were starting. Charlie hadn't been to the cinema for a year or so, so most of the ads were new to him. One of the old ones that he recognised, for a local optician, featured a woman who reminded him of Joy. The ad was years old, so it couldn't have been her. But the likeness was striking.

'Looks a bit like Joy,' Angela murmured.

'Yes,' he said. 'Doesn't she?'

As the ad ended, he realised that he'd felt a sudden jolt when he'd seen the woman on the screen. He found himself thinking of Joy more and more these days. Perhaps he and Stuart had got the wrong women. Angela seemed much more Stu's type. Joy wasn't his type, she seemed very fond of Stuart, and she hadn't shown any interest in him.

'Do you know much about Joy, then?' he asked Angela, as the ads came to an end.

'Not really. Only that she's infatuated with Stuart. I've met her a couple of times since we went to Westbourne Cove, and she rings every few days or so. She isn't what you'd call a feminist. All she talks about is Stuart. As far as I can tell, she just sits by the phone every day waiting for him to call.'

'They make a good couple, don't they?' Charlie said.

18

Charlie was beginning to wish he'd never given Stu that reference. 'What did you do?' he asked, putting the latest letter back in the envelope. 'Photocopy it and hand it out to every bank and estate agent in town?'

Stu sipped his coffee and smiled. 'Come on, Charlie. It's not as bad as all that.'

'No?' Charlie scratched his head. In the last week he'd received eight letters from financial institutions. 'I never thought of you as an entrepreneur, I suppose. I don't mind saying you're a trustworthy citizen and all the rest of it, but I'm sorry, I can't act as loan guarantor.'

'I wouldn't ask you to.'

'Most of these letters and forms do.'

'Take it easy,' Stu soothed. 'The banks are going through the formalities, that's all.'

Charlie wasn't so sure. He'd never so much as seen a loan guarantor form until Stuart had turned up – or Matthew Frazer, as some of the forms referred to him. 'What have you been doing for the last few days, anyway?' Charlie asked. 'I've hardly seen you.'

'Trying to get a business venture off the ground. You should be pleased.'

'I am. So what sort of venture is it?'

'All in good time. It may be superstition on my part, but I hate to talk about deals until I've pulled them off. Don't worry, Charlie boy. You'll be the first to know. Wangling the finance is proving tough.'

'Sorry I can't help you out on that side,' Charlie said.

'You've helped me more than enough already, Charlie. I owe you.'

Charlie felt strangely at sea with Stuart. He was being very secretive about this business venture. 'I wish you'd give me a hint at least. What type of business?'

Stuart ignored the question. 'If I can get it off the ground, it can't fail. Anyway, I must go. Got a possible investor lined up.'

Charlie felt deflated by Stu's imminent departure. 'See you later, then.'

'Want to meet for a quick drink at The Pig in Paradise before you go in to work? If I've persuaded this guy to cough up, I'll tell you the whole deal.'

'OK. One o'clock?'

'See you there.'

'By the way,' Charlie called after him. 'What should I say if Joy phones? She's rung two or three times already.'

Stuart returned. He thought for a moment. 'Tell her I'll see her at her place tonight. Six – no, seven o'clock.'

'Good luck,' Charlie grinned. 'You've certainly dressed up for it. You look like a true executive.'

Stu grinned back. 'Must make an effort to look the part.'

When he'd gone, Charlie busied himself in the kitchen for a while. After his bout of cleaning, there wasn't that much to do, apart from washing up. He hummed as he did it, feeling content.

The phone rang at twelve-thirty, just before he was due to leave for the pub. It was Joy. 'Is Stu there?'

'You missed him again, I'm afraid,' Charlie told her.

'He always seems to have just gone out, lately,' she complained.

'Sorry. But he did ask me to tell you that he'd be round at your place at seven this evening.'

'Oh. Thanks,' Joy sounded brighter. He imagined her smiling at the other end of the line. 'Thanks, Charlie.'

When he got to The Pig in Paradise, Stuart was already there. He didn't look too happy, though. The meeting hadn't gone well. The man wasn't prepared to back him. The frustrating thing was, Stu said, that he'd already raised enough money for the business. All he needed was premises. 'I'll keep searching,' he said.

'What kind of premises do you need?'

Stu sighed. 'I might as well tell you what this is all about.' He took a swig of his beer as Charlie sipped an orange juice. 'My plan,' he leaned forward and spoke conspiratorially, 'is to work as an agent for companies advertising their products on cable and satellite TV. You know, TV shopping. The punter sees a product advertised, along with a phone number, and rings to order it.'

'Sounds a bit specialised,' Charlie muttered.

'But very simple. Suppose you were a company that wanted to sell videos of 1960s music. I'd organise the advertising slot on TV, book it – even arrange to have the advert made, if necessary. At my premises, I'd have telephonists waiting for the orders to come in. We'd pass on lists of the punters' details to suppliers so that they didn't need any sales staff themselves. Everyone's happy. The videos sell. I make my percentage. Simple.'

'What is it that you make the money on, then?' Charlie asked.

'Everything. That's the beauty of it.' Stuart drained his beer. 'I get a cut from the goods supplier, a cut from the TV channel and a percentage of sales. All I need is a couple of big sellers and I'll be in the money.'

'It sounds great. There must be a hitch somewhere.'

Stu shook his head. 'It's such a new market that not many people have cottoned on yet. Very big in America, TV shopping. Everyone I've talked to is excited about it, but none of them have had sufficient funds to get the project off the ground.'

'Be careful, Stu,' Charlie warned. 'It's a good idea, but

there is no such thing as a sure-fire winner. Anyway, how can you get people to lend you money if you've got a criminal record.'

'I'm keeping quiet about that.'

'Is that wise? I mean, what if people find out?'

'When this succeeds, it won't matter if they find out or not. They'll get their money back. That's all that matters.'

'I suppose so.'

'Like I said, I want to put all that prison business behind me, Charlie. And I value my freedom too much to risk anything illegal. So there's no need to deliver a pep talk, if that's what you were planning.'

'I wasn't.' Charlie understood why Stuart wanted to keep quiet about his criminal record, but deceit of any kind made him feel uncomfortable. 'It must have been a terrible experience, prison,' he said.

'It was. But one thing I realised,' Stuart said, 'is that it can happen to anyone. There were loads of ordinary people in there. We're told, all our lives, that there are ordinary people and there are criminals. We think that criminals are different, but it's not true. There is no difference.'

Charlie wasn't quite sure exactly what Stu meant by that, or whether he agreed. But as Stuart went to the bar to fetch another beer and fruit juice, Charlie found himself wishing he could help more. 'Would it help if I let you stay on rent-free for a while?' he asked when Stuart returned.

'That would be brilliant.' Stuart sat down and grinned. 'Are you sure, though?'

'I wouldn't have offered otherwise.'

'Only until I'm up and running, OK?'

'Whatever you say.'

'Cheers, then.' Stuart held out his glass to toast Charlie. 'To the future.'

'To the future.'

Charlie felt a little embarrassed, but he was touched by Stu's obvious gratitude. 'By the way,' he said. 'Joy phoned. I told her you'd be round.'

'Blast, I forgot about that.'

'Is it a problem?'

'Not really. I like her, but she's a bit clingy. I feel as though she's hounding me sometimes. Besides, I met a couple of interesting girls at the Town Hall business exhibition this morning and I tentatively arranged to meet them later. I thought you might want to come along, after work.'

'No, thanks.' He thought for a moment. 'I thought you were going out with Joy.'

'Going out with her, yeah, not married to her. These two girls are from London. They're staying at the Great Western for a couple of nights and wanted someone to show them the town. It's only a one night stand, for God's sake, Charlie. Why don't you come along? It'll do you the world of good.'

'I may not be finished till late tonight,' Charlie pointed out.

'OK, OK,' Stuart said defensively. 'But don't say I didn't ask.'

As Charlie set off from the pub, he whistled to himself. Stuart was incredible! He was exactly the same, as far as Charlie could tell, as when he was a student in his twenties. There was something almost grotesque, he thought, in Stuart's schoolboyish attitude to women.

19

'Charlie?' A head popped through the cubicle curtain. 'There's someone at Reception for you.'

'Who is it?'

Duffy, who was busy readjusting a saline drip for an unconscious RTA victim, glanced up at him.

'She says her name's Angela.'

'Angela? Tell her I'll be with her as soon as I can.'

Duffy smiled across at Charlie. 'In the end they always get curious about exactly what it is we do,' she said with a grin. 'I knew she'd turn up one of these days.'

Charlie smiled shyly, almost embarrassed, as he finished applying a dressing to the patient's shin. He was pleased that Angela had come in. Was pleased that Duffy had noticed. But she hadn't chosen the best of times.

'I can manage for five minutes,' Duffy said.

'Are you sure?' Even as Charlie asked, he knew the answer. They'd fixed the patient up as best they could for the moment, and Mike was waiting for the x-rays to come back.

'Go on. It's not every day you get visited by a lady friend.'

'I'll be in the coffee bar then. Five minutes.'

He walked quickly down to Reception. Angela sat uncomfortably wedged between a noisy, blood-smeared drunk and a distressed young teenager. In the corner, a porter argued loudly with a volunteer sandwich lady about the price of a bar of chocolate. The noise level fell slightly as the teenager was led away towards a cubicle by a nurse.

Charlie was pleased to see her. He could do with being cheered up this evening, which had been busier than most. Angela looked a little shocked and, as he approached, he became concerned. 'Are you all right, Angela?'

'Fine,' she said, with a slight smile. 'I've never been in a casualty department before. I didn't think there'd be injured people sitting around like this.'

'It is pretty busy tonight,' he told her. 'But it can get worse, believe me.'

'I was in the area,' she explained. 'I thought I'd pop in and see where you work. I don't suppose you can get any time off?'

'I can manage five minutes.' He led the way through to the coffee bar. As they walked, people rushed past them in the corridor.

'Are you sure? It seems hectic.'

'They know where I am. If they need me, they'll bleep me, don't worry.'

They bought a couple of coffees and carried them over to a free corner. 'I'm glad you came,' he told her. 'It's the first chance I've had to get off my feet for hours.' He sat down opposite her and smiled. She was looking good tonight in a pair of jeans and a pale mauve sweater. 'Are we still on for tomorrow?' he asked as he relished his first sip of coffee.

'Mmm.' She looked down at her drink for a moment, then up at Charlie. 'Well, actually, no. What I really came here for was . . . I don't think this thing between us is working out.'

'What?'

'You must have noticed it too, Charlie. We like each other well enough, but we don't exactly spark off each other, do we? It dawned on me this morning that I don't actively look forward to our dates. And we haven't got very far, romantically, have we?'

'It needs a little time, Angela, I . . .'

Charlie was so taken aback that he couldn't find the words.

'I'm not blaming you, Charlie. Both parties have to want to take things further. But it's not there between us. I think that's true for you as much as for me. You've been honest with me, it's the thing I've admired most about you. You deserved some honesty in return.'

'But I had no idea.'

'We have almost nothing in common, Charlie. You have your nursing,' she paused and looked around her. 'And your dedication is admirable. But I'm ambitious. I couldn't have a successful relationship with someone who didn't want to push for bigger and better things.'

'We have different approaches to life,' he said. 'So? I can accept yours if you accept mine.'

'This shift work is another problem. What time is it – nine o'clock? – and—'

Ash interrupted them. He smiled hello at Angela and leaned over to talk to Charlie. 'Susan and Jackie from the night shift have broken down out at Hewley Down on their way in,' he explained, rolling his eyes. 'They're stuck thirty miles outside Holby and the break-down truck can't get to them for an hour and a half, minimum.'

Charlie was still looking at Angela in disbelief. He blinked a couple of times, then turned to Ash and took a deep breath. 'OK. Organise a couple of agency replacements, could you?'

'I'd love to, Charlie, but Forbes has removed all the agency files.'

'What?' Charlie frowned. 'Right. Give me a minute and I'll be through.' He watched Ash's receding back for a moment or two before turning to Angela.

'Sorry about that. Just another routine hassle at work.'

'I'm sorry. This is an insensitive time and place to broach this subject. I had no idea that it was going to be like this or I wouldn't have come here. We can still go to the cinema tomorrow, if you like. So long as you realise that it's as friends and not as – whatever it was that we were.'

Charlie shook his head. 'I'm glad you told me,' he sighed. 'You're right to stop things before they get too far. It's my fault. I shouldn't have told you about the therapy.'

'Don't be silly. No one's to blame.'

'Let me phone you in a few weeks' time,' he suggested. 'See how you feel about things then.'

'No, Charlie. Let's call it quits. The whole dating scene is a gamble anyway, isn't it? Very few dates turn into successful relationships, otherwise there wouldn't be so many dating agencies.'

Charlie couldn't think what to say to that. He sat feeling utterly forlorn. 'I'm sorry.' He got to his feet. 'But I have to get back to work.'

She held out her hand. 'Well, I hope you find someone who's right for you. You deserve it.'

They shook hands, then she leaned forward and kissed his cheek. 'Goodbye, Charlie.'

As he walked back to Reception, he realised that it was the first time she'd kissed him.

On the way past the waiting area, he spotted Ash, calming the drunk with the bloodied face. Even Ash had a broken relationship. Why couldn't people get on with each other? It made no sense. Charlie and Angela were both honest, sensible people. But that, it seemed, wasn't enough. So, what *did* it take?

Charlie was washing his hands when Ash found him. 'Well?' Ash asked. 'Have you found a solution?'

'I think,' said Charlie, bewildered, 'I think we've got to learn to understand one another better.'

Ash frowned. 'Eh?'

'What? Oh, sorry. The nurses. Right. Come along to my office and we'll sort it out.'

But they found they couldn't sort it out. Charlie got his address book out and rang a couple of off-duty nurses, but they all as good as laughed at him. He couldn't get agency nurses in, and he wasn't able to pay his own staff to work overtime. His hands were tied. There was nothing he could do – except allow a busy casualty department to become mayhem. 'Forbes should see the place when it's like this. He's happily tucked up in his cosy bed, oblivious. It makes me sick.' Charlie picked up his address book and hurled it across the office.

20

An hour had passed since Charlie had talked to Angela. He was in his office trying to fill in some of his patient report forms. The only problem was that he kept reading the same forms over and over again, without taking them in. It was infuriating. He had more than enough work to be getting on with, without sitting around doing nothing. He put his head in his hands, briefly, and thought of Elizabeth Corley. How he wished he could talk to her now! His next appointment seemed an age away.

She'd been right. It was good to confide in people. But in this case, with Angela, it had backfired. Deep down, he knew it wasn't his fault, but that's the way it appeared at the moment. If only he'd approached it differently. Made an effort to be more solicitous. What if he'd been more forceful, outgoing? Perhaps he would have been more successful.

But then, he thought, raising his head and staring at the wall, that wouldn't have been me. Not really. So what good would it have done in the long run? No, he'd done the right thing. It hadn't worked, that's all. Nobody was to blame. It worked out that way sometimes. Then why did it feel as if he was to blame for Angela's reaction?

Let's face it, Charlie thought, there's not many women who'd happily fit in with your lifestyle. You work too hard, and people like Gavin Forbes are trying to ensure that you work even harder.

Duffy knocked briefly, then entered the office. 'Hi,' she

smiled cheerfully. 'The nosebleed in cubicle five is under control, so I won't have to pack it after all.'

She sat down with a sigh and put her feet up on the side of the wastepaper basket. Despite the fact that she was also overworked, she looked vibrant, dynamic – thriving, in fact. It amazed Charlie that she could be so lively. But then, that's how he'd been as well – until they'd lumbered him with all the extra responsibility of being clinical manager. The extra workload had worried him when he'd accepted his new job description. But then, what choice did he have? Maybe it wasn't a question of the workload, as much as his attitude to it.

'Bliss,' she sighed. 'To get the weight off my feet for a minute or two.' It was only then that she looked at Charlie properly.

'Problems?' she asked, noticing his expression.

Charlie shrugged.

'Did Angela bring bad news? I saw her leaving earlier. She looks nice.'

'She is nice.'

'Well, that's good then, isn't it?'

'Not really. She's dumped me.'

'You're joking! Surely not?'

'Do I look like I'm joking? She came all the way here to tell me. I suppose it does her credit that she told me to my face. Still, given my history with women, why am I surprised that she decided to pack it in before it got started?'

Duffy reached out and placed her hand on Charlie's shoulder. 'It must be a blow for you Charlie. I don't know what to say.'

'Neither do I.' He shuffled the papers on the desk. 'The thing that really got me,' he said, 'is that I didn't see it coming. It didn't occur to me, when I saw her in Reception, that she might have come all this way to ditch me.'

Mike Barratt opened the door. 'Greetings,' he said. 'Sorry to interrupt, but have you got the patient notes for David Greig?'

Charlie flicked through his pile. 'Yup. One of the few I've managed to complete. Just as well you don't want any of the others.'

'I heard that your girlfriend came in to see you this evening.' Mike tapped the door frame with the notes. 'You don't seem that happy about it.'

'Girlfriend,' Charlie laughed grimly. 'People are quick with the gossip, aren't they?' He took a deep breath. 'She isn't my girlfriend. She's looking for someone who's a high-flier. Someone who wants to bulldoze their way to the top of their profession. Someone forceful and probably a bit ruthless. I'm definitely *not* her man.'

Mike exchanged looks with Duffy and got the message.

'Why am I such a failure with women?' Charlie sighed.

'You can't win, sometimes,' Mike told him. 'Most women complain that pushy men are too macho, or sexist. When we try to be understanding or sensitive, they brand us wimps. Don't take it too badly, Charlie, we've all been through it.'

'The stupid part of it is,' Charlie shook his head sadly, 'that at the back of my mind I knew all along. I knew it wasn't working, but didn't want to face it or accept it. The signs were there from the start.' He gave a tired smile. 'Why do I feel so upset?'

'Pride?' Mike suggested.

'I doubt it. Sometimes I feel as if I have no pride left.'

Mike's bleeper went off. 'Got to go,' he said, switching it off and smiling ruefully at Charlie. 'You'll be OK. This woman obviously wasn't for you.'

'How's it going with Stuart?' Duffy asked, with the air of someone changing the subject, as soon as Mike had gone.

'Fine. Though I haven't got as much in common with

him as I thought I had. In the old days we were too busy going out and getting drunk to notice. But Stu's all right. It's good to have the company.'

'I'd better get back,' she said, getting up.

'Thanks for listening.'

'I wish you'd confide in me more often, Charlie.' She paused at the door. 'We all care about you, you know. Listen, do you fancy coming round to my place tomorrow? A light lunch before the shift. How about it?'

'Thanks Duffy, but I'm too busy. Really. It would be too much trouble for you, anyway, with little Peter and Andrew—'

'There you go again,' she interrupted. 'Assuming that it would be a trouble and not a pleasure for me. You're wrong. I wouldn't have invited you if I didn't mean it. I'd love to see you away from work for a change. Please come, or are you doing something more important tomorrow lunchtime?'

'I haven't got anything on.'

'I'll expect you around twelve, then.'

'Right,' he smiled. 'You've got me there. I'll come.'

'Good.'

'How is Peter?'

'Great. He's three now, getting into everything. Won't stop chatting. But you'll see for yourself tomorrow. Andrew's going to be there, too.'

'It'll be nice to see him again. Hang on,' Charlie pushed his reports aside and stood up. 'I can't concentrate on these. I'll come with you.'

'It's going to be a long shift,' sighed Duffy. 'It feels like I've been here forever already.'

'Thanks for agreeing to stay till Susan and Jackie get here.'

'It's no more than you're doing.'

As Charlie walked down to Reception to call the next patient, Susan and Jackie burst through the flap doors of the walking wounded entrance, looking breathless but cheerful.

'You got here then?' Charlie laughed. 'You look like you've run all the way. We weren't expecting you for another half-hour at least.'

'A police car stopped and picked us up,' Jackie explained. 'They brought us into Holby and dropped us at the ambulance station. Josh and Jane brought us over in the ambulance – sirens, flashing lights, the works!'

'Good luck. It's busy, busy, busy and I don't mind admitting I've had a hard day.'

21

Charlie sat on Duffy's sofa, watching Andrew jiggling Peter up and down on his knee. Peter was squealing and giggling with pleasure. He was a lovely child, happy and smiling every time Charlie saw him. Duffy came in with a tray of coffee and a glass of freshly squeezed orange juice for Peter.

The signs of their relative affluence were everywhere – in the quality of the food they ate, the dining chairs they sat on, the clothes they wore. Of course, Andrew was a consultant, so his salary was considerably higher than Charlie's. 'Thanks for lunch,' he said. 'It was delicious.'

As well as being aware of how happy Peter was, Charlie couldn't help notice how well Duffy and Andrew got on together. And he knew it wasn't just a show being put on for his sake. This was a genuinely happy family. Earlier, Charlie had sat and watched as both Duffy and Andrew played with Peter. At one point, Peter had come over to show him one of his books, and his fresh, excited smile had touched Charlie deeply.

In other circumstances, he'd thought, I might have had children, perhaps a son like Peter.

It would be wonderful to be a father, he thought. He remembered when Euro Disney had first opened. He'd thought to himself that he would never go there unless he had a family. It had made him yearn for children, an emotion that he'd never felt so strongly before. Perhaps the feeling had been so powerful because, for the first time, it had occurred to him that time was beginning to run out.

'You're looking thoughtful,' Andrew remarked as Peter ran across the thick carpet to Duffy.

'I was thinking how lucky you two are,' Charlie said. 'Peter is a wonderful boy.'

'Yes,' Andrew smiled across at Duffy. 'We count our blessings, don't we, darling?'

'Absolutely,' she agreed. 'But you'll have kids one day, Charlie.'

'I'm not so sure now,' he said. 'I'm getting on. Approaching middle age.'

'It's simply a case of finding the right woman,' she told him.

'And you may find one where you least expect it,' Andrew added. 'It may very well turn out unexpectedly, too.'

Charlie had almost forgotten. It hadn't been lovey-dovey all the way for Duffy and Andrew, although it was easy to imagine that they'd always been blissful, seeing them like this. But they'd had tough times, too. Duffy, he remembered, had walked out on Andrew when she'd found herself pregnant. She'd brought Peter up on her own for more than two years before they were reconciled. And now, here they were, married. Happy.

Perhaps there's hope for me yet. I shouldn't be so negative about my prospects, Charlie told himself. Duffy had struck rock bottom a couple of years ago, and look at her now.

'I could imagine you as a father,' Andrew told Charlie. 'And a grandfather! You have just the right bearing. Approachable but in control.'

'I've got far too much on my plate to think about having kids,' Charlie lied. 'Even without people like Gavin Forbes making life difficult for me.'

'Gavin Forbes?'

'You know,' Duffy reminded him. 'That administrator who took over from Simon Eastman. He came waltzing in from nowhere and started dictating to everyone what they should and shouldn't be doing.'

'It's all very well to treat a hospital as a business,' said Andrew. 'It is nowadays. But administrators don't have any hands-on dealings with the patients. It's easy for them to lose sight of the fact that patients are not units of measurement, they are real human beings that require human input as well as medical attention.'

'Tell that to Gavin Forbes,' Charlie muttered.

'And why haven't they found a new SHO yet?' Duffy wanted to know. 'Joyce is all very well, but she's a temporary stop-gap. I wonder if Forbes has deliberately left the post unfilled in order to save money?'

'Unlikely, I should think,' said Andrew. 'That wouldn't be within his jurisdiction.'

'Besides, Joyce is being paid, isn't she? Though it wouldn't surprise me if Forbes has been whispering in a few ears.' Charlie sipped his coffee. 'I suspect that man has a finger in more pies than we know about.'

'By the way,' Duffy told Charlie. 'We've heard a bit more about Rob.'

'Yes,' said Andrew. 'He's getting on splendidly. The skin grafts have taken very well. And he's coping admirably. Cheerful and joking with the staff. I can't tell you how much I admire him.'

'On the subject of people we haven't seen for a while,' said Duffy. 'Have you heard anything of Julian and Sandra?'

'All I know about Sandra is that she moved back up to Scotland to be closer to the oil rigs where her husband works. And as for Julian . . .'

'I know about him,' said Andrew. 'He's doing extremely well for himself at the Royal Victoria, Nuneaton. He's a big hit there, apparently, with both staff

122

and patients, despite the fact that he can be somewhat abrasive at times.'

Charlie smiled. He had fond memories of them both.

'On that note,' said Duffy, 'I think we should get going.' She picked up her jacket and bag.

As they left, Andrew shook Charlie's hand. 'You should come round more often,' he said.

It was shortly before ten in the evening when Charlie got home, tired after the shift. He'd assumed that Stuart would be out, but the kitchen light was on, so he went through to say hello.

It wasn't Stu, however, but a woman he'd never seen before. She was wearing Charlie's dressing-gown and was pouring boiling water into the teapot. 'You must be Charlie,' she said as he entered. 'Just in time! Do you want a cup?'

'Yes,' he said.

'Yes you want a cup of tea, or yes you're Charlie?'

'Both, I suppose,' he said, still stunned at finding her there.

'I'm Christina, by the way.'

'And, er, how do you know Stuart?'

'I've been working at the business exhibition in the Town Hall. It closed at lunchtime today, so we spent the afternoon together. He was there when it opened and we met then.'

He vaguely remembered Stu mentioning two women from the exhibition. Christina handed him a mug of tea and carried another towards Stuart's bedroom. As she left, he realised how attractive she was. Tall, straight-backed, fair-complexioned. Not unlike Joy in fact, though not in terms of personality. As he thought of Joy, he felt a jolt of anger on her behalf. She didn't deserve Stuart playing around like this.

Charlie took his mug of tea through to the living-room.

After a minute or two, Stuart entered, wearing his own dressing-gown. Christina followed and sat in one of the armchairs, feet tucked up beneath her.

'Guess what!' Stuart said with an excited smile. 'It looks as though I've found myself some premises. Christina and I looked at them this afternoon.'

'It's a very prestigious place,' she said. 'Exactly the sort of office that clients will love to visit.'

Charlie frowned. 'I thought you said that you only needed a bunch of telephone operators. You don't need prestigious offices for that.'

Stuart seemed a little thrown by that. 'No, you're right. Where the operators sit is of no importance, but I still have to sell the concept to clients. I need a reasonable office for that, Charlie. No one's going to be impressed by some of the chipboard and frosted-glass affairs I've been looking at over the last few days. No, a decent office inspires confidence.'

Charlie shrugged. He supposed so.

'Sorry,' Christina turned to Stu. 'I must be going. I've got an early train in the morning and I have to get back to the hotel to pack.' She disappeared into Stuart's bedroom.

Charlie didn't want to mention Christina while she was still around, so he talked of other things. 'So when are you taking on these premises?'

'I've already signed the lease,' Stuart told him. 'I'll be in business as soon as I can organise the fittings.'

Charlie nodded. Stuart always liked things to happen fast.

Christina returned, wearing tight jeans and a revealing top. She crossed to Stuart and kissed him briefly. 'Thanks,' she said. 'I'd've had a boring week if it wasn't for you.'

'Pleasure.'

'Bye Charlie, nice to meet you.'

Stuart got up and showed Christina out. When he got back, Charlie shot him a black look and picked up the empty mugs. 'How could you do that? What would Joy think if she knew you were jumping in and out of bed with Christina?'

Stuart grinned. 'It was only a bit of fun. I won't be seeing her again. And Joy won't find out. So what's the harm?'

'Joy shouldn't be treated like this,' Charlie insisted. 'It's irrelevant whether she finds out or not – the fact is, you're being dishonest with her and that stinks.'

'Oh, for God's sake,' Stuart sighed. 'Grow up, Charlie.'

'I was going to say exactly the same to you. I thought you'd have grown out of this kind of thing years ago. I can't believe you're still treating women like this.'

Stu looked confused. 'I don't understand why you're getting so upset about this. It has nothing to do with you.'

'Except that I know Joy,' Charlie pointed out. 'I know what kind of person she is, and that she doesn't deserve this.'

'Oh really? D'you know, Charlie, you'd almost think she was *your* girlfriend, the way you're going on about her.'

22

'She said that it wasn't my fault,' Charlie told Elizabeth. 'But looking back, there's so much I could have done to make things different. I didn't make an effort to alter my shifts when Angela wanted to do things.'

Elizabeth leaned back in her leather swivel chair. She held her pen against her lips, thoughtful. 'But that wasn't practical in the long term, was it?'

'With a bit of effort I might have juggled the odd evening free. I've swapped shifts with other people enough times. I'm owed the favours.'

'But how much of an answer would that have been in the end?'

'That's the whole point,' Charlie sighed. 'Maybe I didn't need long-term solutions. If only I'd established our relationship on a workable level, Angela might have come to accept my shift work. There might not have been any long-term problems if I'd dealt with the short-term ones.'

'What you are saying is that if you'd invested more in the relationship, in terms of time, approach, etcetera, that it wouldn't have failed? That it would have stabilised and developed?'

'Possibly.' It didn't sound as likely when Elizabeth put it like that. 'Maybe what I mean is that there's no point in starting a relationship in the first place if you're thinking in advance that it may not be worth it.'

Elizabeth nodded. 'Sometimes, though, relationships

simply don't work, not because of lack of commitment from either partner, but because the individuals concerned are plainly incompatible. You must have had experiences of that kind in the past?'

'You could say that.' Charlie resisted the temptation to laugh. It was the story of his life. 'If I let past relationships get to me, I wouldn't bother with new people at all. I haven't exactly got a past littered with happy love affairs.'

'Hence your cynicism. But what I'm trying to establish here is whether or not what has happened with Angela is your fault.'

'You think it is?'

Elizabeth raised her eyebrows, refusing to be drawn. 'What intrigues me is why you should be so keen to blame yourself, when it is so patently no one's fault.'

'Maybe I wouldn't if it was the first time it had happened.'

'Well, that's a little more objective,' she said. 'We're going in the right direction. This Angela business has set you back somewhat, Charlie. Still, you're willing to discuss it, which is a sign of progress.'

'I suppose it is,' Charlie agreed.

'The very fact that you were willing to enter into a new relationship was a positive step in itself.'

'I guess that's an improvement, isn't it?' Charlie scratched his head. 'Yeah.' He shifted in his seat. 'Actually, I was pushed into it by my flat-mate.'

'But you felt confident enough to go along, to attempt it.'

Charlie smiled shyly. That was true.

'And having met Angela once, you were under no obligation to see her a second time.'

Charlie thought back to that afternoon at Westbourne Cove – the sea, the wind, the pier. He remembered those toasted teacakes, and how lively and new and interesting Angela had seemed. What had gone wrong? Elizabeth was studying him. He looked up and met her gaze. They both smiled.

'Charlie, have you noticed how much calmer you are since you started coming to see me?'

'I suppose I am,' he admitted.

'You are. In spite of this bad experience with Angela.'

'I suppose that's an improvement, too, isn't it?'

'Absolutely, and you need to recognise that.' She drew a breath. 'Now, leading on from this whole business of fault and blame, I want to talk about anger.'

'Anger?'

'Specifically, about your problem with anger.'

'But I don't have a problem with anger. I'm not angry at all. Not with Angela, anyway.'

'That's my point,' she said. 'Most people would be furious if someone broke off a relationship unexpectedly.'

Charlie crossed and uncrossed his legs. Sometimes this minute examination of his feelings got a bit much. 'Depends whether you feel that they were right to leave you or not,' he said. 'Angela saw me as inadequate, and if you look at it from her point of view, I suppose she's right.'

'Look carefully, you will find anger. Instead of blowing a fuse as some people do, or even shouting and calling Angela names behind her back, you have internalised it all, even going so far as to deny its existence.' Noticing Charlie's expression – disbelief mingled with a touch of fear – Elizabeth softened. 'Don't worry, this is surprisingly common. We English are taught to suppress our emotions, often with unfortunate results.

'You're also angry and frustrated at the cyclical way in which things go wrong in your relationships with other women. It seems to happen again and again until a pattern evolves that you feel you can't break. The situation now is that you've come to expect this self-inflicted pattern of failure, therefore you are helpless to change it.

Instead of saying, "It didn't work out with Angela. Never mind, it could have happened to anyone," you've said, "It's all my fault, no wonder she dropped me." '

This was too much for Charlie all at once. He leaned forward, ran his fingers through his hair, silently appealed to Elizabeth. 'I'll have to think about that,' he said at last.

'I'm sorry if this makes you uncomfortable. It's a natural reaction. But you are strong enough to confront this now. Please bear with me a little longer.'

Charlie nodded. He wanted to stand up and walk out, but what choice did he have? Elizabeth went on. 'Your situation at work is similar. Now, it's becoming more stressful each day because you're being burdened with more responsibilities and less time in which to carry out your duties. There's more work, fewer staff, and you're being expected to achieve better results. But you don't express real anger about this, Charlie, just a world-weariness and a cynical, "oh, well, there's nothing I can do about it" attitude.'

'But there *is* nothing I can do about it.'

'That may well be the case. How you are dealing with it is the problem.'

'My workload won't be reduced if I go round ranting about it. What's the use of complaining?'

'It will externalise your anger. Get it all out from inside, where it can do a great deal of damage. In other words, by allowing yourself to get angry – to voice your frustrations and fears – you are also confronting them. When problems are confronted head-on and shared with others in this way, you'll be surprised how they diminish in scale.

'Not only do they become workable, but all that emotional energy is released, and pressure decreases.' She laughed. 'The phrase "letting off steam" is very appropriate.'

Charlie stood up and walked over to the window. 'I

know all that,' he said. 'It's fine in principle. But I don't like troubling people with my problems.'

'Do you mind listening to others when they talk to you about things that are bothering them?'

'No.'

'So why do you think people won't want to listen to you, if you say you don't mind listening to them?'

Charlie stared out of the window. He could think of no answer to this.

'Here's an exercise. Think of your friends and colleagues. Choose two who you respect as normal, well-adjusted people.'

Charlie thought of Duffy and Ash.

'Have you ever seen them cross? Angry? Shouting?'

'Often. When things go wrong, or people let them down.'

'Have you ever seen them in tears?'

Charlie remembered Ash crying, just after Nikki had had the abortion. And Duffy had cried with relief when she'd discovered that Peter was all right, after a scare.

'Yes,' he said, slowly.

'So, why do you think *you* are afraid to get angry when, by your own admission, respected colleagues do, and with constructive results? And why are you afraid to cry?'

'I don't know.'

'You must have some idea, Charlie? Think.'

He stared out of the window, watching passers-by outside, hurrying busily to their destinations. 'I suppose I don't want to bother people. Embarrass them.'

'All right.' She swung her chair round to face him. 'But Charlie, haven't we just established that normal, well-adjusted people express fear, anger or tears as a matter of course?'

'Yes.'

'Yes. And you had no problem with that. So here's the

crunch. Why do people have the right to bother you, yet you haven't got any right to bother them?'

Charlie was annoyed with Elizabeth. Why was she pushing him like this?

'Answer please, Charlie.'

'Confidence, I suppose.'

'Finally!' Elizabeth sighed with relief. 'We've reached the bottom line. The only problem you have, Charlie Fairhead, is a simple lack of self-confidence.'

23

Charlie returned to his chair and sat down. He frowned at Elizabeth, who was beaming expectantly, waiting for his reaction.

Could it really be that simple? He knew that he habitually took on board things that were in fact none of his responsibility. He'd always thought of it as a weakness, but pinpointing it to confidence seemed logical enough. Was it only lack of confidence that caused Charlie to blame himself for the break-up with Angela? OK, Stuart was still seeing Joy, but that was no indication of the success of their relationship. Charlie had at least treated Angela honestly, whereas Stu was being deceitful. The fact that it hadn't worked out with Angela didn't affect that. They hadn't been right for each other.

And it wasn't his fault! Being able to see the truth of that statement for the first time was a revelation. He felt a sense of amazement flow through him. It registered itself as a tingle that travelled up his spine. He grinned at Elizabeth.

'It's true,' she said. 'You are not inadequate, nor are you doomed to flounder in and out of relationships for the rest of your life. So you can forget about what has or hasn't gone wrong in the past, it's irrelevant to how you tackle the future. All these expectations of failure are false ideas that you have planted in your own head, and which have no basis in reality.'

Charlie nodded in agreement. She was right. He could

see now that the whole thrust of their sessions so far had been leading up to this moment.

'Good. Now we have identified the nature of the problem' – Elizabeth pushed her notepad away and clasped her hands on the desk in front of her – 'another couple of little exercises.' Charlie pulled a face. She smiled. 'The others have worked well for you, these will too. They are confidence-boosting exercises.'

He leaned back in his chair and steeled himself. Elizabeth's little exercises seemed to grow progressively more difficult.

'When you are next out shopping – it doesn't matter where, or what for – I want you to make a point of talking to the shop assistant who serves you. Have a quick chat about the weather, something that's been in the news, whether it's busy in the shop or not – that sort of thing is fine. Then I want you to talk to people you don't normally talk to at work. Ask them how they are, pass a few pleasantries. It may sound superficial, but it's important to get a sense of yourself being able to interact easily with strangers and people you don't know.

'On top of that, I want you to choose a confidante. Not necessarily one individual, but a person or persons you can trust. Go to them and tell them about something that really bothers you. It is vital that you realise the abundance of support on offer, if only you're prepared to ask for it. Both these exercises foster openness and trust – the foundation of all truly successful relationships.'

'I'll give it a try.'

'Not a try, Charlie,' she corrected. 'You *will* do it. Think positively.'

'All right, all right,' Charlie laughed. Elizabeth joined in. It was incredible how she had the knack of making him feel better about himself.

'And one last thing before you go,' she said. 'Who is Joy?'

'Joy?' Charlie sat up. What did Elizabeth know of Joy?

'The name keeps cropping up, that's all. More regularly than Angela's.'

'Oh?' said Charlie. 'I wasn't aware . . .'

'Weren't you? Perhaps you'd better tell me about Joy.'

As Charlie walked home after the session, he felt lighter than he had in months. Elizabeth saw things in him that he wasn't aware of. As he approached his flat, he noticed Joy waiting on the pavement. 'Hello,' he said. 'Been here long?'

'Just a couple of minutes. I'm looking for Stuart. I came round on the off-chance. I've been trying to think what to do next.'

'Come in, now that you're here. Have a coffee.'

As he let her into the flat, Charlie pondered the curious coincidence of meeting her now. He showed her into the living-room and went to put the kettle on. 'When did you last see Stu?' he called through.

'Ages ago,' she called back, then walked through to join him in the kitchen. 'He said he'd come round the other night, remember? You passed the message on. Seven o'clock, he said. But he never turned up.'

'Strange.' Charlie spooned out the coffee.

'Mmm. Something else must have cropped up.'

Yes, Charlie thought. And probably her name was Christina. He wondered whether Stuart had been with her that night, too.

They carried the coffee through. Charlie sat opposite Joy who smiled at him for an instant, before staring fixedly into her coffee mug. She was clearly upset. Carefully made-up, smartly dressed, she had obviously made an effort before coming here. She looked as though she might be on her way to a dinner party. Charlie thought how pretty she looked, even though her eyes were downcast. Suddenly he felt overwhelmingly sorry for her, an emotion tinged with the desire to protect her from the pain that Stuart would undoubtedly continue to inflict on her.

'What am I going to do, Charlie?' she asked. 'Stuart is the first man for ages who has taken any interest in me, and now he's stopped coming round to see me. He hasn't even phoned. I've been messed around before, and I can't bear it to happen again. I'd rather be on my own.' She cupped her hands round her coffee mug and took a sip of the warm liquid. 'Stuart is honourable. I can't believe he'd deliberately hurt me. I just can't understand why he hasn't been in touch.'

'It's very bad of him,' Charlie sympathised.

'All I want to know is where I stand.'

Charlie saw her misery, and felt torn in the most painful way about what to say to her. On one hand, he wanted to tell her about Christina, to warn her about what Stuart was doing; on the other hand, Stu was his friend, and to tell Joy what he knew would be a betrayal of their trust. Then, of course, there were his own feelings for Joy, which he now realised went far beyond friendship. He longed to tell her to drop Stuart – so that she could go out with him instead.

'What do you think I should do?' Joy asked him. 'You know Stuart better than I do.'

He shrugged, feeling like a heel. 'All I know is that he's been very busy lately – although I'm not trying to make excuses for him.'

Elizabeth had told him to be more open about his feelings for Joy, and here she was asking for his opinion. But this was Stuart's girlfriend. Stu might have treated her badly, but that didn't alter the fact that they were still, technically, going out together. How could he justify trying to steal his friend's girlfriend? 'Look. Do you want something a bit stronger?' he indicated her coffee mug. 'I'm going to have a whisky.'

'Thanks,' she said. 'I'll have a very small one with a splash of water.'

Hell, he thought as he fixed the drinks in the kitchen, I must tell her how I feel. She can make her own mind up about what she wants to do about it, if anything. I'll do it, he decided. Take the chance. He'd risk losing her, but he had to try and tell her how he felt. If she didn't feel the same, then at least he'd know. And he wouldn't mention about Stuart two-timing her. He returned to the living-room and handed over her whisky.

'Thanks, Charlie,' she smiled.

'That's OK,' he said. 'Actually, there was something that I wanted to say.'

'Oh?'

He took a deep breath, but as he was about to speak he heard Stuart's key in the lock. He couldn't believe it! He closed his eyes, briefly, in frustration.

'Is that Stuart?' Joy leaped up and moved towards the door. Stuart entered, surprised to see her there, but pleased. 'Hello,' she grinned. 'I've been wondering where you were.'

Stuart crossed to her and gave her a kiss.

'Can I talk to you?' she whispered.

'Sure.' He took off his jacket and tossed it over the arm of the sofa. 'I'm glad you're here. I've been meaning to come round and see you, but I've been rushed off my feet the last week, haven't I, Charlie?'

'Mmm.' Charlie raised his glass to his lips.

'Setting up a business is so time-consuming! I kept on thinking, I'll see Joy this evening, but when the evening came, I always found that I hadn't got anywhere near finished. I'm sorry I've neglected you. But it's only temporary, I promise. I'll make up for lost time soon, don't worry.'

'It would have taken two minutes to phone me, Stuart.'

'I know.' He looked contrite. 'You're right. All I can do is apologise.'

Charlie was stunned by Stuart's charm and apparent

sincerity. It was like seeing an electronic gadget being switched on. As soon as he had seen Joy, he'd turned on the gallantry and the smiles. 'Please forgive me?' He sat on the sofa beside Joy and slid his arm round her shoulders.

'All right,' she told him. 'But in future, if you're going to be frantically busy, please tell me.'

Charlie downed the remainder of his whisky and stood up. 'I'll leave you two to it, then.'

'Thanks for inviting me in,' Joy chirped. 'And for the drink.'

'Yes,' said Stu. 'Thanks, Charlie.'

Feeling like an intruder in his own home, Charlie went through to his bedroom and, closing the door, leaned against it with a groan.

24

At work the following day Charlie had a tough time keeping his mind on what he was doing. He kept on thinking of Joy and Stu as he'd left them the previous night; of Joy's almost unbearable trust in Stuart, of her vulnerability, and Stu's ability to be so off-hand about people. He was caught in a conflict of loyalties. How much honesty did he owe Joy? It was up to Stuart to either make or break the affair. It wasn't Charlie's place to interfere. But that didn't take into account his feelings for her.

Given that Stu had always had so many girlfriends, perhaps it was impossible for him to be serious about Joy – at least, in the way that she wanted him to be. There had already been that episode with Christina, and it was only by chance that Charlie had found out about that. Were there others?

He was in his office working through some staff rotas when Mike rang. Could Charlie come to his office immediately? This was a little unusual in itself, but Charlie wasn't worried. He'd delivered several patient reports to Mike and one of them was pretty complicated, so he assumed that it was about that. Mike greeted him warmly enough. 'Come in. Close the door, Charlie. Sit down.'

Being asked to sit down was the first inkling Charlie had that something was wrong.

'This is in the strictest confidence,' Mike began. 'I shouldn't even know about it yet myself, but I've been tipped off by another consultant.' He took a deep breath.

'Gavin Forbes has submitted a written complaint about you to the Board of Trustees. Apparently he has accused you, in writing, of theft. Of a computer terminal, of all things.'

'What!' Charlie got to his feet.

'OK, OK, Charlie. Sit down. I know this is a shock. But I thought you'd better have advance warning. The Board is going to write to you, requesting an interview.'

'This is ridiculous,' said Charlie.

'Of course it is. It's obvious to anyone who knows you that you didn't do it. But crazy though it seems, this has to be taken seriously.'

Charlie couldn't understand why Gavin Forbes was so convinced that he was a thief. No one, as far as he could tell, had come up with any evidence as to who the culprit was. So how could Forbes point the finger at him? He might just as well accuse Duffy, or Ash, or Norma on Reception.

Mike tried a wide, sympathetic grin. 'The thing to remember is that Forbes is working on speculation at the moment.'

'Well, what else has he got to go on? There's no evidence, because it doesn't exist!'

'I know, I know,' Mike placated him. 'Sorry. That came out wrong. What I meant was you'd better be on your best behaviour. He'll be looking for the slightest breach of working practice or discipline. Play everything by the book for the time being, OK?'

'Sure,' said Charlie. 'It's nice to know I lead such a charmed life.'

He made his way back to his office and looked at the new monthly rota on his desk. The thought of going through it again was too much – he didn't have the concentration after what he'd just been told. Instead, he wandered along to cubicle two to check on the progress of an elderly female patient who'd been brought in earlier with concussion and a suspected broken hip.

Duffy was adjusting the patient's position on the trolley as he entered. She looked up and smiled.

'Hiya.' Charlie moved across to the trolley to help her. The patient, Mrs Stubbs, was now semi-conscious, and hooked up to an IV drip. Charlie cast a questioning glance at Duffy.

'Mike put in the IV,' she said softly, aware that the patient might very well be able to register their conversation despite her apparent semi-consciousness. 'Mrs Stubbs here was badly dehydrated, but her hip is fine. No fractures, so that's good news. We're trying to arrange a bed for her upstairs. Mike thinks she should stay in for a day or two, just for observation.'

Charlie nodded. He saw now that Duffy had been changing a soiled sheet when he came in. Together they finished the job swiftly.

'Any chance of you relieving me here for a couple of minutes?' Duffy asked. 'I sent that new HCA for Steristrips five minutes ago and she hasn't come back.'

'Sure.' Duffy disappeared, leaving him looking at Mrs Stubbs, who appeared, as she lay there, to have nothing wrong with her at all, but to be sleeping peacefully. Charlie could imagine her waking at any moment, feeling fine. There was even a slight smile on her lips, he thought, taking a step backwards to admire her gentle features.

Charlie cursed silently as a tray of instruments clattered to the ground. He hadn't noticed it on the unit behind him. Mrs Stubbs seemed undisturbed. Her fragile white eyelids didn't even flutter. After checking her pulse briefly – it was normal for her age and condition – Charlie crouched down and started picking the instruments up from the floor as quietly as he could.

When Duffy returned he was on his knees trying to retrieve a scalpel from under the trolley.

'Charlie?'

'Sorry,' he said. 'I'll fetch some more from the steriliser.'

She seemed concerned. 'It's not like you, Charlie, to knock things over.'

'I've had a bit of bad news,' he admitted, getting to his feet.

'Not again!'

They stepped just out of Mrs Stubbs' hearing. Charlie explained about Forbes and his official complaint.

'It's a joke!' Duffy cried. 'It must be.'

'I wish it were. See you later.'

As he walked along the corridor, Charlie was seized by rage. Forbes' office was just upstairs. Why shouldn't he confront the man? Impulsively, he raced up the stairs, taking them two at a time, not stopping till he reached Forbes' door. Elizabeth would be proud of him, he thought, knocking hard. It was about time Forbes explained himself anyway. He knocked again, but there was no answer.

Mike came out of his office to see what all the commotion was. He frowned when he saw Charlie and beckoned for him to come in. 'What I told you was strictly confidential,' Mike said sharply, before Charlie could sit down. 'I meant it. I'll be in serious trouble if anyone finds out that I told you.'

'Sorry, Mike.' Charlie scratched his head. 'I didn't think of that.'

'Please. I know this is hard on you, but take care not to let Forbes see that you know. Not yet, anyway.'

By the end of the shift, Charlie had calmed down. He'd come across Duffy in the storeroom about an hour earlier and had joined her for a moment, closing the door behind him. 'That poisonous git Forbes!' he'd shouted. 'I bloody hope he suffers for this! I'd like to stuff his budget sheet down his throat until he chokes on it!'

Duffy looked at him, stunned for a moment. Then she caught his eye and they burst out laughing. It felt good to laugh for a while about something so stupid that had become so serious. They laughed for a long time. Duffy had to wipe away the tears.

'I'm glad you can see the funny side of it,' Charlie had snorted, and they'd both cracked up again.

When he'd left the storeroom, he'd felt much better – even up to doing a stint of paperwork.

Stuart arrived home that evening in celebratory mood: his loan had come through and his business was about to be launched. 'At last it's all coming together for me!' he exclaimed. 'I'll be up and running almost immediately.'

'Won't it take time to set up all those telephone links? And what about finding clients?'

'No worries.'

'Our computer system had a few hiccups at first,' Charlie remembered. 'Multiple operator terminals are horrendous to get working effectively.'

'We'll only need one computer.'

'Oh. I thought your telephonists would be working with VDUs. Surely computer ordering's intrinsic to what you're doing.'

'Eh . . .? Oh, yes.' Stuart nodded. It seemed to Charlie that he'd been caught out for a moment, but if so, he covered it up quickly. 'We'll have one central computer. The other VDUs can run off that,' he told Charlie. 'We can add inputs almost indefinitely as we expand.'

Charlie shrugged and left it at that. He wasn't ready for what Stuart said next.

'So how about having a party to celebrate?'

'A party? Where?'

'Here.'

'Sorry, Stu. No way.'

'How about Friday?'

'The one time I ever had a party, the place was a disaster area for weeks. The carpet was dotted with cigarette burns, the furniture damaged. *And* I spent half the evening trying to get rid of gate-crashers.'

'Sounds like fun,' Stuart grinned. 'But seriously, Charlie, you're talking about student parties there. This one would be the height of sophistication.'

'I don't think so.' Charlie pulled a face. 'Besides, I'm on early shift on Saturday morning.'

'Come on. You're not geriatric yet, though you're behaving like it. I'll be responsible for any damage, how's that? If there is any – which there won't be.'

Charlie wished people wouldn't push him into things. He'd never been the party type. But he felt mean, not letting Stu celebrate his new success. 'Oh, all right,' he said at last. 'But keep it low-key.'

'Bring all your mates from Holby City,' Stu said immediately, filled with enthusiasm. 'Invite as many as you can!'

'Most of them will be working. Or sleeping.'

'Bring them anyway,' Stu laughed.

Charlie had to smile at that. He could just imagine it – the graveyard shift turning up, tired, blood-spattered, but ready to party. Maybe Stu had the right attitude. If they were going to have a party he might as well try to get into the spirit of it.

He wondered, suddenly, if Joy would be there. Perhaps now was the time to broach the subject. 'Stu?' he said. 'Are you going to invite Joy?'

'No. So keep quiet about it if you see her. She's not the party type. She wouldn't enjoy it, anyway.'

'You two not getting on?'

'I've got better things to do than spend my evenings with Joy, pleasant though that is every now and again. And she's a bit stand-offish, if you know what I mean.'

'You mean she won't jump into bed with you?'

'I don't always expect a woman to do it on the first date, but there comes a time, usually.'

'So it's not serious? You and her?'

'It never was,' he said. 'She's weird sometimes. She's had this traumatic past, or something. Maybe that's why she gets so clingy. To be honest, Charlie, I'm more interested in my business right now. Plenty of time for women later.'

Charlie tried to hide his elation. Stu wasn't serious about Joy, which left the stage empty for him to make his entrance. But what did she think of him? She might be too upset over Stu to even begin to look around for someone else. It was terrible to think that she'd be hurt. Still, he thought, she'll be better off with me than with Stuart.

25

It was Friday evening, and the party was all set. Charlie, despite his initial misgivings, decided that it wasn't his responsibility. It was Stuart's party. He would attend it as a guest and not feel any obligation as a host.

He'd invited one or two people from Holby City, but wasn't sure if they'd come. Duffy had a previous engagement – a dinner party for some of Andrew's consultant friends – so she couldn't make it, which Charlie was secretly relieved about. He couldn't imagine Duffy at a party organised by Stuart. He felt she'd see Stuart as a jack-the-lad type, with no redeeming features.

The letter from the Board of Trustees still hadn't materialised, which was frustrating, but a relief at the same time. He wished he could forget about Forbes. He decided he was going to put Holby City to the back of his mind and enjoy the party.

Stuart, who had been out, arrived back at eight o'clock carrying a heavy cardboard box. 'Booze.' He dumped it on the table. 'I brought it over by taxi. Could you go and get the other box from downstairs?'

Charlie went down to get the rest of the drink. Stuart had certainly gone to town. There was gin, whisky, Southern Comfort – Angela's favourite he remembered – vodka, wine and beer. And that was only in *this* box. As he staggered upstairs with it he saw Stuart coming down.

'I'm off to the corner to get some mixers and soft

drinks,' Stu said. 'Could you dump all that stuff in the kitchen?'

Charlie nodded and staggered on.

By the time Stu returned, Charlie had laid out all the bottles on the kitchen table, and filled bowls with nuts and crisps.

'Great.' Stuart surveyed the goodies. 'We're all set. The beginning of the end, eh?'

Charlie knew what Stu meant. It was the launch of his new business on Monday, and they both knew he'd have to put in a lot of hard graft to make it work. But Stu was optimistic and motivated.

'Here's to the business,' Charlie toasted before the first guests arrived. 'I wish you every success.' And he meant it, too.

As the guests started arriving, shortly after half-past eight, Charlie couldn't help wondering where Stu had dug them up. Half of them seemed to be casual acquaintances from the pub, plus the man who was lending Stu money, and a few shifty-looking types. It was a strange mix of people, but lively enough. Stuart had bought several new music tapes, bands which Charlie didn't recognise, but they helped give a buzz to the atmosphere.

When Angela turned up, Charlie felt OK about it. There was a brief nervousness as they shook hands, but Angela was as confident and assured as always. She chatted to Charlie about his work, asked about Gavin Forbes. It was curious, Charlie thought, how they got on better now that there was no underlying agenda to their relationship.

Joy arrived too, looking unsure of herself, but stunning in a floaty emerald dress.

'I invited her in the end,' Stuart whispered to Charlie. 'Though I'm beginning to see that it might have been a mistake.'

Perhaps he was right. Joy certainly didn't look at home

here. He took her through to the kitchen and poured her a whisky and ginger.

'You don't look like you're in a party mood.' Charlie took a gulp of beer from his can.

'I'm not really,' she admitted. 'I thought I might liven up after a couple of drinks, but I've never been brilliant at parties. I came to see Stuart, mostly, but I realise now that he'll have to spend most of the evening talking to other people – especially the people who are going to help him with his new business.' She drained her glass and handed it to Charlie for a refill.

Charlie felt so sorry for her that he could hardly speak. She seemed so vulnerable. When Angela came through to say hello to her, he used it as an excuse to wander off himself. He was finding it difficult to remain at a polite distance in Joy's company. Instead, he went through to the living-room.

A woman was talking to Stuart. She was slightly shorter than the usual women Stuart went for, but there was no mistaking the type: loud, attractive, lively, joky, attentive. There was an unmistakable intimacy about the way they interacted. It was clear to Charlie that if they hadn't slept together, they soon would. 'Ah. Charlie.' Stu grabbed his elbow. 'I'd like you to meet Sandy.'

'Hi,' she said with a huge, false smile that sent shivers of dislike up his spine.

'Hello,' he said. 'How'd you meet Stuart?'

'I'm a PR rep. I was working at the—'

'Business exhibition at the Town Hall?'

'Did Stu tell you?'

'No. I guessed. I don't know how.'

Fortunately, the doorbell rang, so Charlie excused himself and went to open the door. It was Ash, with another member of staff from Holby City – Edward, a porter who was saving up to go to university. Charlie knew him only slightly.

As he served them both a drink, he noticed that Stuart was talking earnestly to Joy, who was standing there with yet another glass of whisky and ginger. She looked upset.

'This party of yours is the first one you've invited me to,' Ash said.

'It's *not* my party,' Charlie told him. 'It's just being held in my flat.'

'Well, cheers anyway,' Ash smiled and took a sip of his lager.

Stuart disengaged himself from Joy and came through to talk to Charlie, steering him into a corner of the kitchen. 'You've got to help me with Joy,' he said. 'She's asking awkward questions about Sandy. I need you to corroborate this story I told her—'

'Hang on a minute,' Charlie interrupted. 'I'm not going to corroborate anything. You've messed Joy about enough as it is. I don't want to see her hurt.'

'That's the whole point. I'm trying to *save* her from being hurt.'

'Yeah? Why invite Sandy here tonight, then?'

'I can't do anything about that now.'

'You'll get no help from me,' Charlie told him straight. 'You've treated her badly enough as it is.'

Charlie turned and walked away. He felt breathless with annoyance. A moment later, Joy intercepted him.

'Can I have a word?' she asked.

'I need to get out for a breath of air,' he said. 'I'll be back in a couple of minutes.'

'I'll come with you.'

It was refreshingly cool outside. There had been a shower recently, and rain was dripping from the leaves of the trees in the avenue off the main road. Joy looked fragile in the half-light and Charlie had to stop himself from putting his arm protectively round her shoulder.

'I don't understand Stuart,' she said, slowly. 'He seems

so different tonight. So cold. I don't know what I've done wrong.'

'You haven't done anything wrong.'

'Then why is he so off-hand? And who is that Sandy woman?'

Charlie wanted to tell Joy how he felt. He wanted to tell her the truth – that Stuart wasn't capable of conducting a serious relationship, but that he, Charlie, was. But it wasn't a good time, not when Joy was upset with Stuart. It would be unfair on both of them.

'I'd rather not see Stuart at all than have this sporadic on-off business. Even when he arranges to see me he doesn't turn up.'

They walked along the quiet avenue in silence for a while. Her shoulders seemed slightly stooped as she carefully avoided the puddles. 'I don't know why I'm telling you all this,' she went on. 'Stuart's your friend. But I need to tell someone, and I feel comfortable talking to you.'

This was too much. Charlie thought of Elizabeth, of how she had encouraged him to be honest about his feelings. Well, if there was a good time for putting her theories to the test, this was it.

'I feel comfortable talking to you as well,' he said quietly. 'In fact, I feel more than comfortable.'

He stopped by a glistening privet hedge and looked earnestly at her. 'Look, Joy.' He hesitated. 'When we first met, back in Westbourne Cove, I felt almost from the beginning that things were the wrong way round – that Stuart should have been with Angela and I should have been with you.'

He searched her face, trying to gauge her reaction, but it was too dark for him to see her expression. 'I shouldn't be telling you this, because you're still fond of Stuart, and anyway, I don't suppose I'm your type at all . . .'

He felt suddenly miserable. Of course he wasn't her

149

type. He was making a fool of himself because he had drunk a few beers.

'But Charlie,' she said. 'That's not true. You are my type, more so in some ways than Stuart. You're dependable, for a start, which may not be glamorous, but it's the most important attribute a person can have, as far as I'm concerned. And you're kind. And understanding.'

Charlie couldn't believe it. In his amazement, he took her by the shoulders and drew her towards him so they could kiss in the shadow of a tree. She kissed him back briefly, then broke their embrace. But not immediately.

'They'll be missing us at the party,' she said.

As they strolled towards the flat, Charlie marvelled at his luck. Joy reciprocated his feelings! He took her hand as they walked and she squeezed his fingers gently. When they reached the flat, Joy slipped her hand out of his and entered the room ahead of him.

The party was still noisy and smoky. Joy immediately went off towards Angela in the living-room, leaving Charlie in the hallway to talk to Ash and Edward.

'I saw you,' Ash whispered with a grin. 'Slipping out with that woman.'

Charlie could only smile back at him. He couldn't remember ever feeling this elated. His all-time high was short-lived, however. Joy seemed to be ignoring him. He didn't know why. Perhaps not to arouse Stuart's suspicions? Or did she regret what had happened? At one point, he smiled at her across the room and she pointedly turned away.

Confused, Charlie felt like hiding. But instead he went into the kitchen to get a drink for Ash. There were a couple of blokes in there fooling around. One was swinging a dead vodka bottle from his fingers.

'I'm going to count to ten,' the first one sniggered. 'And you're going to go into a deep sleep, a deep, deep sleep. One, two, three . . .'

'Hi,' said Charlie wearily. He didn't want his kitchen wrecked by drunks. 'I'm Stuart's flatmate. Who are you?'

'Fitters,' the second man drawled. 'We're doing Stu's office for him.'

'Oh.' Charlie relaxed slightly. Not gate-crashers, then. 'It's specialist stuff, putting in those phone lines.'

The men looked blankly at Charlie. One was swaying slightly. 'Are you BT then?' he asked. 'Or are you doing the computer?'

'No,' said the sober one. 'It's just a regular consultancy job. You know, make it look as expensive as possible so the patients think they're getting their money's worth.'

'Patients?'

'Patients, clients, whatever you call the punters who go for hypnotherapy.'

'Eh?'

The tipsy man rummaged in his back pocket and produced a crumpled leaflet. 'Here.' He flattened it out and handed it to Charlie. 'Pretty smart, ain't it?'

'Are you sure it's hypnotherapy?' Charlie asked.

'Private clinic,' the other man said, rubbing his thumb and forefinger meaningfully. 'Not a bad business for a doctor these days.'

26

Charlie dragged himself out of bed at six the next morning. He'd had a sleepless night, full of disturbing dreams that he couldn't remember. When he padded through to the kitchen, he noticed that the mail had already arrived. He recognised the official letter from the hospital immediately and, with a sinking feeling, ripped it open. The Board of Trustees requested his presence at 2.30 pm the following Tuesday. The letter gave no indication of what the meeting was about, though of course, Charlie knew all too well. The Board was taking Forbes' accusation seriously after all.

'How do I get into these situations?' he groaned as he topped up the kettle. He had to leave for work in half an hour.

He picked up the crumpled leaflet advertising Stuart's hypnotherapy practice, wandered into the living-room and flopped onto the sofa. He felt lousy. And not because he'd drunk too much at the party the night before. He hadn't drunk much at all, in fact. Not enough to give himself a hangover. He was always careful when he had to get up for early shift.

No, it was the way Joy had virtually ignored him after they'd come back from their walk. After all they'd said! That, and the discovery of Stuart's pseudo-hypnotherapy business. Charlie had been so upset at the revelation that he'd quickly said goodnight to Ash and Edward, cursorily indicated to Joy that he was going to his room, and then he'd stayed there. The party atmosphere had gone sour for him and if Joy wasn't interested in talking to him, then there was no reason for him to stay up. She hadn't come to knock on his door, to ask how he was or to say goodbye, so now he had no idea where he stood.

He looked at the leaflet in his hand. The heading read: HOLBY HYPNOTHERAPY CLINIC, and beneath:

Assistance with all problems, emotional or psycho-logical. We use hypnosis as a tool to relieve – Stress, Anxiety, Depression, Insomnia, Smoking, Sexual Problems, Phobias, Weight Anxiety, Migraine. Improve your self-confidence. Free initial consultation.

There was no mention of names or qualifications. How could Stuart do this? He was no more a hypnotherapist than Charlie was! It didn't make sense at all. And why was he always the last to know? Thinking back over the last week, Charlie remembered Stu's blank looks when he'd talked of telephone operators and VDUs. No wonder!

Stuart, still tousled and sleepy, appeared at the living-room door. He was carrying a glass of water and looked bleary-eye but cheerful. 'Great party,' he said. 'I'll just get this water down, then it's back to bed for me. What happened to you last night? You went off early.' He looked down and saw that Charlie was holding the hypnother-apy leaflet. 'Ah.'

'What is this, Stu?' Charlie asked.

'I was going to tell you today, anyway.' Stuart sat down on the arm of the sofa. 'But I wanted it to be a surprise. I was going to take you round there when the fitters had finished. It's going to look brilliant, Charlie. See, the problem with a lot of these alternative therapies is they're being done in private homes. But the suite I've got is guaranteed to appeal to the professional classes, people who expect to pay good money for good treatment. I've done my research, too. There are hypnotherapists galore in most towns, but not in Holby. That means I've got a large, untapped client base.'

'And you've got no training, no experience,' Charlie pointed out. 'It's just another rip-off, Stu.'

'I know how people tick. I was a nurse, don't forget.' Stuart bristled defensively. 'That gave me a real insight into people and how to treat their problems. Physical and emotional.'

'But you need qualifications.'

'Not legally, you don't.'

'I can't believe that.'

'It's true. When I said I wasn't going back to prison, I meant it. There is no law in this country that says you have to have a qualification to practise hypnotherapy.'

Charlie glanced at his watch – he couldn't be late for work. 'Even if that's so,' he said, 'a person needs training before they have a *moral* right to practise any kind of therapeutic treatment.'

'But Charlie, it's incredibly straightforward. I've bought in a stock of hypnotherapy tapes - that's basically all I need. I tell the client to relax, I talk to them, play an appropriate tape, and *voilà!* fifty pounds an hour.'

'That's wrong, Stu.'

'Come off it,' said Stuart. 'You know as well as I do that the placebo effect is as good as any drug.'

'But if people have confidence in you, you have a duty to them to know what you're doing. You can't abuse their trust.'

'I won't,' Stuart told him. 'I can almost guarantee that my clients will be helped by the treatment they receive. The fact that they come to me and are willing to pay means that they want to deal with their problem – the tapes will do the rest.'

Charlie shook his head. 'Listen. I've got no time at the

moment, but you're making a mistake with this.'

Stu lowered his voice so it sounded sincere and confidential. 'No, you listen. There's plenty of money to be made, believe me. I could offer you a partnership. Think what that would mean. You could leave Holby City, where they work you like a dog, and you could come to the Holby Hypnotherapy Clinic and earn twice as much working half the hours.'

'What happened to this TV shopping business?'

'That didn't work out, although it's an on-going idea. Maybe, if I can make enough money out of the clinic, I could set up in telesales as well. Wait,' Stuart said, as Charlie moved to the door. 'Think of the future. Our own alternative therapy clinic, catering to every pseudo-science that you can think of: aromatherapy, acupuncture, acupressure, shiatsu, reflexology – all harmless, all popular and all fifty quid an hour.'

Charlie's hand rested on the door handle. 'For a start, Stu, hypnotherapy is not harmless. I know, I've seen the victims.'

'What victims?'

Charlie was longing to go, but it was important that Stu should know. 'All right,' he said. 'A few years ago, we had a bad RTA. Some half-wit larking about had convinced a young girl that she was in a burning building. She freaked out, ran from the house and got hit by a car.'

'Obviously it can be abused, but how often does that happen? The tapes explain all that. You just have to apply some common-sense rules along the way, that's all. Anyway, if you wanted to come into business with me, you could do as much training as you liked. Go off and do course after course. I suppose it adds a bit of extra credibility if you can put a few letters after your name. Of course, we could make up some letters and no one would know the difference. I could call myself Stuart Stonehouse, FHHS or something – Fellow of the Holby Hypnotherapy Society.'

'But there isn't one.'

'There would be if I started one.'

'That's criminal.'

'That's one thing it's not, Charlie, criminal. Which is the beauty of the whole set-up.'

'I think you're mad.'

'Your problem is that you have no sense of opportunity. No wonder you're stuck in Casualty, up to your neck in work.'

'At least I have a clear conscience,' Charlie told him grimly.

'Relax. You take everything too seriously. Why don't you come along and see the premises?' he suggested with a grin. 'Consulting rooms, I call them. You check out the set-up. You'll see it's all above board and it'll make you feel better.'

'OK,' Charlie agreed. 'As long as you realise that my coming along to look doesn't mean I approve.'

'Sure. I really will be helping people, Charlie, qualifications or no qualifications. When do you want to see the place?'

'Not today, anyway. I must go now.'

As he rushed about, preparing to leave, Charlie wondered whether he should talk to Stu about Joy. He might well have noticed that they had left the flat for a time the previous night. But then again, there was no point in talking about it until Charlie was more sure of what was going on, if anything. First of all, he had to interpret Joy's behaviour during the second half of the party. Her offhandedness made him doubt that she'd meant what she'd said. After all, she'd drunk two or three whiskies one after the other. Maybe her judgement had been impaired.

What made her actions difficult to understand was that she'd seemed so genuine and sincere. Charlie couldn't imagine her being in any way devious. But then, he'd trusted Stuart too, and look what had happened there.

27

When Charlie walked through the doors into the Casualty Reception, he sensed that something was different. Everything appeared the same on the surface: there was a queue of patients, the bustle, the builders wandering through. But Norma seemed to hesitate before saying hello, and she didn't do so in quite her usual spontaneous way.

He walked down the corridor to Admin. Duffy and Ash were already there, deep in conversation. 'Yes, but we'll have to be careful . . .' he heard Duffy saying.

He was about to say hi, but she noticed him out of the corner of her eye and jumped with fright. 'Charlie!' she cried. 'You startled me.'

'Good morning. You seem a bit jumpy,' he said. 'Is everything OK?'

'Fine,' she said. 'Ash was saying that the party last night was pretty good.'

'Yeah, thanks for the invite, Charlie. Edward came in a few minutes ago. Hangover's not the word to describe the state *he's* in.'

'We were also talking about holidays.' Duffy cleared some space on a work surface. She was beginning to sound more her usual self. 'Andrew and I were thinking of going off to the Norfolk Broads, or maybe even splashing out and going somewhere like Copenhagen. How about you?'

Charlie shook his head. 'It's been so long since I had a holiday I've forgotten what it's like. I don't really enjoy them, anyway,' he added. 'I miss my work too much.'

'There's dedication for you.' Duffy smiled, but there was something unsettling about the way they both seemed so wary of him.

'Got a letter this morning,' he told them. 'From the Board of Trustees. I've got to see them on Tuesday.'

'About this Forbes business?' Ash asked carefully, glancing across at Duffy.

'Looks like it.'

'We're all keeping our fingers crossed, Charlie,' Duffy told him.

'Yeah.' Charlie frowned. They hadn't seemed surprised when he'd mentioned the letter. Had they known? And why were they acting so out of character? He'd known them for too long. He could tell when they were hiding something.

But he shrugged it off. It was too early in the morning and he had enough to think about. Much better to get on with his job. Janice would be waiting for him in the office, keen to get home to her kids. He turned back down the corridor, bumping into Mike on the way.

'Morning,' Charlie said.

'Morning. And how are you today?'

Mike's over-cheerful greeting alarmed Charlie slightly. Mike was usually miserable early in the morning.

'Is there some kind of conspiracy?' Charlie asked. 'I seem to be the focus of attention all of a sudden.'

'Oh? I wouldn't know.' Mike looked blank. 'People don't tell me anything.'

'Thanks.'

'Don't look so glum,' he said. 'This Forbes business will blow over soon enough.'

'I hope so,' Charlie said with feeling.

The shift change-over went smoothly and he was soon busy. Saturday morning was always one of A and E's busiest times.

'The train had already started moving,' a middle-aged patient told Charlie, presenting a crushed hand. It had been trapped in the train door. 'It was stupid of me.'

'And dangerous. People die from doing that sort of thing.'

Charlie couldn't help wondering, as he worked, if Gavin Forbes had somehow got to some of the staff. Everyone seemed oddly wary of him this morning, and he couldn't think of anything else it could be. Or was he just paranoid – imagining that he couldn't even trust his friends?

While Joyce was examining the crushed hand, Forbes passed the cubicle. 'Excuse me a moment,' Charlie said, and dashed out to catch him.

'Mr Forbes,' he called as he caught up with him. 'Can I have a word with you about this meeting on Tuesday?'

Forbes didn't break his stride. 'I'm too busy,' he said. 'Anyway, I don't wish to discuss it. Everything will come out at the meeting.'

'Thanks,' Charlie said bitterly to Forbes, retreating. He stopped in the corridor and sighed, looking up at the ceiling and taking several deep breaths, before returning to Joyce and the patient.

Later, after directing the same patient to x-ray, Charlie approached Norma at the Reception desk. She had her back to him, talking to one of the porters. The porter glanced up, saw Charlie, and froze briefly, signalling with a look to Norma that Charlie was behind her. She turned. 'Hello Charlie,' she said. 'Busy?'

'What is this?' he asked. 'Everyone seems to be talking about me behind my back.'

Mike, passing, smiled at Charlie and shrugged sympathetically. Norma said nothing. She seemed temporarily lost for words. The ringing telephone came to her rescue. She turned to answer it and Charlie headed for his office. This is ridiculous! he thought, slamming the door. And it's not my imagination. He set to work on some reports to try and distract himself.

Thank goodness he had an appointment with Elizabeth that afternoon. But she would probably think he was paranoid. 'Everyone is talking about me behind my back' sounded absurd, but it was true. Most likely she'd say he was imagining it because he subconsciously believed people didn't like him.

The phone on his desk rang and he sighed before picking it up. 'Hello?'

'Charlie? It's Joy.'

'Joy!' He tried to sound casual, but failed completely. 'This is a surprise.'

'I'm sorry to bother you at work,' she said. 'I know how busy you are, but I had to phone to apologise for last night.'

'You don't have to apologise.'

'I do,' she insisted. 'And I want to explain. When I got back to the party, after our walk, and Stuart was there, I felt so guilty.' Her voice was thick with emotion. 'I didn't want to humiliate him – it was his celebration, after all.'

'I thought that might have been what it was,' Charlie said. 'But it was difficult to tell.'

'I know, Charlie. I'm sorry. I wanted a chance to talk to Stuart alone first. Then, when you went off to your room like that, I felt dreadful. You see, I've never been in a situation like this before and I wasn't sure how to handle it.'

'It's all right.'

'I did mean it last night,' Joy continued. 'You are very special to me.'

'I feel the same,' Charlie said softly.

'I went round to see Stuart this morning,' she said. 'Explained how I felt. He was very good about it. I think he might have been relieved, I'm not sure. Anyway, we've broken it off.'

'Oh. So that means you're free . . .'

'To see you.'

Charlie felt a surge of elation. 'Great. I mean . . . Look, why don't we meet up later? I'll be finished by two. We could spend the afternoon together.'

'I was hoping you'd say that,' she said. 'It's why I rang, really.'

They both laughed. From nervousness and relief.

'I wish you were here,' Charlie whispered. 'So that I could give you a hug and a kiss.'

'You can do that this afternoon. How about three o'clock in Carlton Gardens? By the open air café?'

'Fine. See you then.'

'Bye.'

'Bye.'

Charlie put the phone down. He could feel himself beaming from ear to ear. This was the best possible thing that could have happened! How could he have doubted Joy, even for a moment? He had known instinctively that she was sincere, and he had been right.

Mike knocked and entered. 'Did I leave the Baxter file here?' He crossed to the pile of paperwork on the cabinet, but did a double-take when he noticed Charlie's ecstatic expression. 'What's happened to you in the last ten minutes?' he asked. 'Have aliens invaded your body? Have you been at the drug cabinet?'

'A girl just asked me out,' Charlie sighed.

'Must have been some girl.'

'Yes. She is.'

28

As Charlie made his way to the park, he felt an exhilarating sense of *rightness* about what was happening. His worries were suddenly insignificant. Forbes could go and stuff himself. Charlie would survive.

It was a cloudy day, but the light breeze was warm and made Charlie feel bright. The faint scent of flowers wafted by and he smiled because it reminded him that he was about to see Joy. Even the traffic on the busy road didn't bother him. It amazed him afresh that one person had the power to lift his emotions to these heights. Joy was exactly what her name implied. He pictured her waiting for him in Carlton Gardens, her hair perhaps pulled back from her face as she smiled. It occurred to him then, that Angela had been absolutely right. Their relationship had never made him feel remotely like this. He had simply clung to her because he was lonely and any company was better than none. But with Joy . . .

A sudden realisation stopped him dead. He was due to see Elizabeth Corley in twenty-five minutes! Hell, he thought. Bad timing or what?

Fortunately he had his pocket diary with him, which contained his important phone numbers. The first telephone he came across had been vandalised and he ended up having to go and buy a phonecard from a newsagent before he could make his call.

The receptionist kept him waiting for a couple of minutes before Elizabeth could speak to him. 'Lara tells me you want to cancel our appointment,' Elizabeth said when she finally came on the line.

'Yeah, sorry. Something important's cropped up. I know I'll have to pay for a session. But that's OK.'

'Is it work?'

'No, it's personal.' He couldn't keep the excitement out of his voice, so he continued. 'You know that girl, Joy, I've kept mentioning to you? Well, she wants to see me. She's broken things off with Stuart.'

'I see.' Elizabeth sounded thoughtful. 'You should come in and see me, Charlie.'

'But I've arranged to meet her in ten minutes.'

'It's not like you to throw up a therapy session just like that.'

'I know,' he said. 'But it went right out of my head this morning. Elizabeth, this relationship could be *the* one for me. Joy has already made real sacrifices so that we can be together. I know she's committed.'

'I hope this works out,' Elizabeth told him. 'But I don't want you to wait a whole week before your next appointment. Can you come in on Monday?'

Charlie checked his diary. 'Sorry. Wednesday?'

'Fine. Four o'clock again?'

'Yup.'

'And Charlie,' she said. 'Remember the highs and lows. Be careful. Don't worry if you feel a commensurate depression later on.'

'That won't happen,' Charlie told her.

'Bear it in mind, anyway. See you on Wednesday.'

Charlie hung up. It was kind of Elizabeth to be concerned about him, but unnecessary. He felt better than he had in years. This was how life *should* be. He'd be able to stop going to see Elizabeth soon, anyway, if things went on like this. He made a mental note to tell Elizabeth how much she'd helped him before he finished.

He hurried to the gardens and made it on time – just.

Joy was already there, sitting on one of the benches by the ornamental fountain wearing a pale cream top and a green skirt. She beamed up at him as he came to sit, breathlessly, beside her. She looked radiant with her wide eyes and full smile.

'Hiya,' he said. 'Thought I was going to be late.'

She checked her watch. 'Spot on.' She took his hand. 'Hello, Charlie. What a lovely afternoon.' She sighed and stood up, pulling him up too.

'If you call cloudy weather lovely.'

'I don't like it when it's too hot. With my pale skin I have to be careful,' she told him as they strolled down towards the river. 'I have to cover up, which is the last thing anyone wants to do when the sun is blazing.'

'I like lying in the sun,' he said. 'Or I used to. I haven't done it for ages.'

'I can see that,' she said with a grin.

'It's not something I think of doing any more.'

'Good,' she said.

They walked on, chatting about nothing in particular. Joy explained that a lot of the trees and shrubs were planted in the time of Sir Thomas Carlton, the Victorian landscape artist who had laid out this municipal park.

'Which is why it's called Carlton Gardens.'

'Sharp!' she laughed.

As they walked, Joy hummed occasionally to herself, running her fingers over the pleats of her skirt. 'You know,' she said at one point. 'I can't remember ever feeling as happy and contented as this.'

'Snap.' Charlie was too caught up in his own contentment to notice the almost desperate way that Joy had spoken.

'I don't feel any pressure with you, Charlie. I feel safe.'

'And you didn't with Stuart?' He suddenly wished he hadn't mentioned Stu's name. He felt that he'd been insensitive as he saw her face pinch slightly.

'He wanted to do things his way,' she said. 'He wasn't interested in what I wanted to do. He didn't understand my views on sex before marriage. He told me that nobody felt that way any more. But it's amazing how many women do feel like that. They get pushed into sexual relationships by men, when they'd rather wait until the time was right.'

Charlie wasn't sure what to make of all this. He hadn't thought specifically of how and when their relationship might develop, sexually, but he had imagined it as a natural progression. Joy was, more or less, asking him to keep his hands to himself until they were absolutely sure of their relationship. It was a tall order, in some ways, given how attractive she was, but his own libido had been so flat lately it was refreshing not to have to worry about that side of things yet.

'What I hope for, is a long-term, trusting relationship. How about you?' she inquired with bright eyes.

'The same,' he said.

'It's difficult, though. I've learned not to be too optimistic.' She said this sadly, and Charlie was sensitive enough not to ask what she meant. Clearly she'd been through some bad times. 'I tend to trust people too much,' she said. 'It's my nature, which is a pity because, sooner or later, I usually get hurt.'

Charlie realised how completely unsuitable Stuart was to handle a relationship with someone like Joy. No wonder the whole thing had been a non-starter. As far as Charlie was concerned, it was important to make sure of a firm footing with a person before making a commitment. Joy's attitudes towards sex would cause no problems if they turned out to be as right for each other as he hoped. 'I'll respect your boundaries,' he said.

They ended up sitting by the river. A weeping willow leaned out over the water beside them. A group of ducks swam along the bank. 'Tell me something about yourself.'

Charlie lay back on the grassy bank and looked up at the pale sky. 'I know you don't come from round here, because you've got a slight northern accent.'

'Oh, you noticed,' she said. 'Not many people do.' She sat with one hand in her lap, and one hand clasped in Charlie's. 'This will take about two minutes,' she said. 'I come from Guisborough, which is just above the North York Moors. It's a beautiful place.'

'I think I went there once,' Charlie frowned. 'Isn't it near Middlesbrough?'

'That's right. I lived there until I was eighteen. I have three brothers, one sister and seventeen cousins. My father is a train driver, so we used to go all over the place with concessionary rail tickets when I was a kid. My mother runs a pet shop.'

'I wish I had a large family. I always envy people who have lots of relatives.'

Joy's face darkened as he said this and she looked away, taking her hand from his and running it through the grass.

'Are you OK?' he asked.

'Families aren't always happy.'

'No, of course. There are always bad times, in every family.' He was sorry he'd asked her to talk about herself, now. He'd obviously reawakened some painful memory.

'Look,' he tried to lighten the mood. 'It's after six. Why don't we go somewhere for a bite to eat?'

'How about the café in the gardens?'

Charlie remembered seeing a sign. It closed at six. 'Perhaps we could go to The Colonnade. You know, the restaurant with the pillars. It has a terrace that overlooks the river.'

'That would be lovely, Charlie. I've never been.'

'Then it's time you did.' He took her hand and led her back the way they'd come. 'Where do you go, then, when you go out to eat?'

'Usually somewhere inexpensive, Indian or Chinese.'

'There used to be a brilliant Chinese restaurant down there.' He pointed down past the river. 'I had Peking duck there a couple of times. It was delicious. You had to order it twenty-four hours in advance, because it takes so long to prepare. Something to do with overnight marination, I think. Sadly, it closed down.'

They came to The Colonnade and Charlie opened the door for Joy, who seemed suddenly shy as she waited for him to summon a waiter. 'By the way,' he told her. 'Guess what Stuart's been up to? He wasn't setting up a TV shopping service after all. That fell through, apparently. He's going into business as a—'

'Hypnotherapist,' she said. 'Yes, I know.'

29

'Everyone else knew about this but me,' Charlie complained as Stuart showed him into his new premises.

'Not everyone,' Stuart told him brightly. 'Joy only knew because she was around when I found this place. And Sandy knows, of course.'

Charlie smiled at Sandy as they passed her desk. Stuart had taken her on as his receptionist. She looked very glamorous, as usual, sitting at her uncluttered matt-black desk. As Stuart opened the door to his office, her phone rang. Sandy waited a couple of rings before answering. 'Good morning. Holby Hypnotherapy Clinic, Sandy speaking, how may I help you?'

Stuart ushered Charlie into the office and closed the door behind them. The carpet was the same as the one in the reception area – thick, darkly patterned wool that contrasted with the pale muted colours of the walls. Stuart's desk was enormous, obviously designed to impress. Even his chair was studiously executive – dark leather with chrome sides, not unlike Elizabeth's but more expensive-looking. Stuart sat down and swung his feet on to the desk. 'Well?' he asked.

The office was part of a Victorian building in an expensive area of town. Stuart was surrounded by accountants and law firms. With the brass plaque on the front door, the video entryphone and all the expensive decor, it could have been a Harley Street clinic in London. Charlie said as much. 'It is impressive,' he added. 'But how did you come up with the capital?'

'Borrowed. Financiers know what a high profit margin there is in a business like this. It's a pretty safe bet.'

'But it looks so – medical,' said Charlie. 'Almost like a high-class GP's consulting room, or where you'd go to see a psychiatrist.'

'That's deliberate,' Stuart pointed out. 'It's designed to inspire confidence. People who come in here to see me must believe they are in safe hands.'

'But what if you get someone who's genuinely disturbed?' Charlie wanted to know. 'I mean, OK, if you're talking about playing tapes to help people stop smoking, that's one thing. Or if they want to lose a bit of weight. But what if someone has a serious psychological problem?'

'I know what I can and can't do, Charlie. If someone like that came in, I'd just tell them that I didn't have time to take them on, and send them elsewhere. I'd say my patient register was full.'

'Patient register!' Charlie was alarmed. 'You make yourself sound like a doctor.' He was reminded of the fitter at the party who'd automatically assumed that Stuart was qualified.

Stuart shrugged it off. '*Patient* was the wrong choice of word, that's all. Slip of the tongue. Come over here, let me show you all my gear.'

With obvious pride, Stuart guided Charlie through his array of hi-tech equipment. There was a sophisticated tape-deck and a supply of large earphones and eye patches for blocking out light if necessary. There was also a wide-screen Nicam stereo TV for visual stimuli. At one side of the room there was an electric reclining chair which made Charlie feel uncomfortable. It reminded him of newspaper stories about pseudo-therapists who sexually abused their clients. It was a disturbing image, but he resisted the temptation to say anything. Stuart wouldn't do anything like that. As far as Charlie knew, he had no strange sexual hang-ups.

'Sorry,' he told Stu. 'I still don't like it. It makes me uneasy. And in a way, it's true what I said earlier. You're conning the public. Even worse, you're tinkering with something that nobody really understands.'

He stood in front of an array of tapes and read their titles: *Confidence Booster*, *Meditation*, *Inner Enlightenment*, *Stress Reduction*, *Ambition*, *Overcoming Shyness* . . .

'Those tapes work,' Stuart told him defensively, an edge of irritation in his tone. 'It's been proven.' He'd been trying to infect Charlie with his enthusiasm all afternoon and the fact that it hadn't worked was getting to him.

'They're really popular in America,' he added. 'In California everybody uses them.'

'That's no recommendation,' Charlie said coolly. 'The Americans go in for every fad under the sun. It doesn't mean they work. Even if they do work, no one knows *how* they work. If I were you I'd steer clear of these tapes. And some of them have subliminal messages, don't they? Very dodgy, Stu.'

'Thanks a lot,' Stu moaned. 'I brought you over here to show you my big business venture, the best thing that's happened to me in years. I've worked hard, setting this up. But you've managed to make all my work seem like nothing at all. It's good to know your friends are behind you when you need them.'

'If only it was something other than this,' Charlie said a little guiltily. 'I'd be a hundred per cent behind you. Or if you'd done some training first.' He looked around and sighed. 'I'll be honest with you. If you weren't a friend of mine, Stu, I might go to the authorities about all this. It's just not right.'

'Go ahead. Report me.' The anger in Stu's voice was unmistakable. 'Some friend you are. It may come as a surprise to you, Charlie, but I actually *want* to help people. I want to make money while I'm doing it, but that doesn't mean I don't care about the clients that come here. Luckily everyone isn't as miserable as you!'

'OK, OK,' said Charlie, 'I didn't mean to be so . . . Let's just forget it, shall we? You know how I feel.'

'And I know why you're so uptight,' Stuart pointed his index finger at Charlie. 'It's because I've borrowed all this money, isn't it?'

'No.'

'You think I won't be able to pay it back.'

'It's nothing to do with that,' Charlie said. 'Really.' He made an effort to be conciliatory. 'Do you fancy going for a pint and a sandwich?'

'Great idea.' Stuart looked decidedly relieved that Charlie had stopped having a go at him.

Sandy was just finishing a phone call as they came out. 'Off to lunch?' she asked.

Stuart nodded. 'I'll be back by two.'

'OK. Bye. Bye, Charlie.'

As they left, the phone rang again. Charlie could hear Sandy answering the call: 'Good afternoon. Holby Hypnotherapy Clinic . . .'

'Looks like it's busy already,' Charlie said.

'I've taken out some high-visibility ads in the local press,' Stuart grinned. 'I've already got three appointments for tomorrow alone.'

As they sat in the pub, Charlie plucked up the courage to speak to Stu about Joy. He seemed unconcerned. 'Who she goes out with now is her business, not mine. I hope you have better luck than I did.'

Charlie helped himself to peanuts from the little dish on the table. 'I was scared you might be pissed off,' he admitted. 'Think I'd stolen her from you.'

'Hah.' Stu took some peanuts too. 'There was never really anything there. I only kept it up with her because she's such a looker, but she doesn't make the most of herself. And, like I said, she's a bit clingy. You'd better

171

watch out, Charlie – she's the marrying kind.'

Charlie was secretly pleased to hear this, because he'd thought the same thing. 'I was surprised to see Sandy as your receptionist,' he said.

'It seemed like a good idea.' Stu crunched on some more peanuts and smiled. 'People say that you shouldn't mix business with pleasure, but I can't say I agree.'

'It takes all sorts,' Charlie remarked philosophically.

'Too right. Maybe Joy is your sort. She needs someone like you. Someone . . . stable. She's a nice girl. Nice, but a bit screwed up.'

'What do you mean?'

Stuart laughed. 'It was a joke, Charlie, a joke. Forget it.'

30

As Charlie walked upstairs to the plush new boardroom, he wondered what was in store for him. He'd been dreading this meeting, but he was also curious. What was going to happen? The accusations of theft were ludicrous – there was no way they could prove anything. All he had to do was be honest, and deny everything. What could they do? They'd be better off conducting a serious investigation into the disappearance of equipment than pointing the finger at random, which was what Forbes seemed to be doing. They'd be more likely to catch the real culprit that way, for a start.

Reaching the door, he took a deep breath, knocked, and entered. All the trustees were there. Dalgleish, Royston, Peters, Anne Mackay, a couple he didn't know, plus, of course, Gavin Forbes. Predominantly male, middle-aged management. As he took the only vacant seat, there was hardly a glance in his direction.

He sat down with a sinking feeling. Dalgleish, at the head of the table, had Charlie's personnel file in front of him. Gavin Forbes sat opposite him, looking smug and self-satisfied.

'Good afternoon, Mr Fairhead,' Dalgleish said. 'Thank you for coming. Let's get straight to it, shall we?' He looked at Charlie with a neutral expression and consulted the notes in front of him. 'You are aware, Mr Fairhead, that there have been, and continue to be, unacceptable levels of pilfering and theft of medical supplies and equipment from your department.'

'Isn't that true of all departments?' Charlie asked.

'Not at all,' Dalgleish replied. 'At least, not to anything like the extent that it is happening in A and E. And even if that were the case, it wouldn't excuse it in your own department.'

'A and E is the only department that has such open access to the general public,' Charlie pointed out. 'We can't do anything about that. Some people are skilled at dashing into offices and cubicles as soon as they see the medical staff head off in another direction.'

'Nevertheless, even taking that into account, the situation is unacceptable.'

Dalgleish glanced at Gavin Forbes, who nodded back. 'In the last two weeks alone,' Forbes began, producing a list, 'four cervical collars – two hard, two soft – have disappeared, plus a stethoscope and a portable ventilator. And that's not even taking into consideration the assorted medical supplies.'

'Are you sure?' asked Charlie, surprised. 'Has anyone checked whether they are up in other departments?'

'I've investigated this whole matter most thoroughly, and have concluded that these thefts are highly organised' – Forbes paused for effect – 'by someone who knows what they are doing, and who has an outlet or connections to sell the equipment. Holby City simply can't afford to fund replacements.'

'Quite.' Royston spoke up for the first time. 'The thief has to be someone who has access to all areas, who is on the premises for long hours, someone who can bring a car into the loading bay without causing suspicion.'

'And,' Forbes added pointedly, 'someone who has the authority to order nursing staff to other areas whenever convenient.'

Charlie began to realise what was coming. He wished Mike could have been there, but the meeting had been called at short notice and Mike was already committed to something else.

'The thief would have to have the ability to divert staff from exit doors, so that cars could be loaded up with stolen goods,' Forbes told him. 'There is no other way that the culprit could have got away with so much for so long.'

'How do you mean, for so long? This isn't a long-term problem. I've only heard of it recently.'

'Because equipment was replaced as a matter of course under the old system,' said Forbes. 'Nobody cared much, as far as I can tell. Nowadays it isn't possible to endlessly fund departments in that way. Each department is working to a strict budget.'

As silence fell round the table, Charlie realised that the only other people who fitted the bill, as described, were Joyce, the SHO, who could be discounted because she was new and temporary in the post; and Mike, the consultant, whose high salary would surely mean he had no reason to risk his career for such relatively small gains. After all, how high a price would a second-hand ventilator command on the black market? No more than a month's salary for someone like Mike, he was sure.

'In addition,' said Dalgleish, 'Mr Forbes has kept a careful record of the exact dates and, as near as possible, times, that things have gone missing. And they all coincide with your shifts, Mr Fairhead.'

Charlie snorted. 'No one can be that precise unless they do a full stock-taking every hour on the hour.'

'True, to an extent,' Dalgleish agreed.

'I can't believe you're listening to what he's saying.' Charlie pointed an angry finger at Forbes. 'Do all my years in this department count for nothing? All my hard work? I've practically devoted my life to this hospital. Why would I want to jeopardise that?'

'I agree with Charlie,' said Royston. 'It *is* very difficult to believe. His record is exemplary; he has an excellent reputation within the hospital and the department, with doctors and nursing staff alike.'

'I don't like this any more than you do, Mr Fairhead,' said Dalgleish. 'But I had to call this meeting in order to voice Mr Forbes' concerns.'

'Rumours are already spreading in the department,' Charlie retorted, angry. 'And I won't stand for it. They undermine my authority, the trust that my staff have in me. I'm sick of being labelled a criminal by people who haven't produced a shred of real evidence to support their accusations. If this is how the system treats its long-standing staff members, perhaps I'll be better off elsewhere.'

'I'm sorry, Mr Fairhead,' said Dalgleish. 'Please don't take this personally. But we must take this problem seriously. I, for one, can't believe that you or any of your staff are to blame for this, but someone is stealing from us and we have to find out who it is.'

'Well, I wish you luck,' said Charlie. 'And I hope you find them soon. Because if I'm harassed much more, by people who have no right to be smearing my name—'

'I can assure you that my facts and figures are correct,' Forbes said in his most slimy voice. 'If Mr Fairhead isn't responsible, what other solution can you offer?'

There was silence round the table.

'Then I'll offer one,' Charlie said, white with anger. 'I never thought it would come to this and it's the last thing I would ever want to do, but unless this is sorted out soon, I'll have no other option but to hand in my resignation.'

A flicker of a smile played round Forbes' lips as Charlie stood up and walked out in disgust.

31

'Everyone has a limit. Once you've reached it, that's it.' Charlie was talking to Joy as he sat on an ancient armchair in her bedsit. 'I didn't think I'd ever feel like resigning. But I can't work when people are suspicious all the time, and when the hospital management think I'm a crook.'

'It's terrible,' Joy told him. 'People are so mistrustful.'

Joy was perched on the edge of her bed. Her room contained a single bed, a wardrobe and a chest of drawers. There was an armchair by the fireplace, which had an ancient two-bar electric heater in it. A TV stood in the corner on a semi-circular gate-legged table. The dowdy dark green carpet was threadbare by the door and in front of the fire. Joy had tried to liven the place up by painting the walls white, which made the room light enough, but there was something dingy about it, too. There was a door at the far end which led into a tiny kitchenette that smelled of stale grease. It was a smell that Joy had apologised for as soon as Charlie turned up. She told him she'd tried time and again to get rid of it after she'd first moved in, but had failed. It was probably old cooking oil, she reckoned, that had got behind the skirting boards, or under the lino at the back of the cooker.

'How are your colleagues reacting to all this?' Joy asked

Charlie became thoughtful. 'Ash, Duffy and Mike have all been supportive to my face. But I can't shake the feeling that they're talking about me behind my back.'

'I know that feeling,' said Joy. 'A kind of stiffness in the way people talk to you, as though they're pretending to be spontaneous.'

'That's exactly right.'

'They must all have worries on their own account, about what's going on,' she said. 'If people were stealing things from where I worked, I'd be wondering if the finger was going to be pointing at me next, rather than worrying about the person who'd been accused. Especially if I knew they hadn't done it. I'm sure it'll blow over.'

'I wonder.' Joy's optimism was comforting, but she didn't know how the hospital worked. She always seemed to see the bright side of everything. He liked that about her, just as he liked her slender arms and her fine, expressive hands.

'It's so unfair. I hate to think of you being treated so badly.'

'I wish they'd just let me get on with what I've been trained to do,' said Charlie. 'Doctors and nurses are trained to help people, not administrate them. Health care standards are dropping because too much time is being wasted on non-medical business. All I ever wanted to do was *care* for people.'

'I care for you,' said Joy quietly.

Charlie got up from his chair and sat beside her on the bed. He slid his arm round her shoulder and kissed her gently. Up close, he realised that her eyes, which he'd previously thought of as green, had flecks of light brown around the iris.

'And I care for you,' he said. 'It's amazing how close we've become, so quickly. It's made all the difference to how I've handled this Gavin Forbes affair.'

Joy kissed him back, then stood up. 'How about some tea? I'm not being a very good hostess. I should have offered as soon as you came in.'

'You've done fine,' Charlie told her. 'And yes, tea would be great.'

She disappeared into the kitchenette. Her lithe movements were extraordinarily graceful, and Charlie felt a powerful sense of the need to protect her. From what, though? He didn't know, but her air of vulnerability was one of the things about her he found irresistible.

As she was making the tea, Charlie had a look round the room. On the mantelpiece was a trio of photographs. One was of Joy on the beach aged, perhaps, ten or eleven, swinging a beach ball and smiling directly at the camera. One was of a dog, a Golden Retriever, its front paws up on a low garden wall as it panted. The last photo was a more recent one of Joy, taken perhaps a year or two before. She wore a pale pink bridesmaid's dress and held a small bouquet of carnations. She looked bright, light-hearted. Her hair was pulled back, a curling tendril winding its way down in front of each ear.

Other than that, she seemed to have very few possessions. A dozen or so books in a pile beside her bed. Three or four framed prints of seascapes hung on the wall. It was the room of someone romantic, unworldly.

Joy came back in with the tea and saw Charlie holding one of the photos. 'That's me at my friend Alison's wedding. We were at school together. We always said we'd be bridesmaids at each other's weddings. I thought I'd be married first, because we both got engaged at the same time. Her parents thought she was far too young. My mum and dad wanted to get me out of the house.'

'What happened to your fiancé?' Charlie was curious.

'Nothing. We split up. He had . . . a hidden side to his personality. I didn't discover until later that he had a violent streak.' She smiled sadly, handing him his tea. 'Please, sit down again.'

'You have the chair,' he told her.

'No, I like it on the bed.' She ran her hand across the crocheted bedspread.

They sipped their drinks for a while before Joy spoke

again. 'What will you do if you have to leave your job?'

'I'm not sure. Get another one, presumably.'

'As a nurse?'

'Probably. If I wanted to work in casualty it would mean moving to another town. Still, a new area might do me good – blow the dust away.'

'Like London, you mean?'

'Too big,' he grimaced. 'I've gone off cities. Maybe I could get work out in the country; something rural.'

Joy smiled at the mention of the countryside. 'I used to love it when my family went out for picnics on the North York Moors. I really miss the outdoors. Heather. Going for walks with the dogs.'

Her wistfulness made Charlie smile. Her expression had softened and she looked dreamy and distant.

'But rural communities tend not to have Accident and Emergency departments.'

'There are rural hospitals.'

'Not that many any more. It's a possibility, I suppose.' Charlie closed his eyes and tried to imagine himself living in a small cottage surrounded by fields. He couldn't picture it.

'Would you miss your colleagues if you left Holby City?' Joy broke into his thoughts.

'Yeah. I think I would. There's a good bloke there called Ash. And there's Duffy, one of my oldest friends. She's often said how much she'd like to live in the country. She's started house-hunting now she's settled and got a husband to help with the income. Funny. But it always comes back to the problem of making a living. Especially if you've a family to support.'

'I'd love to have children.' Joy brightened. 'How about you?'

'I always hoped I'd be a father one day,' Charlie mused. 'But lately, I've begun to wonder if it'll ever happen.'

'Oh, don't say it like that. It sounds so sad.'

Charlie shrugged and smiled. He didn't feel sad

when she was around. 'There's nothing I can do about it. Either it happens or it doesn't.'

'I wouldn't go that far,' Joy disagreed. 'There are always choices to be made. Look at me. I'm on income support. Okay, I get temporary work from time to time, but I wouldn't think of having kids until I had some kind of stability. One of these days I'll have to get myself a good job, or go on a training course. Learn a skill.'

Charlie nodded. The mention of training made him think of Stuart. 'Stuart seems to be doing OK,' he admitted. 'No shortage of clients as far as I can tell. Makes you wonder if it's worth all the trouble to do any training.'

'But hypnotherapy is different. It's a wonderful thing – using your own mind to cure yourself.'

'I'm not keen.'

'Why not?' she asked. She seemed non-plussed by Charlie's negative reaction. 'There's no harm in what Stuart does. He's helping a lot of people. And that can only be good, surely?'

'Maybe,' Charlie muttered. 'I'll see how it goes.'

'I'm all for different types of therapy,' she said. 'Aren't you? Stuart said you were seeing a stress counsellor yourself.'

'Did he?' Charlie was shocked and a little embarrassed to discover that Joy knew about it. He drank his tea and wondered why Stuart had mentioned it to her. But then, why shouldn't he? And seeing as Joy didn't mind – positively approved, in fact – there was no problem.

'My counsellor is a professional. A qualified doctor,' he said. 'I'm not against alternative forms of therapy, but the practitioners must be qualified.'

He looked at his watch and changed the subject. 'Look, I noticed on my way over that there's something on at the Theatre Royal this evening. A whodunit. Fancy going to see it? I've hardly ever been there, but it looks fun.'

'I'd love to, Charlie, but I haven't got any money.'

'I'll pay.'

Joy looked perturbed at this.

'No, it's not fair,' she said. 'You pay for everything.'

He laughed. 'I'd like to pay for you. It'd be a pleasure.'

'No. You've bought me enough as it is.'

Charlie wondered how he could persuade her. He remembered the notice outside the theatre – gallery tickets were half-price.

'How about if we sit right up at the top then?' he asked. 'It's half the price of a seat in the stalls, so it would be like having two seats for the price of one.'

'Well . . .'

'It wouldn't be costing me extra that way.'

She looked doubtful for a moment, then smiled. 'OK, Charlie,' she said. 'I'd love to.'

As they walked to the theatre in the cool evening air, Joy held Charlie's hand. It was a lot smaller than his own, fragile. It made him feel protective.

'Being with you makes me realise that it's high time I put some real effort into finding a job,' she told him. 'I'll do anything. Cleaning, filling shelves. I should start to build a future for myself, instead of drifting. You've been so good for me, Charlie.'

'I haven't done anything.'

'Being around has been enough. You've helped me get my priorities right.'

'That's true about you, too,' he said. 'If it wasn't for you, this trouble at the hospital would be getting me down. Right now, I couldn't be bothered.'

'It's a good sign for the future when people get on so well.'

Charlie nodded, suddenly filled with hope. Joy squeezed his elbow as she walked, and echoed his smile.

The theatre was bustling outside when they arrived, but they managed to get tickets. 'Tell you what,' said Joy. 'I'll buy us both an ice-cream in the interval.'

32

In Admin, Charlie hummed happily to himself as he opened a new carton of Steri-strips. Duffy, who was walking past, heard him and stopped. 'Hi,' she said cheerily. 'You sound chirpy. Must be this new woman of yours. You were pretty quick off the mark this time, Charlie. How long is it since the last one?'

Charlie grinned. 'That's how it happens sometimes. Who am I to complain?'

'Judging by your blissful expression, I'd say it must be true love.'

Charlie knew she was joking, but there *was* something new about the way he felt towards Joy.

'If it is true love, grab it quick,' Duffy advised. 'People don't realise how rare it is.' She looked serious for a moment, contemplative. 'All you have to do is look at Andrew and me,' she said slowly. 'At how happy we are. Just think how close I came to losing him.'

It was something worth thinking about.

Charlie decided to go to the storeroom to pick up some extra supplies. Mr Hodson was due in half an hour to have the dressing changed on his leg, which was badly abscessed. Charlie's conversation with Duffy had made him feel more confident than he had for a long time. Perhaps he *could* become a family man. He knew it was too early in his relationship with Joy to be thinking in this way, but there was no harm in speculation, surely, as long as he wasn't taking it too seriously?

Perhaps he ought to invite Duffy and Andrew over for a meal to meet Joy, he thought, as he unlocked the storeroom door. He had always respected Duffy as an excellent judge of character. She'd tell him honestly what she thought of her. He knew instinctively that the two women would get on well together.

For a moment he allowed himself to enjoy the silence of the storeroom. Then he collected the dressings and took them down to Admin. Duffy was on the phone and he caught what she was saying. 'But there's no way of checking whether these stories are true or not, and . . .'

As soon as she noticed Charlie, she turned away from him. 'I must go,' she hissed into the receiver. 'Talk to you later.' She put the phone down and turned back to Charlie with a sheepish smile.

'What was all that about?' he asked.

'A couple of queries from Mike. Nothing serious.'

Charlie had never known Duffy to act in this way and it made him feel – rejected, almost. Surely she was close enough to let him know what was going on; what people were saying about him?

He'd been about to invite her over for dinner, but suddenly the idea had lost its appeal. He knew Duffy wouldn't turn against him. Surely that wasn't possible. But she was certainly wary, and that put a distance between them. He remembered the brightness with which she'd teased him about Joy only a few minutes ago, and all at once felt sad. He could cope with as much rubbish as Forbes could sling at him, but when it began to come between friends, it was hard to take.

At the end of Charlie's shift, Gavin Forbes came to his office to talk to him.

'I hope this is going to be quick,' said Charlie. 'I'm about to leave.'

'Your shift doesn't end for another fifteen minutes,

according to my watch,' Forbes countered. 'What I want to talk to you about shouldn't take much longer than that.'

Charlie sighed. 'I've got to tidy up in here, check the department before I go. You're not going to be unprofessional enough to suggest that I work unpaid overtime are you?'

'I believe you used the storeroom earlier, is that correct?'

'I got some dressings. Why?'

'Was it unlocked when you got there?'

'No.'

'And you locked it up after you'd used it?'

'Of course. I'd never leave a storeroom open. Especially now, with all these accusations flying.'

Forbes' expression was grim. 'A number of items have gone missing from that room since I checked the stock yesterday. Three boxes of surgical gloves, a hundred hypodermic syringes and forty five-centimetre bandages. I have already checked. None of the other keyholders have used the storeroom in that time. Which leaves only you.'

'Maybe there's something wrong with the lock,' Charlie suggested, trying to keep his anger under control.

'The lock is fine, Mr Fairhead. If you doubt my word, kindly accompany me to the storeroom and we will check it together.'

'OK, I will.' Charlie felt defiant.

They marched down the corridor to the storeroom. Confidently, Charlie took out the key, one of a number which hung from his key-ring. The door itself was sturdy and didn't look as if it had been tampered with. Charlie unlocked it and looked inside. Everything was as it had been when he'd visited it.

'And you're sure that you didn't leave the door unlocked so that a third party could sneak in and help themselves to supplies?'

Charlie ignored Forbes' question. 'The missing stock had already gone by the time I came for the dressings,' he said evenly.

'How do you know?'

'Because everything is the same as when I left it. It stands to reason.'

'Why don't you just admit that you took it yourself?'

Charlie laughed grimly. It sounded dull, echoing into the storeroom. 'You're ridiculous, Forbes. But you're not going to get away with your pathetic little campaign against me.'

'Wrong. I'm going to see you sacked,' Forbes sneered. 'I won't rest until I've proved you guilty and seen you kicked out of this hospital.'

'Too bad,' Charlie said defiantly. 'You're going to be awfully tired. Because I'm staying put. I did consider resigning, but there's no way I'm going to do that now – I wouldn't give you the satisfaction.'

Charlie checked his watch. 'How inconvenient!' he exclaimed. 'It's one minute past two. I'm off duty. If you don't mind getting out of my way, Mr Forbes, I'd like to go home.'

As he left, Duffy was gathering her coat. He wondered, briefly, if he should tell her about Forbes' latest trick but, remembering her behaviour when she'd been on the phone, he decided against it. What he really wanted to do was to go round and see Joy – she'd be understanding and sympathetic – but he had an appointment with Elizabeth. He wasn't inclined to go, but he'd missed the last one and felt obliged.

As he walked the familiar streets, he saw a couple of pigeons sitting high up on a window ledge, close together. He smiled, and realised he didn't feel too bad, despite Forbes' efforts to get to him. He reflected that he'd probably be able to stop seeing Elizabeth soon. His emotional problems were under control, thanks to Joy. Forbes was still a pain, but Charlie could cope with that. No, Elizabeth had done her job, and a good one, too. He no longer felt exhausted all the time. His sleep was improving; he had a sense of proportion again. Perhaps he should just cancel it today and phone her to call off future appointments.

What stopped him was the fact that Joy was such a great believer in counsellors like Elizabeth. Besides, he thought, it was only an hour. He could go on to Joy's after that.

Charlie spent the first half-hour talking to Elizabeth about Joy. It was easy. Once he started, he could go on and on. He talked about her appearance, her personality, her likes and dislikes. The Forbes incident seemed trivial by comparison. Elizabeth listened thoughtfully without comment until, eventually, Charlie petered out.

'What a difference, Charlie!' she exclaimed, impressed. 'I'm pleased that you have recovered your energy and enthusiasm. But I do have one concern: that you are investing so much hope in a person that you have only known for a short time.'

'But it seems like months since we met at Westbourne Cove. I know she's right for me. I can feel it.'

'That's my point,' said Elizabeth. 'You are making assumptions about this relationship that are premature. You think you're sure of things that you haven't had either the time or the opportunity to test.'

'I know why you think that,' said Charlie. 'But this is different.' No one could understand unless they had met Joy.

'I'm sorry to have to remind you, but you said more or less the same thing about Angela.'

'Oh, Angela . . .' Charlie laughed. 'I said those things about her because I wanted them to be true. Not because I believed them. Now that I feel this way about Joy, I realise that my feelings for Angela were shallow.'

'I wish you all the best, Charlie,' she said, her voice heavy with scepticism. She looked straight at him. 'There's nothing I like to see more than a good, stable relationship. But all the same, be aware that your new emotional state is a precarious one. You must know, and your medical training will have taught you, that yours is a perfectly natural reaction for someone in your situation. You are learning to deal with stress, and are coming out of a bad period in your life, it's natural to fall for the first sympathetic person you meet; the first person who is willing to give as well as to take. Remember, you are apt to see the world in an overly optimistic way at the moment.'

'You mean like a fairy story,' Charlie laughed. 'Eating something and then falling in love with the first person you see, no matter how ugly they are?'

'Yes,' she said. 'That's precisely what I mean. This stage of recovery is crucial. People tend to think they are completely back to normal when it isn't the case. Believe me, there is usually at least one relapse. I've seen it too many times not to warn you of it.'

Charlie smiled wryly. Why not humour her? He liked Elizabeth and appreciated her straightforward manner. She had helped him a lot, but if she knew Joy she would know that this case was different.

'OK,' he said, without sincerity. 'I'll think about it. So you think I should slow things down a bit with Joy?'

'Don't jump into anything too quickly,' Elizabeth advised. 'It's important to get a clear perspective on new relationships before you commit yourself too deeply.'

'Fine,' Charlie smiled. Privately, he was counting the minutes until he could see Joy again.

33

Charlie hurried round to Joy's place straight from Elizabeth's. There was a lightness to his step which made him feel even more buoyant and optimistic. When he arrived, Joy was preparing a meal of Peking duck. The TV had been pushed into the corner and she had opened up the gate-legged table. It was old and shabby, with brown formica on top and bits missing round the edge. Typical bedsit furniture, Charlie thought. But now it looked festive. It was covered with bowls and packets. The duck, uncooked, was by the tiny window in the kitchenette, marinading in what looked like syrup.

'This is impressive,' he said, kissing her.

'I don't often get the urge to cook something elaborate, but today I've been inspired,' she indicated the duck. 'It's been marinading in honeyed sherry. To turn the skin sweet and crispy. I'm preparing some iced water too, to make the spring onions go curly.'

Charlie was moved by her kindness. She'd gone to so much trouble, because he'd mentioned it was one of his favourite dishes. No one had done as much for him, ever – except perhaps his mother, when he was small.

'If you were going to do all this, you should have come round to my flat. There's much more room there.'

'I'm not that comfortable about being with both you and Stuart together,' she admitted with a shy smile. 'I know that sounds silly, but somehow it's difficult.'

'Right. Fine. I can understand that,' Charlie reassured

her. 'About this cooking. Is there anything I can do to help?'

'You could make us both some tea, while I get these ingredients organised.'

It was amazing how much he felt at home here, in her bedsit, with her things around. He suddenly resented Stuart staying with him. He still wasn't paying rent, which had been fine previously – but now that Charlie needed time alone with Joy, Stu seemed to be more and more in the way. If he moved out, Charlie thought, Joy would feel as much at home in his flat as he did here. As it was, there was no privacy. Stuart was bringing Sandy back to the flat, too. Charlie was happiest when he was alone with Joy, but there wasn't much prospect of that at his place while Stuart was around. Also, at the back of his mind, he had a vague image of Joy moving in with him – not immediately, of course, but sometime in the future when they both felt it was right.

He watched as Joy concentrated on the last stages of the meal. It was hard work for just two people. There were special pancakes to be dry-fried and sprinkled with sesame oil; the duck to be slow-cooked and constantly basted; the vegetables to be prepared. The whole thing had obviously taken all day.

By the time they sat down to eat, Joy looked exhausted. They pulled up the armchair, and positioned the gate-legged table so that one of them could have the chair, and the other could sit on the bed.

The duck was divine. The pancakes were dry and floury, but that didn't matter at all. It was the time and dedication that Joy had put into it that was impressive. It means she genuinely cares for me, he thought.

For pudding, she produced a water-ice from the little freezer compartment of the fridge. It was made with tinned lychees.

'Not completely frozen,' she apologised. 'My ice-box isn't as cold as a proper freezer.'

'Mmm. It's wonderful,' Charlie told her truthfully. It tasted pure and fresh and tangy.

After the meal – and after Charlie had insisted on doing the washing up and preparing coffee – they sat together on the bed. It was awkward and not quite comfortable, perched on the edge of the uneven mattress, but Charlie felt pleasantly calm, almost drowsy. 'I appreciate what you did so much,' he told her. 'A meal like that . . .' He trailed off, lost for words but deeply touched.

They drank their coffee and Joy sighed wistfully as she looked round her cramped surroundings. 'If only I could get a job,' she said. 'I'd be able to afford to do this kind of thing more often. But there's nothing around, Charlie. Absolutely nothing. The hotel trade isn't doing well, and that's the only thing I've got much experience in. Temporary work has as good as dried up, mainly because I'm not a typist. I've been considering doing a course in touch-typing or something. What do you think?'

'If you're going to do a training course, you might as well do something more interesting than typing.'

'Nursing, maybe?'

'That takes years. You'd have to be totally dedicated. It's hard work, *very* unglamorous, and I don't need to tell you that it isn't well paid.'

'Still, I think I'd make a good nurse,' she smiled.

'So do I. Sometimes I wish I could go back to being an ordinary nurse.' He told her of the latest Gavin Forbes incident.

'I'm getting fed up with Holby City.' He shook his head sadly. 'It's not worth the stress, I reckon. The only time I feel happy and relaxed is when I'm with you. Funny how things change. Holby City's always been the main focus of my life, and now it's beginning to take second place. Maybe that's my problem – I always put my job first.'

'If I trained as a nurse, you could leave Holby. We could work somewhere together.'

'If only,' Charlie said. 'Sounds great, but it's a dream.'

She leaned against him. 'It may not be as impossible as all that. I mean, with two salaries coming in, even if they weren't all that high, we'd manage.'

'Nursing takes over your life.' Charlie kissed her again, and she leaned her head on his shoulder.

Until then, he hadn't really thought about Joy's decision not to have sex before marriage, because his libido had been so low for months. But now, as he sat close to her, it occurred to him that he wanted to make love to her. She was so soft and inviting, and it was so intimate in her little bedsit. She looked at him, smiled and hugged him. It was as though she was reading his thoughts and accepting them, but without giving in to them.

It's OK, he thought. I can wait. It'll be worth it.

'Do you want to watch TV for a while?' she suggested. 'There's that series set in Lancashire that I've been watching. It's on in ten minutes.'

'Fine,' Charlie said. It didn't matter what they did, so long as they could be together, be close. That deep, rich sense of contentment spread through him again as Joy positioned her portable TV on the table and tuned it in.

Although the feeling of wanting to make love to her diminished, it still remained as a glow. He was pleased, in a way, that she felt the way she did. The last thing *he* wanted to do was rush, headlong, into a sexual relationship, when he'd been so wary of relationships for so long. No, he was pleased that she took the stand that she did, admired it really. It gave them a chance to get to know each other first.

The programme, a light drama that was diverting without being too much effort, was soon over. Joy had pulled her pillows halfway down the bed so that they could use it as an extended sofa. She was leaning against him, curled up against him, looking thoughtful and absorbed.

It was a quarter to eleven when Joy turned the TV off.

Charlie stretched languidly. 'I've got to go,' he said. 'Yet another early start.'

Joy gave him a cuddle as he stood up. 'Charlie,' she said quietly, hesitantly. 'You could always stay here. If you wanted to.'

Charlie was surprised at her offer. He didn't know what to say, but he sensed her nervousness. 'Thanks, Joy,' he said. 'But I'd be better off going. You don't have to do anything you don't want to.'

'I don't want to lose you,' she whispered, clinging tighter to him. 'All the men I've been out with want to sleep with me before I'm ready for it. Either I go to bed with them, or they leave. Usually that's been a disaster, but I feel safe with you. I think maybe it would be OK, because I love you so much.'

Charlie caught his breath. She'd said it! At last. The surge of emotion within him was overwhelming. He'd never experienced anything quite as powerful before. 'I love you too, Joy,' he murmured. 'Do you think we'd be able to make a go of it? If we got married, I mean?'

34

When Charlie went round to Joy's bedsit again the nex[t] afternoon, he felt strangely nervous. The previous evenin[g] he'd left soon after his proposal. Joy had been taken aback and he'd decided to give her time to think about it. He[r] offer to let him stay the night had been eclipsed by th[e] mention of marriage. But then, he thought, if she says yes that side of it will be cleared, anyway.

'Hi,' she said when she opened the door. 'Come in[,] Charlie, I need to talk to you. About last night.'

Charlie's heart sank. She seemed a little agitated. H[e] wondered if he'd seriously offended her.

'Sit down, please,' she said when they entered the room[.] Charlie did so, placing his hands carefully in his lap s[o] that his own nervousness didn't show.

'First of all,' she said. 'Thank you for your proposal las[t] night. It was wonderful.'

'But?'

'But I can't answer you straight away. I can't make [a] decision like that while I'm still living here in this grotty bedsit. If I say yes, I want to do it on my own terms. [I] wouldn't want you to think I was doing it to escape from[n] here.'

'I wouldn't think that for a moment,' he said. 'You don'[t] have to prove anything, Joy.'

She smiled. 'I've been looking through the papers today,' she said. 'As soon as I've fixed myself up with [a] job, I'll give you your answer, Charlie.' He opened his mouth to speak, but she held up her finger to silence him. 'I'm sure I'll get something soon.'

Charlie shrugged. If that was what he had to wait for, he might as well accept the situation. At least she hadn't rejected him. Her reservation about marriage was valid enough. 'Have you seen anything you could apply for?' he asked.

'There was one.' She picked up the paper. 'For an English-speaking care assistant in the Far East – rural Japan of places. I've always wanted to go abroad.'

'Japan?'

'I'm not saying I'd want to go on my own.' She handed him the paper and pointed out the ad.

He read it, and noticed, printed below the address for applications, the words WOULD SUIT MARRIED COUPLE. ACCOMMODATION PROVIDED.

Joy looked at him meaningfully. 'You said you were thinking of moving away from Holby,' she reminded him. 'Somewhere in the country.'

'But I wasn't thinking of Japan!'

'It might be interesting, though. Very high salary.'

'True, but—'

'Shall I send off for an application form? We don't have to fill it in, even. And if we were asked to go for an interview, we could always decide then.'

'All right,' Charlie laughed. 'I've never thought of going to Japan, but who knows . . . I've had about enough of the power games at work. Sometimes even Japan doesn't seem far enough away from the likes of Gavin Forbes.'

'Maybe a complete break would be a good thing. An ideal way of setting up a life together.'

'But we could do that here in Holby,' Charlie said. 'Once Stuart moves out of my place, you might want to move in.'

Charlie bit his lip, afraid that she'd feel he was pushing her into a decision. She looked thoughtful, her eyes focused on her hands. 'I'd think about it, Charlie,' she said at last. 'But only once I've got a job. And it would only be temporary. I'd want to set up a new home with my partner.'

'Definitely,' Charlie agreed. 'I would have suggested that anyway.'

'You're so kind,' she sighed. 'I don't deserve you at all.'

Charlie smiled. 'You know, the more I think about this Japan idea, the more it appeals to me. I worked myself into the ground at Holby, and it seems to count for nothing. Someone like Gavin Forbes comes along and points the finger at me and, if he succeeds, my career and reputation could be in ruins overnight. I've sacrificed my social life, my friends – and where has it got me?'

'Wouldn't it be wonderful to go somewhere new?' Joy sighed wistfully. 'To move away and live a quiet life, with someone you love.'

'Now you're talking,' Charlie agreed. He could almost see it now, getting up late, sitting out on some subtropical veranda drinking cocktails. Doing an hour or two of gentle nursing, and then spending the evenings walking in the hills while the sky turned orange . . .

'And the countryside is such a good place to bring up children – grandchildren,' Joy added.

'Let's not get too carried away,' he said. 'The chances of that job are remote. Still, it's made me realise. I could do something else. I don't have to slog my guts out at Holby if I don't want to. Perhaps I *should* hand in my resignation.'

'If it were to come off I'd marry you and then we could go off to a new future together,' Joy said excitedly. She took the paper back from Charlie and ringed the ad with her pen.

'I'll send off for an application form first thing tomorrow.'

Charlie pondered the idea. Somewhere deep inside him the concept of getting up and going somewhere completely different, leaving it all behind, had struck a chord.

'I'd have to give at least two months notice at Holby City,' he said. 'And sell the flat. Which might not be easy.'

'Stuart might buy it from you,' Joy suggested. 'Or better still, rent it, so that we still had a base here if we wanted to come back.'

'That would be great,' he agreed. 'The problem is, Stuart and I aren't getting on that well just now. We had a bit of a bust-up yesterday evening.'

'Oh? About what?'

'His hypnotherapy business, again. He mentioned one of his clients, about how he was counselling her for a problem. I didn't like his story for two reasons. First, he referred to her as a patient. The word patient is wrong. Stuart isn't a doctor. And second, what he was telling me should have been kept between him and his client. Talking to friends about the personal lives or medical histories of people who come for treatment is highly unethical. At Holby City it's a sacking offence. I told him it was wrong, but he just made a joke of it. Said he'd stop talking about his work if I stopped talking about mine.'

'You're too hard on him, you know,' Joy said. 'What he's trying to do with hypnotherapy is useful, not harmful. I would recommend it to anyone. Maybe it would have worked better for you than your stress counsellor.'

'Sorry,' said Charlie, as gently as he could. 'But you don't know what you're talking about. Anything like that is dangerous. Hypnotherapy could end up causing a lot of trouble in the hands of untrained people.'

'Actually, I do know what I'm talking about,' she replied. 'Because Stuart is treating me.'

'What!'

'And he's doing a brilliant job.'

Charlie needed a moment to take this in. He sat up suddenly. The romantic atmosphere vanished. 'Why didn't you tell me?'

'Maybe I kept quiet because I knew you might react

like this,' she said. 'I'm not ashamed of it, if that's what you're thinking. Anyway, you didn't tell me you were seeing a stress counsellor, so I don't know why you're upset I didn't tell you about this.'

Charlie shook his head in disbelief. He couldn't put into words how appalling it was to think of Stuart tinkering with Joy's mind when he had no firm idea of what he was doing. Joy had become defensive. She moved away from him slightly, looked away.

'When you told me that you were having therapy I was pleased,' she said. 'I thought you'd be happy for me, too.'

'It isn't the same. Dr Corley is trained, experienced. Stuart's an amateur. I've got nothing against his profession,' he added. 'If you'd only told me you needed – wanted – therapy I could have asked around, found someone well respected. Professional.'

'You don't understand, Charlie. Don't you see? Stuart's been doing it for nothing. I've been a . . . well, a guinea pig, I suppose.'

'What!'

'Oh, Charlie, don't be angry with me!'

'I'm not angry with you,' he told her levelly. 'I'm *furious* with Stuart. Why do you want hypnotherapy, anyway?'

'Because I have a problem!'

'What problem?' He felt a tight band of anger across his chest and had difficulty keeping his voice level.

'Just something from my childhood. Nothing that affects us.'

'Of course it affects us,' he said. 'I love you and I want to help you.'

'Well . . . I used to see my father beating my mother.' Her voice became very quiet. 'He never touched me or any of the other kids, but he used to beat her. It was terrible. I thought maybe . . . Well, anyway, Stuart's been going through it all with me, and it *has* been helpful.'

35

Charlie stood impatiently with his finger pressed on the button of the intercom. Annoyed and upset, he couldn't understand why it took so long to get an answer. Sandy's voice came over after a few seconds. 'Yes?'

'It's Charlie.' He spoke into the stainless steel intercom mike. 'I need to see Stuart.'

The door clicked open and Charlie burst through the little hall into Reception. Sandy, seeing the expression on Charlie's face, became immediately defensive. 'We didn't expect you,' she said carefully. 'Have you got an appointment?'

'You know I haven't.'

'I'm afraid Stuart is with a client at the moment. Would you like to wait here until he's finished?'

'How long will that be?'

Sandy glanced up at the trendy matt-black clock, then at Charlie.

'About fifty minutes,' she said. 'Though sometimes, when he has no appointment immediately afterwards, he runs over a little.'

Charlie sensed that she was lying. She hadn't looked at the clock properly and she sounded insincere. He crossed the expensive carpet to Stuart's door and opened it carefully, just in case there *was* a client in there.

'Charlie! you can't just—' Sandy sprang to her feet, but she was at the other side of the reception area. There was no way she could intercept him.

Stuart was in his office. Alone. Sorting out a stack of tapes. Charlie strode over to him, put his palms on Stuart's desk and leaned towards him. 'What have you been doing behind my back?'

'Charlie, Charlie.' Stuart put the tapes down. 'Calm down. Sit down.'

Charlie didn't want to sit down – he wanted an explanation. 'What have you been doing to Joy?' he demanded.

'It's none of your business, Charlie. If she doesn't want to tell you, then why should I? Weren't you lecturing me about confidentiality only the other day?'

'You shouldn't be treating her, Stu. You've no right. Dealing with past traumas is out of your depth.'

Stuart's brow furrowed. 'Back to the old argument, are we? You are convinced I don't know what I'm doing?'

'You don't.'

'Oh. Did Joy tell you my therapy isn't working? Did she say she was feeling worse, or that she wished she had never come?'

Charlie clenched his jaw. He had no reply to this. He looked at his hands, now curled into fists. Stu sat behind his huge desk and contemplated Charlie for a moment. 'She didn't, did she? Because it's working for her. She's benefiting, Charlie. You should be pleased.'

'That you're using her as a guinea pig? That stinks, Stuart.' Charlie started pacing. He felt so helpless, frustrated.

'It's your own natural protectiveness that's making you angry,' Stuart said, trying to sound reasonable. 'Joy can decide for herself what she wants. She doesn't need you rushing round here like Sir Galahad. Maybe you're angry because business is going well for me, and none of your depressing predictions have come true.' Stuart rocked back and forth in his chair.

'So? I care about Joy.'

'And that's what this whole outburst is about?'

Stuart continued to rock back and forth as Charlie paced, hands thrust angrily into his pockets.

'She's sensitive. I don't want her hurt, Stu.'

'Go home, Charlie.'

Charlie stopped and studied his friend's face. He sensed an anger behind the calm exterior.

'You're my friend and I owe you,' Stu continued. 'But *never* burst in here like that again. Understand?'

Charlie sighed. Maybe he was being a bit extreme. 'What are you treating her for?' he asked, calmer now.

'Ask her.'

'Is it . . . She mentioned she had a violent father. Is that it?'

'Maybe.'

'You said that if someone came to you with a complicated problem, you'd send them elsewhere.'

'It's not complicated, Charlie,' Stuart said, trying to be conciliatory. 'What she told you is about all there is to it. She has trouble dealing with it, that's all. Hypnotherapy helps.'

There was something in Stuart's smooth manner that made Charlie feel he was covering something up. It made him all the more anxious for Joy. 'And you play her your tapes?'

'One in particular,' he told Charlie.

'Which one?'

'Why don't you go back and ask Joy?'

'Because I want to know what you're doing to her. I want to be sure it's not causing harm.'

'OK,' Stuart sighed. 'Here.' He crossed to his tape shelf and picked one out.

'*The Divine Path*?' Charlie said in a mocking tone. 'What the hell does that mean?'

Stu inserted it into the deck and pressed the play button. Eerie sounding music started up, with long soothing notes. Charlie thought it sounded creepy. 'For relaxation only,' Stuart explained. 'It's to get clients relaxed enough to go into a trance. This tape works for Joy.'

'What do you do once she's in a trance?'

'She's afraid of making the same mistake that her mother made,' Stuart said. 'I talk her through it. She's had trouble with previous boyfriends turning out to be violent, and she's afraid that she keeps falling for men who'll beat her.'

Charlie scratched his head. Poor Joy. His anger faded to concern. 'But you're not violent, Stu, and nor am I.'

'Joy joined Compu-Date to try and break the cycle. The fact that it's worked doesn't remove the original fear.' Stu removed the tape from the player and put it away in its case. 'This is one of the tapes I use to help people break a familiar pattern in their lives.'

'And she believes this stuff helps her?'

'It does help. It helps a lot of people – even more than I expected,' Stu insisted. 'Instead of being so cynical why don't you come along to a session? Watch me in action, as it were.'

'No, thanks.'

'About Joy,' Stu said. 'Seeing as you're going out with her, maybe you ought to know a bit more. Although she is very nice, and trusting, she is actually pretty screwed up inside, Charlie. I mean, you wouldn't believe some of the things that she's told me about the past and what she feels about her father—'

'Stop! That's enough!' Charlie exclaimed. 'I can wait until she tells me herself.' Charlie hadn't come here to make Stu break a confidence.

'What this boils down to,' Stuart said, 'is that you're angry with Joy, not me, because she didn't tell you that she was coming here.'

Although Charlie denied it, he knew that Stuart was partly right. He looked at him and sighed. He didn't feel he was getting anywhere. Stuart didn't regret what he'd done, which didn't surprise him. It made him wonder what he'd hoped to achieve by coming here. There was no point in staying any longer. He'd said what he'd come to say. He was about to leave, when he noticed a book on the shelf behind one end of Stu's desk. He leaned over and pulled it down. *Methods of Hypnotic Therapy: A Basic Guide*.

Stuart tried to reach out for the book, too, but Charlie got there first. He opened it. It was an ABC hypnotherapy manual for beginners.

'I don't use that book,' Stuart told him. 'It's just got a useful index of terms in the back.'

Charlie flicked through the pages. One section was titled: 'How to bring Individuals out of a Trance', another 'Hypnotic Suggestions'.

'Give it to me,' Stuart demanded.

'This worries me.'

'You're like a broken record, Charlie. I told you, I use tapes. If you're that worried, come to one of my sessions. See for yourself.'

Charlie considered.

'It would put your mind at rest,' Stu said. 'Listen. There's a woman who's coming for the third of six anti-smoking sessions. I'll ask her if she'd mind an observer. If she agrees, how about it?'

What did he have to lose? 'All right,' he agreed.

Charlie left, and Sandy who'd been listening to the whole thing through the half-open door, stared at him with hate as he passed. It didn't bother him in the slightest – he stared at her with equal venom.

He walked back to the flat feeling down again. The most incomprehensible part of the whole business – and the most hurtful – was that Joy hadn't confided in him. She had sat there and listened while he'd talked to her about Elizabeth and his trouble with Gavin Forbes. But she hadn't said anything about herself. Only when their opinions about Stuart had clashed had she mentioned her therapy. And only then had she mentioned her troubled past. But she'd confided in Stuart. And that hurt.

It must be something about me, he thought. Maybe I bring out the worst in people. He felt his shoulders hunching as he walked, his eyes on the pavement, head bowed. Why couldn't he get anything right? Why was his life such a mess?

36

'Thanks for seeing me,' Charlie said to Elizabeth. He knew he must look a mess. Tired, drawn. He hadn't shaved.

'No trouble.' She stifled a yawn. 'You sounded as though you needed to talk.'

'Haven't slept all night,' he told her. 'I don't know how I've ended up feeling like this. Or why. I feel as if everything has crumbled round me.'

It was five-thirty in the morning. Charlie was shaking slightly as he sat, staring at the floor between his feet.

'Take it easy,' she advised. 'You're here now. I'll get you some coffee.'

He hadn't noticed before, but there was a filter coffee machine at the far end of the room on a trolley. Jars of coffee, sugar, and powdered milk stood neatly in a row beside it. He watched as Elizabeth measured out some coffee and switched the machine on. She produced mugs from underneath. 'No fresh milk, I'm afraid,' she said. 'Only Coffee-Mate.'

She was wearing jeans and a T-shirt. She looked more informal and approachable like this, Charlie thought. Not as dishevelled as he did, but certainly not her usual neat, professional self.

Charlie waited, picking at his fingernails, not looking up. He felt nervous, strung out. All he'd been aware of was his need to come here, but now he was with Elizabeth, he couldn't think of anything to say.

She handed him his coffee and he cradled it in his hands. It was soothing. 'Decaffeinated,' she smiled. 'You look jumpy enough as it is.' She drew up the second chair and sat down. 'Tell me what happened.'

Charlie haltingly began to explain to her about Joy, how well it had been going until he'd found out that she'd been going to see Stuart professionally. 'Why did she keep it from me?' he asked, frowning deeply. 'How could Stuart be so stupid? And why did I let it happen? I knew, when I found out what Stuart was up to, that something like this would happen. But I let it go. I let him off the hook, and he stuck his nose right into Joy's past. He had no right. And I let it happen.'

'Wait a minute.' Elizabeth stopped him. 'Do you know exactly what's been going on between Stuart and Joy in these therapy sessions?'

'No,' Charlie admitted. 'I don't want to think about it. I know I should have stopped him.'

'The first thing to say,' said Elizabeth, 'is something that I have said to you repeatedly, and it's no less true now. You did nothing wrong. Why are you blaming yourself, Charlie?'

'I knew there was going to be a disaster, and I didn't stop it.'

'You don't know if Stuart has done any damage,' Elizabeth pointed out. 'I share your horror that he is practising without training, but you have no evidence of any therapeutic misconduct with Joy.'

'Not yet.' Charlie sipped at his coffee. It was stronger than he was used to, and more bitter. But that seemed appropriate. 'But it doesn't mean he won't. The more Joy trusts him, the more he'll be able to hurt her. Not deliberately, I'm sure. But that doesn't make it all right.'

Charlie wondered at Elizabeth's perpetual calmness. Didn't anything bother her? Perhaps she hadn't understood exactly what Stuart was doing. This was crazy. Her placid approach should help him, but it wasn't. It was getting to him.

'Let's get this into perspective,' she said now, gesturing with her hands for Charlie to wait, slow down, think about this. 'I did warn you that you were going to experience highs and lows. Often, though not always, these highs and lows can be artificially extreme. That's why I was so suspicious when you phoned a few days ago in a state of euphoria. Part of what you are feeling now – this low – is a natural reaction to that high.'

'What are you saying? That my feelings for Joy are a mood disorder?'

'Not at all. But here you are, at this time of the morning, and that surely proves that there was an artificial element to your euphoria? By the time Joy agreed to go out with you, you had already formed an unrealistic image of her in your own mind. To you she was nothing short of perfection. The woman you'd been searching for your whole life. When she turned out to be less than perfect – as everyone is – your fragile sense of stability came crashing down around you.'

'Joy isn't perfect. No one is. But she's a wonderful, unique woman,' Charlie told Elizabeth defiantly. He looked her full in the face. 'I've asked her to marry me.'

'Congratulations.' Elizabeth seemed genuinely pleased for him. 'I hope you can build a happy and secure future together. Look at the progress you've made already. No doubt Joy has been a part of that. You are succeeding admirably, and without the aid of medication.'

Charlie laughed hollowly. 'Succeeding,' he croaked. 'Look at me. I'm as bad as ever.'

'Hang on, Charlie. As I just explained, you are merely experiencing the down side of your emotional high. Think of a piece of elastic that's stretched too far. It has to snap back. This is a short-term reaction, I promise. You have achieved so much, you have Joy, supportive colleagues –

think about it. You have lots going for you, more than many people have.'

He ran his hand across his chin, felt the roughness of stubble against his palm. Maybe she was right. Elizabeth had an extraordinary capacity to make him see things in a rational way – even at a quarter to six in the morning. He began to feel his pulse slowing. It had been out of control all night. 'Maybe I did overreact.' He leaned back in his chair. 'It was the shock. And then I felt that I'd failed.'

'You have to recognise that this sense of failure is an exaggerated form of a feeling you have habitually experienced. If you accept that, then it won't present a long-term problem. You haven't failed, Charlie. I hope you can see that.'

'I suppose I can,' he sighed.

He felt light-headed with fatigue, his body uncontrolled. At last the anguish of the night seemed to be evaporating. 'I need to talk to Joy to try to sort it all out. I was too busy with my own worries. I didn't think that she might have problems of her own. I didn't allow her the time to open up to me, let me try to help her. By listening, at least.'

'Maybe that's all you need to do,' Elizabeth nodded. 'Listen to her.'

'Why am I so self-centred? I feel so guilty. Poor Joy.'

'There you go again,' Elizabeth warned sternly. 'That is so destructive. Watch your language. Look out for words like blame, guilt, fault – anything self-denigratory. Examine the emotion you have attached to it. Nine times out of ten, or ten times out of ten more likely, you'll find that you are being unnecessarily hard on yourself.'

Charlie shifted uncomfortably. Elizabeth's words were hitting home, as usual. Making him face up to hard realities. He looked out of the window at the empty street beyond.

'You *must* cultivate a positive attitude. You must

believe in yourself, in the fact that you behaved in the best way that you could in the circumstances.'

'Perhaps,' Charlie grinned wryly. 'But I'm still worried about what Stuart is doing. Maybe I should contact the authorities. I'm afraid someone will get hurt.'

'You must decide what to do,' said Elizabeth, getting to her feet and clearing the empty mugs away. 'And as for Joy, you're right when you say that you should speak to her.'

Charlie took a deep breath and let it out slowly. He ran his fingers through his hair and shook his head to clear his thoughts. 'I feel calmer now,' he said slowly. 'And I know what to do. I'll go and see Joy after work. I'll have a word with Stuart, too. Bursting into his office like that was a bad idea. I need to be level-headed with him. With Joy as well.'

He laughed gently as he thought back to how he'd reacted to her news that she was seeing Stuart for therapy. 'She must have been horrified. I was well over the top.'

He closed his eyes for a moment. It was incredible how his head, so recently full of clamouring and contradictory emotions, was now composed. 'It's amazing,' he told Elizabeth. 'How different things can seem in the morning.'

She nodded. 'Let's arrange our next appointment.'

'Fine. And then I must dash home to have a shower before work.'

37

Charlie was still calm when he arrived at work. Although he hadn't slept, he'd come to work in the past feeling more tired than this. He was no stranger to lack of sleep. At least this time it wasn't part of a pattern. He'd been kept awake by a problem, and now he knew what he had to do. He'd apologise to Joy for his reaction to her news of the previous evening. He had to make it clear that he took her seriously. He'd be sympathetic about her problems if she wanted to talk them through with him. And he had to make her understand that his feelings for her hadn't changed – that he still meant, and would stick by, his proposal.

The department was frenetic as usual. Today, it felt good to lose himself in the tasks at hand. He was able to cope with the rush, the stress and the open displays of emotion as people were brought in. It left him with little time to think about himself.

He marvelled at how smoothly A and E worked, the way people were mobilised into action at a moment's notice; by the emergency bleeper, crash alarm, or the ambulance radio. This was what he liked best – working in a busy department where staff functioned together as a team. He wondered, as he worked, how many lives they had saved over the years. It was a satisfying feeling, and it made him realise how much he would miss Holby City if he ever did leave. There had been good times over the years. When things were going badly it was easy to forget that.

One thing troubled him. Duffy, Ash and Mike were still

behaving strangely, clamming up when he came into the room, or as he passed in the corridor. Maybe they were being careful with him, knowing what he was going through with Forbes. Maybe they were anxious about his future, given how much Forbes wanted to get rid of him, and didn't want to upset him by talking about it. Whatever the reason, it was upsetting, because they were long-time friends.

During a brief lull, Duffy put her head round Charlie's door. 'How's it going?' she asked.

'Fine. Just taking a few minutes' breather. You?'

'Just finished the fractured femur in four,' she said, entering. 'I've come to hide for a moment before I go back to the fray.'

She fanned her face with an x-ray envelope she was carrying, then sat on the edge of Charlie's desk and smiled at him. Her manner was so friendly that he began to wonder whether his previous impression had been imagined.

'Look,' he said. 'You must think I've been acting strangely lately.'

There was a knock on the door and the new HCA came in. She was only seventeen, with pale skin and large eyes – very keen although not particularly efficient. 'Charlie?' she asked. 'When's the best time to talk to you about taking time off?'

'Never,' he told her. 'What do you want time off for?'

'It's a friend's wedding the Saturday after next. And a big party afterwards. It'd be great if I could get the time to go.'

'OK. I'll see what I can do.' He noted down the date.

'Thanks, Charlie,' she said happily, and left.

Duffy smiled after her. Oh, to be seventeen again. Charlie smiled too. There was something about a day like today, when everything went according to plan and none of the problems were too complicated. No one had died, either. It put everyone in a good mood.

'Anyway Duffy. As I was saying, I wanted to apologise. The last few days. I've been up and down like a yo-yo. You see—'

Another knock on the door. It was Edward, the porter. 'Charlie,' he said. 'What's all this about a new system of tea breaks that Forbes is bringing in?'

Charlie shrugged. It was the first he'd heard. 'Probably a rumour,' he said. 'You know as well as I do that tea breaks aren't his jurisdiction.'

'Maybe he could pass an edict,' said Duffy. 'Telling the public not to have accidents. That would save time and money.'

They laughed. Edward spotted a wheelchair-bound patient zooming past, heading for Reception. He pulled a face and hared after him.

When they were alone again, Duffy put her hand on Charlie's shoulder. 'Sorry, Charlie. What were you saying?'

'Oh,' he said, 'nothing. Don't worry about it. I've got a better idea. Tell me something cheerful about you.'

'That's easy,' she said. 'Andrew and I are going to look at a house this evening. Out in the country.' She rolled her eyes.

'That's great.'

'Isn't it? We picked up the details of several at the weekend and we've narrowed it down to one.'

'You didn't say anything before.'

'I've been busy talking Andrew round to the idea,' she said, unable to hide the excitement in her voice. 'Just think. Away from the grime of the city. It would be lovely for Peter. Safer. Cleaner. And this house has a huge garden.'

'Sounds great.'

'And I've picked up our tickets to Copenhagen today, so that's a weekend to look forward to. I never thought I'd enjoy the perks of being married to a consultant so much.

Here,' she said, opening the envelope, warming to her subject, 'I've got a brochure about the place for you to feast your eyes on. So you'll know what you're missing.'

'That's disgustingly cheerful news,' Charlie grinned. 'I wish I'd never asked.'

She laughed. 'I'd have told you anyway, whether you wanted to hear it or not.'

She drummed her fingers against the door for a few moments before shrugging slightly and leaving the office. After she'd gone, Charlie wondered if he ought to break his no-holiday rule and splash out on a break for himself and Joy. Once he was finished with Elizabeth, he'd be able to save a bit. Maybe they could grab a last-minute bargain. It didn't matter where to. The prospect of a holiday was suddenly a cheering thought, he needed something to lift his mood now that his lack of sleep was catching up on him.

He sighed pleasurably and opened the Copenhagen brochure. The shiny pages were covered with touristy pictures, and smelled of printer's ink. He was reading about the statue of the Little Mermaid when Forbes looked in. 'Aha,' he said as he noticed the brochure. 'Thinking of going abroad? Denmark's an expensive place, you know. Come into some money, have you?'

'If you've got something to say, say it,' Charlie told him. 'Otherwise, bog off.'

'I was just passing,' Forbes smiled. 'I wondered if everything was OK.'

'Everything's fine.' Charlie put the brochure down and stood up. 'Now, if you'll let me pass, I've got to get back to work.'

He left Forbes standing in the doorway of his office and made his way along the corridor towards crash. Anything to get away from that creep. Josh and Jane, the paramedics, were in there conferring.

'Hi, Charlie.' Jane sounded concerned. 'You look tired.'

213

'I'm being harassed by Forbes,' he said.

'Who isn't?' Josh commiserated as he sponged down a stain on the front of his jacket.

'Do I look that bad?' Charlie frowned.

'Only today,' Jane smiled. 'You've been a lot brighter, lately, it's been a boost for the department. Everyone picks up when you're cheerful, Charlie. You have that effect.'

Charlie was chuffed.

'I hear there's a new woman on the scene,' said Josh, raising his eyebrows.

'Correct,' Charlie admitted. 'I've asked her to marry me.'

'Charlie!' Jane cried. 'That's marvellous!'

'She hasn't said yes. Yet.'

'But you're in love.' Josh did a little dance.

'I suppose I must be.'

Josh and Jane's radio crackled to life, and they dashed off, but not before they'd both patted Charlie on the back.

'Take it easy.'

Charlie was exhausted when he finished his shift and left the hospital, but he'd been worse. A strong coffee when he got to Joy's, and he'd be OK for a while. Then an early night, and he'd be fine.

Besides, it didn't matter that he was tired. Tomorrow was his day off. Charlie was really looking forward to having some time to himself at last. After the events of the last twenty-four hours, he felt he'd never needed a break more.

As he walked, bright white clouds passed overhead so that the light changed from dappled sunshine to shade from one moment to the next. He was glad to be out in the fresh air. He passed a travel agent and, on impulse, went in. All the destinations looked equally inviting, so he picked up a stack of brochures. He'd go through them with Joy and they could decide together.

It was only as he neared Joy's house that he remembered he'd left it in anger the previous day. He'd tried to phone her from his office earlier, but her line had been engaged. He found himself flushing with embarrassment at the thought of seeing her again, and having to explain his ridiculous over-the-top behaviour. He might as well explain that these mood swings were normal – and temporary according to Elizabeth. Had it only been this morning that he'd been sitting in Elizabeth's office? It seemed such a long time ago.

He assumed that Joy would be expecting him, since he'd been round straight after work every day for a week. Today, he thought, it would have been better to talk to her first. Make sure that she realised he was no longer angry. But still.

He stopped off and bought a bunch of pink carnations. They looked great, in full bloom, and he hoped she'd like them. He decided he'd insist on paying Joy's share of the holiday too. He knew she wouldn't be able to come otherwise. Given that she was so keen to travel, he felt sure she'd be thrilled by the whole idea.

It took her longer than usual to answer the doorbell. Charlie was about to ring again when she opened the door.

'Charlie.' She seemed pleased, but subdued, as she accepted his proffered flowers.

'Aren't you going to ask me in?' he beamed.

'Come in.'

Charlie had prepared himself for almost anything. Anger, silence, tears. But he wasn't prepared to find Stuart sitting in the armchair with a mug of coffee in his hand.

215

38

'Why shouldn't I come round to see Joy?' Stuart asked. 'I was worried about you after yesterday. We both were. You flew off the handle – not your style, Charlie.'

'Aren't you going to sit down?' Joy asked, returning from the kitchenette. She'd arranged the carnations in a milk bottle filled with water and she carried it carefully to the table. 'They're lovely.' She admired the flowers for a moment. 'D'you want a coffee?'

'Thanks,' he said gratefully. 'But let me apologise first. To both of you. I overreacted yesterday and I'm sorry.'

'That's OK,' Joy said quietly.

'Let's just forget it happened. We all get upset from time to time,' Stuart smiled. 'Why don't I treat you to an Indian meal this evening? Both of you. Business is booming already, I can afford it. And we all need to relax.'

Charlie glanced at Joy before agreeing.

'Thanks, Stu,' he said as Joy smiled enthusiastically. 'That'd be great.'

'In that case, I'll get back to the office.' Stu got up and headed for the door. 'I'll see you at about eight at the Taj Mahal on Brook Street.'

'Brilliant,' said Charlie.

When Stuart left, Charlie approached Joy and kissed her gently. He wanted to make sure that she'd forgiven him. He still felt awkward. 'Sure you're OK about last night?' he asked as she hugged him, pressing her cheek against his chest. 'I've been feeling guilty and embarrassed about it all day.'

'Ssh,' she whispered before smiling up at him.

'Listen,' he said, handing over the travel brochures. 'I thought we could have a look at these. See if we wanted to go away somewhere. Maybe the end of the summer.'

'Oh, Charlie,' she said. 'That's sweet, but I can't afford—'

'My treat.'

'You can't go on paying and paying for me. I feel dreadful.'

'You'll get a job. You can pay your full whack in future.'

She laughed. 'I suppose there's no harm in looking at them.'

'Right.' Charlie looked at his watch. Ten to four. 'I'm sorry, but if we're going out for dinner, I've got to go home and get some sleep. I'm knackered.'

He hugged Joy and kissed her again before he left. She was soft to hold and he felt at peace, closer to her than at any point since they'd met. She had forgiven him so easily and so completely that he was almost overwhelmed with gratitude.

He called for Joy at a quarter to eight, feeling refreshed after a sleep, a wash and a shave. She was lively, intense, and pleased to see him. She had put on a dark dress which accentuated her pale skin and made her look elegant.

'You know,' she said. 'We could probably manage a cheap week in Spain, or even Florida. I hadn't realised that some of the bargain breaks were so affordable. Greece looked lovely too. Some of the islands look like paradise in the holiday guides.'

'So you've been reading up about it?'

'I couldn't resist those beautiful brochures,' she giggled.

As they left for the restaurant, Charlie realised he didn't feel the weird sense of euphoria he'd experienced

217

previously. This time he was rational, in control. He was proud to be with Joy, and they were both happy in each other's company.

Stu was waiting for them outside the Taj Mahal. Charlie realised, too, as they took their table, that he was no longer angry with Stuart. Elizabeth was right: Stuart's professional conduct wasn't his responsibility. He'd voiced his opinion, and that was enough. Besides, getting angry with Stuart solved nothing. He was in business now, and Charlie's opinion couldn't stop that.

His strategy should be different in future, he thought. If the subject arose, he would encourage Stuart to do some training in hypnotherapy, rather than implying that he shouldn't be practising at all. He could point out that it would be in Stu's interests to gain a better professional standing by gaining a recognised qualification. That, in conjunction with hands-on experience, would be very much to his advantage.

When Stuart left the table to make a phone call, Charlie leaned forward and refilled Joy's wine glass. She was smiling – had been all evening – and looked radiant.

'Have you thought any more about my proposal?' he asked, as sitar music twanged in the background.

She became serious. 'Of course I have. I've hardly stopped thinking about it. But my answer is still the same. Wait till I've got a job, then I'll feel happier about taking decisions for myself.'

'If you wanted to, we could make this holiday of ours into a honeymoon.'

'What a lovely thought,' she said gently. 'But please, don't pressure me, Charlie.'

Charlie had to accept that as an answer of sorts. It made no difference to him whether Joy had a job. But he could see that it was important to her, and so he nodded his agreement and continued to eat his lamb pasanda.

'Charlie . . .' she said tentatively.

'Yes?'

She looked almost breathless, as if she was about to tell him something important. But Stuart arrived back at the table at that moment, and Joy masked her expression of frustration by picking up her wine glass and taking a sip.

It was clear to Charlie, as the evening progressed, that Joy was still fond of Stuart. She had been the one to call the relationship off, so he'd never bothered to think about it. But he remembered how infatuated she had been with him at first. She hadn't ended the relationship because she'd begun to dislike Stuart, but because he wasn't the marrying kind. Now that he watched them, talking and laughing together, Charlie felt a brief pang of envy that Stuart could be so easy-going, relaxed and conversational.

'You know, Charlie,' Stuart said, looking up. 'That job of yours is wearing you out. You're not as young as you used to be. I'm going to be needing someone to come into business with me in the not-too-distant future. Especially if I'm to offer other forms of treatment as well as hypnotherapy. What would you say to joining my team?'

'That's an interesting idea,' said Charlie, tearing at his nan bread and thinking privately that there was nothing he'd like less. He didn't want to upset Stu though, so he decided to wriggle out diplomatically. In any case, the following afternoon after work he'd be sitting in on a hypnotherapy session himself. He'd keep quiet until then, at least. In the meantime, the thought of working as a subordinate to Stuart was a nightmare. His flippant attitude to work would be unbearable. 'But I don't know anything about these therapies.'

'You could be the one who does the research,' Stuart said, helping himself to more rice. 'You could find out about what they all are, and how they work. I've been thinking of changing the name from the Holby Hypnotherapy Clinic to the Wyvern County Alternative Therapy Centre.'

'That sounds brilliant,' Joy declared. 'Maybe you could employ me as well. There must be other things I could do.'

'Why not?' said Stuart. 'There should be plenty of work for someone as intelligent and as presentable as yourself.'

Joy laughed with pleasure at the compliment.

When she left to visit the Ladies, Charlie took the opportunity to talk to Stuart. 'Has she told you that I've proposed to her?' he asked.

'No, but I'd guessed, from the way you've been looking at her. What did she say?'

'Basically, not until she's got a job.'

'But otherwise, she said yes?

'I suppose so.'

'You do look happy together, Charlie,' he said flatly. 'I hope it works out.'

'You don't seem pleased.'

'It's not that,' Stu frowned. 'I'm just not sure Joy's right for you.'

'Well, I am,' Charlie told him confidently.

When Joy returned, Stuart made a show of ordering a bottle of champagne to celebrate.

'You can't celebrate what hasn't been decided yet,' Joy objected.

'Nonsense,' Stuart laughed. 'If we can't celebrate your engagement, we can at least celebrate your relationship. How about that?'

'I wasn't going to tell you about it until I'd made up my mind what to do,' she told Stuart shyly.

'It was obvious anyway.'

'Oh, all right.' Joy broke into a wide grin. 'I might as well tell you both now. I've had a think,' she turned to Charlie, 'and I've decided to accept your proposal.'

'Joy!' Charlie, delighted, reached across the table and took her hand.

'I was going to wait until we were on our own.' She smiled. 'But do you mind?'

It was clear from Charlie's expression that he didn't mind in the least.

'I realised when I was in the loo that I did want to marry you,' she said, squeezing Charlie's hand. He leaned forward and kissed her. He didn't mind that Stuart was there to see it – he wouldn't have minded if the whole of Holby City Hospital had been there to see it.

'Congratulations,' said Stuart with an uncharacteristic lack of enthusiasm.

After the meal, Stuart went off to visit Sandy for a couple of hours, and Joy and Charlie jumped into a taxi back to his flat. 'I'll pay the driver,' he told her. 'And he can take you on to your place.'

'I'd like to come in for a while, if that's OK?' she said, holding on to his arm and resting her head on his shoulder. 'It's been fun to have Stuart around, but it'll be good to have a few moments to ourselves.'

'Too right,' he agreed.

When Charlie let them into the flat, he took her in his arms and kissed her for a long time. She was hesitant at first, but then relaxed into his arms. When they broke off, he laughed. 'What now?' he asked. 'A nightcap? A cup of tea?'

'Tea, please,' she said. 'I could do with it after all that food and champagne.'

She came into the kitchen and put her arms round Charlie's waist from behind as he filled the kettle. 'Let's not wait for me to get a job,' she said. 'Let's get married soon.'

'And go for a honeymoon?'

'Yes, I'd love that Charlie.'

'So would I.' He turned to hug her and stroked the fine hair away from her ear. He loved the smell, the feel of it. 'I love you so much,' he whispered.

'I'm sorry I wasn't sure at first,' she said.

Charlie understood that. He remembered his relationship with Trish. He'd taken a long time to make up his mind about that. 'That's OK,' he said. 'As long as you are now.'

'I am.'

'Oh, before you go,' Charlie remembered. 'I wanted to talk to you about tomorrow. I thought we might go somewhere after I've sat in on this hypnotherapy session of Stuart's.'

'What did you have in mind?'

'I don't know. We could go to Castleby Park, maybe, or for a drive. We could even go back to Westbourne Cove and visit that tea-room.'

'I don't really mind, Charlie. You decide.'

'No, it's your day as much as mine. What do *you* want to do?'

'Please will you choose?' she asked, almost plaintively.

'OK,' Charlie said, surprised that she didn't want to take part in making the decision. 'How about going to Castleby Park if the weather's good? It's got a pretty garden and a lake. Or we could go for a drive if it's wet.'

'Lovely,' she said contentedly. 'I'll look forward to it.'

A short time later, when Joy left to go back to her bedsit, she kissed him and ran her fingers through his hair. Charlie realised with a sense of wonder that after they were married, at the end of each evening, she would be staying home with him.

39

The weather was beautiful the next day, bright and warm. Charlie and Joy spent a blissful few hours in each other's company. They didn't do much in the end, just strolled around the old-fashioned, formal gardens of Castleby Park, admiring fragrant tea-roses and exotic-coloured grasses, then hired a little rowing boat to go out on the lake.

When they were in the boat, Charlie tentatively asked Joy if she'd like to talk about her past, the troubled childhood she'd had. 'I'd rather not,' she snapped unexpectedly, deflating Charlie's buoyant mood with her tone. 'I had a less than perfect father, but he wasn't all bad. At least he wasn't a wimp.'

'I'm sorry, if you don't want to—'

'I don't. That's all behind me now. I've broken out of the victim thing, and I won't be a victim again.'

'Fine.'

Aware that he'd touched a sore spot, Charlie decided to leave it. She'd tell him in her own good time. He continued to row lazily, the oars splashing quietly in the water. Gradually Joy's face cleared and their mood began to lift.

'It's a perfect day,' Joy said after a while, as she lay back in the boat and smiled happily, trailing her fingers in the water. 'Hot and sunny. If I close my eyes I can imagine we're sailing on a sparkling, azure sea off a beautiful Greek island. The beach is smooth, golden and deserted, and on a distant hill I can see—'

'You've been reading those travel brochures again,' Charlie laughed.

Joy opened her eyes and sat up. 'I couldn't help it,' she chuckled. 'There's one photograph, of a Greek island, with tiny white cottages and an intense blue sky. I can't get it out of my mind.'

'We could go,' Charlie said, filled with a desire to give her everything she ever wanted. 'For our honeymoon. Which brochure is it in?'

'No,' Joy shook her head, suddenly subdued. 'It's very expensive. Almost the most expensive of the lot.'

'That doesn't matter.'

Charlie tried to sound cheerful, but he knew it did matter. It would be tough enough scraping together the price of the cheapest holiday. Even the day out at Castleby Park was expensive, what with hiring the boat and a pub lunch.

Later, as they drove back to Holby, Charlie regretted that he had been so careless with money lately. He always seemed to be hard up. It all went so quickly: on take-aways, bills, credit cards – it was hard to keep track. And what about Stu? His business was already a success – he could afford to take friends out for meals, so wasn't it about time that he paid his own way? It was certainly about time he found himself somewhere else to live.

Charlie dropped Joy off. He'd have preferred to have spent the evening with her, but he had agreed to sit in on Stu's hypnotherapy session. He didn't relish the prospect, but he had to admit that he was intrigued as to what actually went on in that so-called consulting room. He resolved, as he made his way there, to bring up the subject of money and digs.

Stuart buzzed Charlie into Reception. It was nearly six o'clock and Sandy had gone home. 'Come through,' he said to Charlie. 'I'll go over the procedure before Mrs Nichols arrives.'

As they entered the office, Stuart glanced towards his desk. 'You can sit there,' he gestured. 'I only use it when I do initial consultations. During the sessions, I usually sit beside the clients, here, so I can talk to them without raising my voice. The clients like me to be close, but not too close, if you know what I mean.'

'I can understand their point of view,' Charlie said, staring at the strangely intricate looking chair. 'And they have to pay for all this gadgetry.'

'It was expensive, but worth it. Business is going well, better than expected,' Stu grinned. 'Clients are happy with the service. Or maybe it's my suave, sophisticated manner that keeps them coming back.'

'Yeah.'

'I encourage them to sign up for a course of ten, sometimes twenty sessions,' he said. 'That way, everyone feels the benefit. Which reminds me,' he slipped his hand into his inside pocket and pulled out his wallet. 'I've been meaning to give you something.'

'There's no need,' Charlie objected as Stu began to count out banknotes. He tried not to gawp at the thick wad of fifty- and twenty-pound notes. There was more in that wallet than he earned in a month. Easily.

'Take it.'

'No.'

'Please.' Stu stuffed a roll of notes into Charlie's pocket. 'Look on it as back rent.'

'You can't give me that much.' Charlie was too embarrassed to remove the money from his pocket and count it, but there must have been close to five hundred pounds there.

'I can afford it.'

'Are you sure?'

'Come on, Charlie boy. I owe you. You helped me out

when I needed it. Would I forget that? Now I'm in a position to pay you back don't go arguing with me. It isn't as though you don't need it – remember, I've seen your bank statements.'

'Thanks very much then.'

'By the way,' Stu added. 'You'll be pleased to know I'll be moving out soon.'

'Oh?' Charlie was taken aback.

'I think I've found a place down by the river. A three-bedroomed flat, luxury fittings, picture windows, the lot. It's just a question of negotiating the right rent.'

'Sounds pretty swish.'

'It is. I should hear within the next few days whether I've got it.'

Charlie studied the electronically operated padded reclining chair. He thought it would have looked equally at home in a super-chic dental surgery or the hi-tech operating theatre of a private medical clinic.

Stuart jumped on to the luxurious black contraption and lay back, gazing up at the ceiling. 'I wonder how much you really know about hypnosis,' he said. The chair whined to an upright position and Stuart swivelled it round so he was facing Charlie. 'Do you know the seven basic steps, for example?'

Charlie looked blank. He knew a bit about hypnosis, but wanted to hear Stu's version.

'All right.' Stu stretched his arm out and produced what looked like a music cassette from a metal cabinet. 'The first step is putting the client into a trance. In my case I precede this by playing a tape of soothing music. This tape lasts about ten minutes.' He handed it to Charlie. 'It helps generate a relaxed mood, so the client is much more open to suggestion. After that it usually only takes a few minutes to get a client into a trance.'

Charlie examined the tape. It looked fairly ordinary. 'How long does it take you to hypnotise Mrs Nichols?'

'Seven or eight minutes. All I do is talk in an even, monotonous tone. When I think they're relaxed enough, I suggest that they go into a deep sleep.' Stuart shrugged. 'It almost always works.'

'And you do this every time they come to you?'

'Ah. This is the clever bit. I don't have to. I implant a post-hypnotic suggestion, a code word, that'll put them back into a trance. It's great fun to see someone clicking into a trance. It gives me an amazing sense of power.' He laughed at Charlie's disapproving scowl.

'Anyway,' he went on, gazing at the ceiling again. 'Step two opens up the limbic system of the brain – that's the area which covers basis survival and emotional responses.'

'Oh yeah? I'd never have known,' Charlie interrupted indignantly.

'Sorry. Forgot who I was talking to for a minute. But things have changed a lot since we trained, Charlie.'

'I know. I keep up.'

'OK, OK. Step three, as you know, is when brain-wave patterns change, breathing deepens, pulse slows, and blood pressure drops. The client is now deeply relaxed. Step four, the trance, leads into step five, when the subconscious is open to influence and ready to receive suggestions. What you can do with a person when they're in that state!'

'Such as?' Charlie looked around. He didn't feel comfortable in this office.

'Not that I've done it myself,' Stuart said. 'But I've read that people can come up in blisters if they're told boiling water's being poured on their arms.'

'Don't believe all you read.'

'Come on, Charlie. People have had operations without anaesthetic.'

'It only works for a tiny minority,' Charlie interrupted. He'd read the medical journals. 'It's not an exact science.

227

That's why I don't like you messing around. No one knows how and why it works.'

'But it does work. That's the thing—' The buzzer sounded from Reception. 'Anyway, you'll see for yourself,' he declared as he got up to open the door.

40

Mrs Nichols turned out to be a nervous-looking woman of around thirty-five. Her frizzy dark hair was pulled back from her face and held in a huge tortoiseshell clasp.

'This is Charlie Fairhead,' Stu said as he took her jacket. 'He's the observer from Holby City Hospital I mentioned.'

'An informal, unofficial observer,' Charlie added quickly, annoyed that Stuart was trying to gain credibility from his presence. 'Thank you for letting me sit in, Mrs Nichols.'

'That's quite all right.' Mrs Nichols smiled and took her place on the reclining chair. Stu selected a tape and inserted it in the machine without switching it on.

'How are you getting on, Mrs Nichols?' he asked.

'I still haven't had a ciggy,' she said proudly. 'But the craving's still there, all right. When I leave here I don't want to smoke. But it comes back.'

'And how long has it taken for the craving to return after each of your sessions?'

'After my first session it was twenty-four hours,' she said. 'After the second it was nearly three days.'

'Definite progress, then.'

'Yes,' she agreed.

'OK,' he told her. 'If you'd like to settle yourself so that you're completely comfortable, I'll start the tape. Try to think of nothing in particular. Let your mind wander, and relax.'

He flicked a switch and a gentle, slightly ethereal music

began to play. It had a subdued beat to it like a slow pulse. Despite himself, Charlie found it soothing him as he watched Mrs Nichols lying inert on the chair.

After a few minutes, Stuart started to speak in a low monotone. 'I'll count backwards from ten,' he said. 'When I reach one, I'll say your catch word and you'll go into a deep sleep. Ten, nine, eight . . .' Stuart kept his voice even as he progressed. '. . . three, two, one.' He paused for a moment. 'Klaxon.' Mrs Nichols' arm, which had been over her stomach, flopped freely to her side and her head lolled away from Stuart, who turned to grin and give the thumbs-up sign to Charlie. 'She's out for the count,' he whispered. 'Impressive, huh?'

He picked up Mrs Nichols' hand and let it flop back on to the chair. 'I have seen someone under hypnosis before,' said Charlie, casting a sceptical look at Stu.

'But not in such hi-tech surroundings.'

'Maybe not.'

'Anyway,' Stuart continued. 'I was in the middle of telling you about the seven steps . . . which one had I got to?'

'You were about to tell me about step six.'

'Ah yes, you're about to get a demonstration of that,' he said. 'It's the suggestion given to the client by the hypnotherapist. In Mrs Nichols' case it's going to be about smoking, but it could be about almost anything.'

That was what worried Charlie. But he kept quiet.

'And step seven is bringing the client out of the trance. That's the easy bit. Now, I'd better get on with the demonstration.'

He turned to Mrs Nichols and took a breath. 'OK, Mrs Nichols,' he said quietly, measuring each word with care. 'You are relaxed. You feel good about yourself. Happy with your progress as a non-smoker. You know your efforts are paying off. You know your success will make you feel happier, healthier, cleaner.'

Stuart went on for some time in this vein. Charlie, who

had been drawn into the music at the start, found himself wanting to drift off to sleep as Stuart's voice droned on quietly, urging Mrs Nichols to give up smoking. He had to make a conscious effort not to listen. He got to his feet and stretched. Stu smiled out of the corner of his mouth as Charlie walked round, studying the fittings in the office.

'When I wake you up,' Stuart told Mrs Nichols, 'the thought of smoking will be disgusting to you. You will go home feeling happy, cheerful and with no craving for nicotine. Your craving is completely gone. Now, I'm going to play a tape, and while it's playing, you'll be relaxed and happy and sure that you'll never smoke again.'

He flicked a switch. This time the music, while still ethereal, was brighter, more upbeat. Charlie wondered, briefly, if he hadn't been partly hypnotised himself. His eyes certainly felt heavy.

Stuart joined him at the bookcase. 'See,' he whispered. 'It's the endless reiteration of the same message.'

As the music died away, Stuart returned to Mrs Nichols, leaning forward so he was close to her. 'When I wake you up,' he said, 'you will feel completely alert. Do you understand?'

Mrs Nichols nodded slightly.

He counted backwards from ten, and when he reached one Mrs Nichols stirred, opened her eyes and smiled.

'How are you feeling?' he asked.

She sat up, looking lively and energised. 'Wonderful,' she said. 'Marvellous.'

'Would you like a cigarette?'

'Euurgh!' she grimaced. 'No thanks!'

'I'm glad to hear it.'

Mrs Nichols eagerly arranged her next appointment before Stuart showed her out. Her mood as she left the office was so buoyant that Charlie almost envied her. He was relieved that Stuart had conducted himself professionally.

'Well?' Stuart asked when he returned. 'Doctor Marvel or what? Impressed?'

Charlie was irritated by Stuart's flippant attitude towards something so serious. 'I'm worried that your subjects are so open to suggestion when they're in a trance.'

'But that's no problem. All I'm doing is repeating a very simple message over and over.'

'I'm sorry. I still have serious reservations.' Charlie had to be honest.

'But I'm only dealing with smoking, weight loss, that kind of thing,' Stuart said.

'Even then,' Charlie frowned thoughtfully, 'you're dealing with delicate issues like self-esteem. There's plenty of potential risk.'

'Not when I'm telling them that they feel good about achieving their goal.'

'So long as that's all you do. Watching you has only confirmed my doubts. Hypnosis is dangerous.'

Stuart laughed. 'Brilliant. I give you a faultless demonstration and you come away more worried than before. It could only happen with you, Charlie boy. Give me some credit for a job well done, at least.'

Charlie stood up and yawned. 'You've made me feel sleepy,' he said.

'You'll wake up in the pub,' Stuart promised. 'Let's go for a pint.'

'Oh, all right,' he agreed. How was it that Stuart always ended up charming him? 'But just one.'

As they were leaving, Charlie noticed a pile of business cards advertising the Holby Hypnotherapy Clinic. On reflex he picked up a couple and slipped them into his pocket.

41

The next morning Charlie arrived at work wearing a smile. He seemed to be smiling a lot lately. He couldn't help it. That was what being in love felt like. It was a fantastic feeling, to love someone and have that love returned. He couldn't wait to tell Duffy and the others his news. He kept seeing Joy's face as she'd said goodbye to him the previous afternoon. It had been open, expressive, hopeful, and he'd seen in her eyes that she loved him. She had changed his life completely.

He was walking along the corridor, buttoning up his white coat, when the paramedics burst through the emergency doors, wheeling a patient on a trolley. Charlie joined Josh and Jane as they rushed towards crash. Joyce and Duffy came running from the other direction.

'This is Maureen Isaac, early fifties we think, possible drug overdose,' Josh told them as they hurried along.

They turned into crash. As Josh filled Joyce in on details of heart and blood pressure, Duffy and Jane immediately set about transferring the patient from the ambulance trolley to the hospital one.

'Attempted suicide, we think,' Jane told Charlie as he checked the unconscious woman's vital signs. He examined her arms under the emergency pressure dressings the paramedics had applied. Both wrists and arms had been deeply slashed, with something like a kitchen knife, by the looks of it. Obviously she had genuinely wanted to finish herself off – and what a mess she'd made. Charlie had to work at keeping a professional detachment from the deep cuts she'd carved into her wrists, but he couldn't stop a creeping feeling of pity at what he saw.

'We were called by a neighbour.' Josh handed a plastic carrier bag to Joyce. 'She found her by chance. Called round to borrow something and spotted her through the window.'

Joyce peered into the bag, grimaced, then emptied its contents on to the nearby work surface. An assortment of pill bottles and blister packs spilled out. Antibiotics, aspirins, sleeping pills, paracetamol, decongestants. Charlie shook his head sadly at the deadly array. 'Looks like she swallowed everything she could find.'

'Wash-out?' Duffy asked.

Joyce nodded. 'Quick as you can.'

Charlie heard the phone in Admin and went to answer it. There were more than enough staff in crash to deal with Maureen Isaac. She looked like an average, respectable sort of woman. He wondered what had happened to make her want to take her own life. He was glad to get out of crash, if he was honest. Attempted suicides always upset him. He'd gone through some tough times himself, but he'd never quite plummeted to the point of giving up all hope. There was no greater tragedy than suicide. And today this poor woman's condition rocked him to the core because it contrasted so starkly with his current happiness.

By the time he returned to crash, Duffy was clearing away the stomach tubing. 'Hi,' she smiled at him.

'Would you like a hand?' Charlie asked. Maureen Isaac's cuts had been cleaned and prepared for suturing. He knew that would be Duffy's next job, as Joyce had been called away to another urgent case.

'OK,' Duffy nodded. 'They weren't as deep as they looked,' she indicated the wrist slashes. 'Sad though, eh?'

At least Maureen was going to pull through. To what, though? Charlie thought. If she'd been that desperate to end it all, she'd be upset to discover that she hadn't succeeded.

'That was messy,' Duffy said later, when they were cleaning up in the sluice room. 'You seem thoughtful today. What's up?'

Charlie pulled off his surgical gloves. 'Joy's accepted my proposal,' he said.

'Charlie, that's brilliant. Talk about quick off the mark!' Duffy called out to Ash who was passing. 'Did you hear that? Charlie's getting married!'

Ash came in and clapped Charlie on the shoulder. 'Hey, well done. Congratulations. Sorry I can't stop. Catch you later.' He waved and was gone.

'So is she going to move in with you?' Duffy asked.

'Eventually. We'll probably move somewhere together. Maybe away from Holby – maybe even abroad.'

'Abroad!' Duffy couldn't believe it. 'But you've never shown any interest in travelling.'

'I'm beginning to realise how much of my life I've given to this department. Especially over the last year. And it's not just this Forbes business. It's more than that – it's all the extra duties I've been lumbered with; the hassle. It's time I lived for myself. And for Joy.'

'I know what you mean,' Duffy conceded. 'I'm beginning to feel the same.'

Charlie had forgotten all about Duffy's house-hunting. 'How was that place you went to see?'

'Gorgeous,' she said. 'But too expensive. It needs so much work. Missing tiles, dry rot, woodworm – it's got the lot.'

He grinned wryly as he threw his paper hand towel in the bin. 'There's always a catch isn't there?' he said. 'It's like this job – high stress but high satisfaction, too. Anything else is going to be a compromise.'

'That's the problem. You can't have everything. Whatever you choose, there is always a down side. But what am I talking like this for? You're getting married!' She laughed brightly. 'And I haven't even met her yet.'

'You will,' he assured her. 'Soon. I promise.'

'What about kids, then?' she asked with a grin. 'Have you thought about that?'

'Give us a chance, Duffy!'

Edward came in. 'Maureen Isaac's husband is in Reception,' he told him.

'Right. Coming.'

As Charlie left, he saw that Duffy was mouthing the news to Edward over his shoulder. He couldn't help smiling. How long would it take to get round the whole department? Five minutes? He paused for a moment to compose himself before approaching Mr Isaac in the waiting area. He was a broad man with a large moustache and thinning grey hair. Charlie introduced himself and showed him into the interview room. Once seated, Charlie quickly went through the preliminaries and tried to reassure Mr Isaac before asking him if he might have any idea why his wife had tried to kill herself.

'It's totally unexpected,' Mr Isaac's voice was dry with disbelief and shock. 'Maureen hasn't been depressed for a long time. Five years ago, maybe. But not recently.'

'Five years ago?'

'Her twin sister died,' Mr Isaac explained, pulling at the corner of his moustache nervously with nicotine-stained fingers. 'Maureen and Gwen went to see their mother in Shropshire. My mother-in-law was ill at the time and they spent the weekend looking after her, so that my father-in-law could have a couple of days off.'

He sighed as he thought back, and rubbed the side of his nose. 'It was exhausting for both of them, and afterwards Maureen had to drive all the way back here in one go. Gwen couldn't drive, you see, so Maureen did it all.'

He took a deep breath. His large, watery eyes made him look doleful as he blinked at Charlie.

'Take your time, Mr Isaac.'

'Ronald.'

'Ronald.'

'My wife fell asleep at the wheel,' he continued. 'Went off the road. Hit the corner of a motorway bridge. Maureen broke three ribs in the crash, but Gwen was killed. It was a terrible shock to us all. Especially Maureen's mother. She only lasted a few days after she was told the news.

'It wasn't her fault. We all told her that. But she blamed herself.'

Charlie nodded. He knew the feeling well.

'It was a year before she could even think of Gwen without crying. She had a hard time coming to terms with what happened, but slowly she got over it. That's why I can't make sense of what's happened now.'

Charlie thanked Ronald and saw that he got a cup of tea He left him in the interview room and went back along to crash, where Duffy was sitting with the still unconscious Maureen. He told her about the death of Mrs Isaac's twin.

'Poor soul,' Duffy whispered, then leaned forwards as a movement caught her eye.

Maureen was beginning to come round. Her head twitched slightly from side to side, as if in denial.

'Maureen?' Duffy said softly. 'Maureen, can you hear me?'

Her eyes opened slowly. Groggily. She tried to focus.

'You're all right, Maureen,' Duffy reassured her. 'Your husband's here.'

Maureen shook her head. 'No,' she gasped.

'It's all right,' Duffy told her. 'You don't have to see him.'

Tears began to roll down Maureen's cheeks. 'I killed

237

her,' she moaned. 'I killed her. It was my fault . . .'

Duffy took her hand.

Back in the interview room, Charlie gave Ronald a brief report, saying that his wife would be fine. He looked so desolate that Charlie didn't have the heart to ask him to wait in Reception.

42

Charlie managed to grab fifteen minutes to do a little urgent paperwork, but as he sat at his desk he found his mind kept wandering back to Joy and their future together.

He still found it incredible that she was actually going to be his wife; that he was going to change from a single man to a husband. The unfortunate case of Maureen Isaac made him realise how lucky he was to have an exciting future to look forward to. He wished he could show Joy how happy she'd made him, thank her in some way. He thought of the money Stu had given him, and suddenly he had an idea. Now he might be able to afford that trip to Greece! As soon as he thought of it, he picked up the phone to ring Joy. She'd be so excited.

He dialled her number, but changed his mind and slammed down the phone before the line connected. Instead, gripped with excitement, he picked up a telephone directory and flicked through it until he found the number he wanted. He pressed the buttons on the phone. 'Wyvern Travel? Look, I picked up some brochures from you the other day . . .'

A few minutes later it was all arranged. Charlie would call round at the travel agency that afternoon and pick up a copy of the Greek brochure Joy had got so excited about. If he found he could afford it, he'd book the holiday as a surprise for her. He was imagining how delighted she'd be, when Gavin Forbes interrupted him by popping his head round the door. 'Handed in your notice yet?' Forbes asked jokingly, with a supercilious smile.

Charlie glared with all his might. 'Another remark like that, Forbes, and I'll submit an official complaint against *you*. For harassment.'

'You won't be here long enough,' Forbes sneered before carrying on down the corridor.

A few minutes later, Charlie took Mr Isaac through to cubicle three to see his wife. She'd been transferred there from resusc, and had finally agreed to see him. Charlie noticed, as they walked, that Ronald was trembling. It was easy to forget that when there was a crisis, it wasn't just the patient who suffered, but everyone close to him or her too. The couple's son and daughter had been informed and were on their way.

Duffy was sitting in the cubicle with Maureen. As soon as Ronald saw his wife, he rushed forward and grasped her hand tenderly. 'Why, Maureen? Why?' he sobbed.

'You know why,' she whispered weakly. 'I can't live with the guilt any more.'

'But after all this time! What happened?' He stroked her coarse grey hair as he spoke.

'I loved Gwen so much.'

'I know you did.'

'Why did you let them save me?' Maureen glanced at Charlie and Duffy. 'I'd be better off—'

'Ssh.' Ronald stopped her. 'I couldn't bear to be without you. Don't you love me?'

'You know I do,' she murmured. 'But you don't understand.'

Charlie nodded to Duffy. 'Let's take a break,' he whispered. They left the Isaacs alone.

Charlie and Duffy got themselves a drink each from the machine, then carried them back to Admin. Charlie took a welcome gulp of coffee.

Duffy was pensive. 'I once tripped over one of Peter's toy trains when I was carrying a hot pan of spaghetti,' she told him. 'The pan went flying. I had this awful vision of Peter with half a gallon of boiling water and pasta flung over him. But he was at the other side of the room, thank God. He hardly even noticed. For days after that, though, weeks even, I kept thinking, what if . . . What if I'd dropped the pan on him? I tell you, Charlie, it's awful to even imagine an accident like that. But for it to actually happen to you . . .'

Later, Charlie approached Ash as he looked up a file on the VDU. 'Hi,' he said. 'Seen Forbes around lately?'

'Not for an hour or so, why?'

'He's snooping. I had a clash with him earlier. I don't want another one.'

'I know how you feel,' Ash told him.

'I wonder if you do.'

'Hey,' Ash said. 'Cheer up. It's not every day a beautiful woman agrees to marry you.'

'How do you know she's beautiful?' Charlie asked with a smile.

'Because I saw you sneaking off with her at your party, remember? Besides I know you've got good taste,' he laughed back. Ash turned to leave, but then hesitated. 'About Forbes.' He looked back at Charlie. 'You know he's into this endless stock-taking?'

'Yeah.'

'He's complaining we're using too many sterile pads now.'

Charlie rolled his eyes. 'That man!' he sighed. 'It's incredible. He'll be expecting A and E to make a profit next! I don't know where he came from, but I wish he'd stayed there.'

'An acquaintance of mine used to work with him. A couple of years ago,' Ash said.

'And?'

'He was notorious, apparently.'

'What for?'

'Well, you won't be surprised to hear—'

Ash was looking over Charlie's shoulder and seemed to freeze. Charlie turned quickly, and glimpsed Duffy signalling at Ash to shut up. She tried to hide the gesture, but Charlie had seen it. 'So why was he notorious?' he repeated.

'Um,' Ash shifted uncomfortably. 'The same as here, basically. Intimidation of the staff. Tampering with the rules.'

'That's not what you were going to say.'

'Sorry,' Ash apologised, moving away. 'Got to go.'

Charlie turned to Duffy for an explanation. 'What is all this?' he asked, but she seemed to have dashed off somewhere, too. He shook his head and crossed to his office. He wished someone would tell him what the hell was going on.

Ash had said that Forbes was a friend of a friend or an acquaintance of an acquaintance, anyway. Was it possible that Forbes had persuaded them to spy on him? Maybe not in so many words. Perhaps he'd told them to keep a look-out to help prove Charlie's innocence? No, it didn't square up. That was the last thing Forbes would do. And, he decided, he should trust more to Ash and Duffy's professional integrity, instead of suspecting. But what *were* they doing? He simply had no idea.

In Reception a couple of drunks were causing trouble for Norma. Charlie went to see if he could do anything to calm them down.

'I've got to be seen now,' the larger of the two slurred angrily, thumping the desk. 'Right now.' He was wearing an old rugby shirt, stained with sweat under the arms.

'Look,' Charlie told them firmly. 'See that sign up there? It says there's a two-hour wait.'

'Nah, I can't wait that long,' the man said. 'It's my arm.'

'Which arm?' Charlie asked.

'This one,' the man said, waving it in Charlie's face.

'It can't be that bad,' Charlie pointed out. 'If you've just been banging on this desk with it.'

This made the man stop and think in an exaggerated drunken manner. Charlie carefully took the man's other elbow and led him away. 'Sit here with your friend,' he said firmly. 'We'll see to you as soon as we can.'

Norma smiled her thanks.

Charlie went back to his office to continue with his paperwork. He'd cleared most of the urgent stuff now, but he wanted time to think. He was still disturbed by Duffy and Ash. Should he confront them, be honest with them? Maybe he could bring up the subject by talking about Forbes' behaviour. Then they could tell him what was going on.

Yes, he thought, he'd be up-front with them and say he was owed an explanation. That would elicit a reaction even if only a denial. More likely, he hoped, he would find out once and for all what all the secrecy was about.

At the sound of raised voices in Reception, Charlie rushed along there to see what was going on. The same drunk was causing a disturbance, kicking at the drinks machine as hard as he could. An elderly security guard was trying to persuade him to stop, but was clearly afraid of physically intervening with someone so large and aggressive.

'Give me a drink!' the drunk shouted, kicking the machine and cursing.

'All right, all right.' Charlie approached from behind, grabbing his arm and pulling him away.

The man turned and lunged, throwing a punch that went wide. Charlie tried to restrain him by the shoulders, but he wrenched free and hurled himself against the machine harder than ever.

'That's enough,' Charlie warned, pulling his arm up behind his back into a clinch. 'Out! Now!' He steered the man towards the exit. He scuffled, but couldn't escape Charlie's grip.

'Get the other one,' Charlie signalled to the security guard. Luckily the second drunk, who was verbally abusive but not aggressive, came without a fuss. Charlie left the first man outside the entrance.

'But I'm hurt!' he yelled. 'I want a doctor.'

'And I want you to piss off,' Charlie told him. 'Come back and I'll ring the police.'

As he walked back into Reception he pondered the lack of decent security in the hospital. He'd brought the subject up many times with the management, but as usual it was a question of budget. Their priorities were all wrong. He hoped something would be done about it soon, after the fire fiasco.

'Well done, mate,' a waiting patient smiled at him. 'It's bad enough waiting for hours, without the likes of them causing trouble.'

Stuart was right, he thought. Holby City was making an old man of him.

He met Duffy in the corridor. 'How's Maureen Isaac?' he asked.

'Joyce has managed to calm her down a bit. I don't know why she's suddenly got it into her head that she deserves to die,' Duffy frowned. 'It's crazy. Something that happened five years ago.'

'Something must have triggered it,' Charlie said.

'You mean a birthday, or the anniversary of the crash?' 'It happens.'

Duffy nodded. 'By the way,' she said. 'There's a son who's just arrived. He's waiting in the interview room.'

'OK,' said Charlie. 'I'll go through and ask about birthdays.' He crossed to the interview room.

Joyce was coming downstairs. 'I've just been talking to Mike about Mrs Isaac,' she said. 'I'm worried about her. We both agreed on a psychiatric evaluation. There's no way we can send her home in this state of mind.'

Charlie agreed. 'Shall I ring the psychiatrist on call?'

'It's OK, I've done it. He's on his way.'

In the interview room Charlie spoke to the son, explaining what was happening. He took the news grimly. When Charlie asked about a significant birthday or anniversary, he shook his head blankly.

Duffy came in. 'We think we might have found out what triggered the crisis,' she said.

'What?'

'She's been seeing a hypnotherapist.'

43

'People will go to any old therapist and give themselves up, mind and body, for treatment,' Mike sighed sadly when he heard the news. 'They don't realise what a delicate mechanism the brain is.'

'A lot of therapists are good at what they do,' Joyce pointed out. Charlie nodded, thinking of Elizabeth. They were having a little conference in Admin.

'Yes,' Mike agreed. 'I know that. But what makes me mad is that it's all so arbitrary. All you have to do is complete some kind of basic, non-standardised training course, and then you can be let loose on the public.'

'You don't even need to go on a course,' said Charlie.

'And that says it all.' Joyce leaned against the work surface.

'OK. You might be brilliant, but on the other hand, you might not be,' Mike said. 'How are people to know, when they're looking for a hypnotherapist, whether they're going to be good, or downright dangerous? If someone went to a doctor and found out that he'd never been trained, there would be a massive outcry – and rightly so. The law's a mess on this issue as far as I can see.'

'And psychological well-being is such a delicate area,' said Joyce. 'Even when dealing with apparently simple matters such as stopping smoking or losing weight, it's important to know *why* people have eating disorders, or compulsions of any kind. You can't properly treat something without first investigating its cause.'

'Absolutely,' Mike agreed. 'It might be extremely complicated, as in Mrs Isaac's case. And it's people like us who have to pick up the pieces.'

Charlie left them to it as Duffy approached and signalled that she wanted to speak to him. She took his elbow and pulled him over to a quieter corner. 'Isn't your friend Stuart a hypnotherapist?'

Charlie paused before replying. Duffy had voiced his own fear. Of course it might not have been him. There must be a number of hypnotherapists practising in Holby. It could have been any one of them. 'Yes, he is,' he said.

'Does he know other hypnotherapists in Holby? By reputation, I mean? He might have some idea of who's responsible.'

'He's new to the business. I don't think he's had a chance to suss out the opposition.'

There was a question hanging between them. Duffy obviously wanted to ask: 'Do you think it was him?' But she was too sensitive to put Charlie under that kind of pressure.

'I might as well tell you now,' Charlie told her, 'that I was against him setting up as a hypnotherapist all along.'

'What are you saying? That you think it might be him?'

'I hope not,' said Charlie, thinking suddenly of Joy. 'Stuart couldn't be that dumb.'

'But if Mrs Isaac had been unstable to start with, and didn't tell him,' said Duffy, 'what then?'

Charlie shrugged. Duffy was right. What then?

'I'm going to talk to Ronald Isaac again,' Charlie decided. 'See if I can find out more.'

'I'll come with you.'

'I'm sorry to put you through this again,' Charlie told Ronald, once they were seated in the interview room. 'But there may be a key piece of information somewhere that will help us to help your wife.'

'I've told you everything,' Ronald said. He sat on the

chair, twisting his fingers nervously. He was pale and drawn and Charlie didn't want to make this any worse than it was for him.

'Let's go back to the accident five years ago,' he began. 'We know the details, but we'd like to know more about the emotional effect this had on your wife.'

'She took it badly, obviously,' he said with a here-we-go-again sigh. 'Gwen and Maureen had always been close. It was devastating for my wife to lose her sister. She went into a deep depression for months. When you lose a twin, it's like losing a part of yourself. Also, the suddenness was difficult to cope with, and the fact that she saw it as her fault. Like I said, it was over a year before she was anything like back to her old self.

'Gwen's husband had a difficult time of it, too. He emigrated to New Zealand the following year with his two children, Darren and Amanda – our niece and nephew. They were eleven and thirteen then. We'd been a close family. Darren and Amanda were always in and out, playing with our children. When they went, it was another deep loss for Maureen. Another part of her life had been blotted out at a single stroke.'

'Did she receive any treatment for her depression?' Duffy asked.

'Yes, from her GP. For three years. She was put on diazepam, and then on anti-depressants, then on diazepam again. She still takes a sleeping pill now and again, but apart from that . . . Like I said, we all thought she had this depression thing beaten.'

It was clear that talking like this was a strain for Mr Isaac. Charlie noticed that his hands were trembling. He glanced across at Duffy, who had noticed it too. 'I'll get some tea,' she smiled, rising and leaving the room.

As Charlie tried to frame a question, he looked out through the window to Reception. Duffy, he could see, was trying to cope with the drunk from earlier on, who had returned to cause further trouble. Charlie was about to go to her assistance when the man staggered outside of his own accord.

'It never stops for you, does it?' Ronald Isaac followed Charlie's gaze.

'No,' Charlie agreed, with a sigh. 'It doesn't. Listen, this hypnotherapist Maureen's been seeing.' He paused. 'Do you know his or her name?'

Ronald shook his head. 'I wasn't that interested. It was one of those hare-brained ideas of Maureen's. She wanted to lose a bit of weight. That's why she went. She's tried all sorts of diets and things, but they've never worked for long. This leaflet was put through our door, offering a free consultation, and she thought it might help.'

Duffy came in with the tea. Ronald took his gratefully. Charlie tried another approach. 'Ronald, do you mind if I ask, what did you feel about your wife having hypnotherapy?'

'I didn't like her going,' he said, sipping his tea carefully. 'Especially as it was so expensive. But she signed up for a course of sessions. She was adamant it was helping her,' he shrugged helplessly. 'It was OK until she became obsessive about it. Last week she began going every day.'

'Every day!' Duffy glanced at Charlie.

'I said it was too much. But she withdrew some of her savings from the bank to pay for it, and it was up to her what she did with her money. I reckoned it couldn't do any harm.' He laughed bleakly. 'She had a lot of faith in this doctor. She said he understood her problems. I was busy at work, so I didn't take that much notice of what was going on, but she seemed lively and cheerful enough. If she could have stayed like that, then it would have been worth every penny.'

'So she was satisfied with her treatment?'

'More than satisfied. Kept going on about the power of the mind to heal itself. It meant nothing to me.'

There was a pause as Ronald finished his tea and reflected on what had happened. They sat in silence for a while before Charlie spoke. 'As you know, we are doing a psychiatric assessment of your wife. I'm sure you understand. If she's still suicidal—'

'I could keep an eye on her at home,' Ronald interrupted.

'Even when you're at work?' Duffy asked.

'Fair point,' he said disconsolately. He looked out through the glass, into Reception. 'Ah,' he said. 'My daughter's here.'

'Let's leave it there, shall we?' Charlie got to his feet. 'Thanks for your help, Mr Isaac. We'll let you know about the report as soon as we hear.'

Mr Isaac left.

'Strange business.' Duffy rose and collected the cups. 'If Maureen was so convinced the therapy was doing her good, how did she end up like this?'

'We'll have to find out,' said Charlie.

'I'll get off,' she said. 'I promised to have a word with Ash when I was free. You'll tell me if anything comes up about Mrs Isaac?'

'Yeah.'

He went to cubicle three. A young nurse was sitting in with Mrs Isaac waiting for the duty psychiatrist to arrive. Charlie leaned forward. Mrs Isaac was facing away from him, eyes closed. 'Maureen?'

She didn't stir for a moment, then gradually turned her head and looked at Charlie. Her face was completely expressionless.

'Maureen,' he said. 'Sorry. I've got to ask you one important question. For our records.' He paused and tried to look as sincere and sympathetic as possible. 'Can you tell me the name of your hypnotherapist?'

Maureen closed her eyes slowly. She appeared not to have heard Charlie, but as she turned her head away, she whispered: 'Dr Stuart Stonehouse.'

44

Back in his office, Charlie wondered what to do about Stuart. His eyes felt heavy and he rubbed them, knowing it would make them more bloodshot than they probably were already. As he shifted papers from one side of his desk to the other, he remembered Stu's business cards. He crossed to where his jacket was hanging and fished out the two cards that he'd picked up. 'Holby Hypnotherapy Clinic' was emblazoned across the top. Underneath was printed: 'Consultant Hypnotherapist, Dr Stuart Stonehouse'.

'Doctor!' Charlie exclaimed under his breath. It was a serious offence, pretending to be a medical doctor. He wondered why he was so surprised. There had been plenty of hints about Stu using unscrupulous tricks, but he supposed he'd chosen to ignore them, believing that Stu had meant it when he said he'd put the past behind him. Letters addressed to the mythical Matthew Frazer still arrived at the flat with frightening regularity, yet Charlie had chosen to ignore that, too.

All his instincts now told him to phone the police. Stuart had to be stopped. How much damage he'd done already, Charlie could only guess at. He'd been worried about Joy before, but now, with a suicidal woman in cubicle three, he felt a surge of panic at the thought of Joy being under Stuart's influence.

He picked up the telephone and dialled a number. The phone rang a couple of times before it was answered.

'Holby Police Station,' a calm voice said.

Charlie hesitated for a moment, then replaced the receiver. He closed his eyes to help him think. It was important that he did the right thing, and not something on the spur of the moment. He wasn't sure what the police would do about Stuart, but they'd be able to do *something* if he told them about the card he was holding in his hand. They would stop him practising hypnotherapy if it was proved he'd been attracting clients under false pretences.

But the police would probably arrest Stuart, or at least pull him in for questioning. And with a criminal record already, this latest misdemeanour would be taken seriously – he might even end up in prison again.

Charlie scratched his neck and tried to think. What would he be letting Stu in for? Would he want to be responsible for wrecking his whole future? He was still a friend, after all. And he wasn't deliberately malicious. Just misguided. He didn't realise or want to accept how dangerous hypnotherapy could be. Perhaps if Charlie went and confronted him with the results of his so-called therapy, Stu would realise his mistake and change his ways. Either he could give up hypnotherapy altogether – perhaps revert to his original TV shopping idea – or he could go and get himself some decent training so that he wouldn't have to lie about his credentials.

After all, Stu had struggled to set up his business and had worked hard to make a success of it. If he was willing to invest the same level of commitment in learning from his mistakes and turning this disaster into something worthwhile, the whole ugly business of involving the police might be avoidable.

But, Charlie had to recognise, warning him of the dangers of what he was doing hadn't stopped Stuart in the past.

Weighing it all up, Charlie decided that the best bet was to go to see Stuart. He felt he owed him that. But he'd be tough. He'd give him an ultimatum: 'Stop practising as a hypnotherapist, or I'll go to the police.'

Duffy broke into his thoughts. 'Hi,' she said. 'I'm nearly finished. Do you fancy going for a coffee in town, or something? I'm meeting Andrew and Peter in an hour. It might be fun – we both need to unwind for a while.'

She noticed his expression and came in, closing the door behind her. 'What's wrong?'

'It was Stuart,' he said. 'I asked Maureen Isaac. Stuart was the hypnotherapist who was treating her.'

'Oh God, Charlie.' She sat down. 'What are you going to do?'

Charlie shrugged. 'And he's been passing himself off as a doctor.'

'It's your duty to report him, really,' she told him, horrified.

'He's been a friend for a long time,' Charlie said. 'I'm not saying that excuses him. But I can't report him without talking to him first. I was thinking of giving him an ultimatum or something.'

'You mean threatening him? He might take that even worse than being reported in a straightforward way.' She frowned slightly as she thought it over. 'Would you like me to report him instead? Would that help?'

Charlie didn't say anything for a moment. Then he shook his head. 'No,' he said. 'I'd better go and talk to him. Thanks, though, Duffy.'

'I understand your dilemma,' she told him. 'But you can't let him off the hook for friendship's sake. All you have to do is think of that woman back there to realise how wrong that would be.'

'I won't let him off the hook,' Charlie sighed. 'I can't anyway, I've already written on her notes that she's under treatment by S. Stonehouse. It'll come back to him eventually whether I talk to him or not.'

'Poor Charlie. I know how difficult it is when there's a

conflict of interests – especially when you're dealing with a friend.'

Charlie left the hospital on his own. He'd declined Duffy's offer of a coffee – he had too much thinking to do. At first he headed for Stuart's practice, but as he walked he changed his mind. He decided it would be best to go over to Joy's first. He could talk it through with her and then decide how to tackle Stuart. He wanted to do this as gently as possible. He didn't want to hurt Stuart unnecessarily. He didn't want to *punish* Stuart. Just stop him from practising.

When he thought of the situation rationally, he found it incredible that he had such a strong sense of loyalty towards Stuart. He couldn't forget when Stuart had first moved in with him and he'd been so depressed. Stu's cheerfulness and company had helped him pull himself out of it, and had been just as important as his sessions with Elizabeth. He owed Stuart a lot. And after all, it was Stuart who'd forced him to join Compu-Date, without which he would never have met Joy.

Charlie had just walked past the travel agent, and now he stopped, suddenly remembering. He almost continued on, thinking this wasn't the right time to be considering holidays but changed his mind and back-tracked to the agency. Wasn't Joy more important than all this? After all, she'd still be there when this whole thing had blown over, and two minutes' delay wouldn't make any difference.

In the end his visit took twenty minutes rather than two, but when Charlie stepped out on to the street again he felt brilliant. He patted the pocket where he'd just put the folded pink slip – the confirmation of the holiday he'd booked. A week for two on the Greek island of Zakinthos! And why not, he thought. Joy was worth it. And he was already looking forward to it himself.

Of course, he'd only gone in to pick up the brochure,

ut when the agent had kindly offered to check the island's accommodation availability on his computer and ound it filling up fast, Charlie had decided he may as vell book it there and then. All it took was his credit card number and there was no going back. Not that he wanted o – he knew Joy would be thrilled.

Besides, on a day like today, with the tragic Maureen Isaac business he needed cheering up.

By the time he got to Joy's bedsit he was satisfied with his decision to speak to Stu and warn him before approaching the police. So it came as a shock when Joy reacted so strongly against his plan. 'You can't do that,' she objected. 'Report him to the police? How could you, Charlie? He's your friend, for a start, and he's helped me such a lot. I'd hate it if he couldn't finish off the treatment he's started.'

'But Joy,' Charlie frowned. 'He's been impersonating a doctor, that's a very serious matter. And he's directly caused a woman to attempt suicide.'

'The doctor business is probably only to help patients have faith in him,' she said. 'And as for that woman, you don't even know the facts. You've only heard one side of the story, and she sounds pretty obsessed anyway. How do you know it's the truth? She's probably just trying to get attention.'

Charlie stared at Joy in disbelief. He couldn't believe that she could say these things. 'But Joy,' he gasped. 'We're talking about someone's *life* here.'

'An unbalanced life,' she countered. 'Stuart didn't make her unstable. He can't be blamed for what she did.'

Charlie tried to explain the situation more fully, but Joy was adamant that Stuart shouldn't bear any responsibility. The only thing they could agree on was that they ought to go and talk to him.

Joy put on her jacket and they left to walk the half-mile to Stuart's practice. 'Please, Charlie,' Joy pleaded as they

walked. 'Don't destroy Stuart. I can't believe that yo
would do that.'

Charlie found it confusing. Why did Joy defend Stuar
so strongly? It was almost as though she saw him as per
fect.

'Imagine what would happen if you did tell the police,'
she went on. 'He'd lose his livelihood, for a start. Hi
record would go against him.'

Charlie looked at Joy in surprise. 'What record?'

'His criminal record.'

'How did you know about that?'

'He told me all about it,' she replied defiantly. 'W
talked a lot, Stuart and me. He's trying to make a fresl
start, Charlie. You can't ruin it all for him now.'

'But I'm not!' Charlie argued. 'I'm giving him a chance
That's where we're going now. Look. He's acted irre
sponsibly and no amount of goodwill—'

'I know what prison does to a person,' Joy interrupted
sharply.

'How come?'

'My father,' she said. 'He went to prison. They called i
theft, but it wasn't. All he did was borrow money from th
shop he worked in every now and then, on a Thursday
when he couldn't make his wages stretch. He'd alway
put the money back in the till on a Friday, so no one knew
He had five kids to support. I was only six.'

'So how was he caught?' Charlie was bemused that Jo
should choose this moment to tell him.

'They did a check one Friday morning and found his til
was out. They fired him on the spot. He got sent down fo
it.'

'That must have been hard for you.'

'For all of us. When he got out, he'd changed. No on
would give him a job because of his record. That's whe
all the trouble started between him and my mother.'

'I'm sorry,' said Charlie. 'I had no idea.'

'People need to be given a chance when they come out of prison. You *owe* it to Stuart, Charlie. You owe it to him.'

The passion with which she spoke was so overwhelming that it made Charlie feel that he was being pushed, somehow, into the wrong. He reminded himself that Stuart had been warned of the possible consequences. And whatever Joy believed, he *was* being fair to him. How fair had Stu been to Maureen Isaac? 'I can't let this pass, Joy,' he said.

'It's the worst thing a person can do,' she hissed. 'Betraying a friend. I thought I knew you, Charlie. But maybe I don't.'

They were approaching Stuart's building. Joy stopped and looked carefully at Charlie. He saw something in her eyes he'd never seen before. A hardness he hadn't known existed. 'So?' she asked. 'What are you going to say to him?'

'I don't know,' he replied miserably.

45

'Charlie boy! Good to see you.'

The warmth of Stuart's greeting, when Sandy showe[d] them through, made Charlie feel even worse, given wha[t] he was about to say.

'Thinking of trying out the services, were you?' St[uart] laughed as he got up from his imposing desk and came t[o] meet them. Joy watched Charlie's expression carefully[.] She looked bitterly disappointed when he told Stu he'[d] come about a serious matter.

'You might want to sit down,' Charlie began. 'In fac[t] maybe you should. Because I want you to listen to ever[y] word I say and take note of it.'

Stuart was immediately defensive. 'What's this a[ll] about?' He glanced from Charlie to Joy.

'It's about a woman called Maureen. Mrs Maureen[n] Isaac.'

Saying the name brought a lump to Charlie's throat. H[e] could still see the knife slashes on her arms and wrists, th[e] plastic bag full of empty pill bottles. He could smell th[e] stench of the stomach-wash bucket, hear her patheti[c] pleading to be allowed to die.

'If you won't sit down, I think I will.' Charlie drew up [a] plush office chair and sank into it. All the showy furnitur[e] in Stu's office disgusted Charlie now. Stuart and Joy sa[t] down too.

'Maureen Isaac, at this moment, is lying in Acciden[t] and Emergency. Recovering from attempted suicide.'

Stuart listened in silence as Charlie explained what had happened.

'I'll admit she was a patient of mine,' Stuart nodded, subdued, when Charlie had finished. 'But I didn't know anything about her depressive state of mind. She came to me to lose weight. That's all I treated her for.'

'Don't mess me around, Stu,' Charlie told him. 'You must have known about it. You were seeing her on a daily basis, for God's sake.'

'Like I said,' Stu shrugged. 'I didn't know anything about her problem.'

'No? Well I've got a problem, Stu. I trust my friends.' Charlie wasn't interested in weak denials. He felt clear about what he had to do. 'You've lied to me all along and I believed you. Even when I should have known otherwise. I believed you when you said you were going into TV shopping. I believed you when you said you'd never treat a client with a psychological problem. How can I believe you now? You're even calling yourself Doctor Stonehouse!' Charlie's voice rose incredulously. 'Doctor!'

'Don't make such a big thing of it,' Joy told him aggressively.

'You're defending him?' Charlie asked, disbelievingly. 'You're defending someone who is a liar and a cheat?'

Her face had flushed a mottled rose colour and her eyes, usually so calm, now looked at him sharply. 'At least I'm loyal to my friends.'

Charlie turned back to Stuart. 'What kind of treatment were you giving Mrs Isaac?'

'Why?' Stuart's question was full of belligerence.

'I'm not asking for personal reasons. I'm asking as a clinical manager in charge of a case. I want information so that, hopefully, I can help save her life.'

'But you said she wasn't in a critical condition,' Stuart objected.

'She isn't. Not physically. But there are still plenty of

indications that she'll make another attempt at suicide as soon as she gets the chance.'

Stuart didn't seem too concerned. Charlie noticed Joy giving him a reassuring glance and began to wonder at her motives. He wondered, too, what their exact relationship was. They seemed to be almost colluding.

'All right, Charlie,' said Stuart. 'I'll tell you. We did a couple of sessions on losing weight, but it wasn't long before she brought up her sister's death. I encouraged her to talk about it, encouraged her to relive the day of the accident.'

'What!'

'What's wrong with that? I simply told her to go through in her mind what had happened and how she felt. She was relieved. She'd spent so long pushing it all away. Next appointment, she came back asking for more of the same.'

'See?' Joy said triumphantly. 'Mrs Isaac *asked* Stuart to do what he did. It was all her own fault.' Joy was so adamant about this that Charlie wondered at her compassion. How could she write off another human being as worthless?

'What happened next?' Charlie wanted to know.

Stuart swivelled in his gadget-ridden chair as he continued. 'I acknowledged her guilt. She was partly to blame. She'd been the driver of the car after all, and she *had* fallen asleep at the wheel.'

'But she wasn't *guilty*!' Charlie cried. 'Of course she wanted to take responsibility for what happened, that's human nature. But it was an accident. She's been punishing herself for years over this, and you've made it infinitely worse.'

'But people are responsible for their actions,' Stuart argued. 'They have to face up to their guilt.' His tone was self-righteous.

'You've got it all back to front. You're talking about

people who have done something wrong.' Charlie spoke slowly and clearly to him, as if he were talking to a five-year-old. 'If a person beats someone up, or abuses them, or murders them, that's wrong. Fair enough. If they've done something like that and they're ever going to mend their ways they have to accept that what they did was wrong. But what we're talking about in Mrs Isaac's case is an accident, Stuart, not a crime.'

'It's still important to face the past.'

'Accept it, maybe,' said Charlie. 'Not blame yourself for it.'

Joy was casting hostile glares at Charlie. This disturbed him, but he put it to the back of his mind. He would deal with it later. 'Don't you understand what you've done?' Charlie asked Stuart. 'Mrs Isaac believed in you because she thought you were a doctor.'

'I've never said I was a doctor. If people want to make assumptions about me, that's up to them.'

'You're lying again,' Charlie groaned. 'What about your business cards?'

'A misprint,' Stuart explained. 'There's only one letter different between Mr and Dr.'

'That's pathetic,' Charlie choked. 'You expect me to believe that?'

'Come on, Charlie. I don't see why you're taking the moral high ground here. The woman was screwed up. That's not my fault.'

'If you admit that this is a case of malpractice, Stuart, then we can decide what to do about it,' Charlie told him, trying to be conciliatory.

'Of course it isn't malpractice,' said Joy.

'Joy's right,' Stuart agreed.

'Listen. If anyone knows about mistakes, it's me. I'm giving you a chance here.'

'That's good of you,' Stuart replied sarcastically. 'But I've done nothing wrong.'

Charlie sighed. 'Then I'm going to have to report you, if that's your attitude.'

Joy was aghast. 'Do you betray all your friends?'

'This has nothing to do with betrayal,' said Charlie angrily. 'Anyway, what about the betrayal of the trust of clients who come here? And what is it between you two? Why are you on his side, and not mine?'

Another look passed between Joy and Stu.

'There isn't more to this relationship than friendship is there?' Charlie asked suspiciously.

'Charlie! How could you ask that!' Joy exclaimed furiously.

'Sorry,' he said. 'Anyway. I came here to warn you, Stuart. I'm not saying you ever meant any deliberate harm, but you're doing harm all the same. Take my advice. Close this place down before the police start investigating it.'

Stuart laughed humourlessly. 'Have you got it in for me, Charlie?'

'Nothing could be further from the truth,' Charlie told him sadly. 'But I have to do what's right.'

'Who says it's right?' Joy grumbled. She sounded like a spoilt child up past its bedtime.

'Look,' he told them. 'This conversation has got about as far as it can go. I'd better leave. I *am* going to report you, Stuart.'

Stuart smiled confidently. 'You wouldn't really do that. Not to a friend, Charlie,' he said.

'Of course you wouldn't,' said Joy.

Charlie made his way back to the hospital, trying to decide what to do for the best. Perhaps they were right. Maybe he couldn't do this to a friend. At the forefront of his mind was the need to find out how Mrs Isaac was getting on. He needed to know before making a final decision about Stuart.

262

When he arrived, he found that the duty psychiatrist had done the emergency assessment, and the verdict was that Maureen was too unstable to go home yet. The psychiatrist had recommended that she spend an initial seven-day observation period in a psychiatric ward or a psychiatric institution – but places were hard to come by, and he was still searching for a bed.

As Charlie passed through Reception, he noticed Ronald Isaac with his son and daughter. All three looked washed out. Ronald looked up as Charlie approached.

'Hello again. Have you been told what's going on?' Charlie asked.

Ronald nodded. 'But everything takes so long, doesn't it? They're searching for a bed for Maureen. And they have no idea how long it's going to take.'

'Have you talked to her?'

'Yes.' He sounded subdued. 'I don't think she understands what's going on. Not really.' Mr Isaac shook his head. 'If only she'd never gone to see that hypnotherapist.'

Charlie walked towards his office with a heavy heart. Jill, one of the consultants' secretaries, passed him. 'Charlie!' she exclaimed, surprised.

'Mmm?'

'I didn't think you were in the building.'

'I'm strictly off duty,' he told her, holding his hands up defensively.

'It's just that there's a senior meeting upstairs – about you.'

'What? When?'

'Right now, I'm on my way there.'

'What's it about?'

'The Forbes case.'

Charlie's heart sank even further.

'You probably have a right to be there,' she said. 'Let me just check. Are you going to your office? I'll call you in a couple of minutes.'

Charlie closed the Venetian blinds in his office. The darkness calmed him. So Forbes had finally succeeded. He was about to be sacked. Would the trustees listen to him? The phone rang on his desk.

It was Jill. 'Hi, Charlie. Would you like to come up? It's the boardroom, first floor,' she said.

Charlie felt indescribably sad as he stood up. But he knew he wasn't ready to give up. He would put up a fight, argue his corner – on principle, if nothing else.

He looked at his desk. His entire working life at Holby had been dedicated to helping people in crisis. No matter what people accused him of, he knew his professional integrity was intact. Or was it? He thought of Stu. And Joy, and how much she meant to him. He sighed. His responsibility was clear, no matter what the repercussions.

He picked up the phone and dialled the number of the police station.

46

Charlie waited impatiently, the telephone jammed between ear and shoulder. What was taking them so long at the police station? He'd been passed from department to department. First he'd got the switchboard, then the sergeant at the information desk, and now he was waiting to be put through to someone else.

He shifted the receiver from one ear to the other, thinking that he could be filling in a report as he waited, if only he could concentrate. He was only too aware of time ticking past, of the people in the board room upstairs waiting for him. Would they start without him? he wondered. And in the end, did it really matter? They were probably going to inform him that his contract was being terminated anyway.

'Oh, hurry up,' he said to the telephone. All he wanted to do was get this over with. He felt bad enough about it as it was – Joy and Stuart had seen to that. But once he'd reported it, his legal duty would be done. He'd fill in the date and time on Maureen Isaac's report form, and as far as he was concerned that would be it. What the authorities decided to do – if anything – was up to them.

He was about to replace the receiver when a voice came on the line.

'Mr Fairhead?'

'Hello. At last.'

'I'm sorry you were kept waiting, sir. I was on the other line—'

'Couldn't someone else have dealt with it?' Charlie snapped. Did these people think he had nothing else to do? It was only a case of writing down a few details, surely.

'Not really, sir. You see, I'm dealing with this case. Detective Constable White.'

'Case? What case?' Charlie grimaced, hoping they hadn't got him mixed up with another caller.

'The case of Mr Stonehouse,' came the reply. 'Now, I believe you are calling on behalf of Holby City Hospital. If you'd like to give me particulars—'

'Hang on. I'm still not clear. Are you saying that there's already . . . that Stuart is being investigated already? Has someone else complained?'

'I'm sorry, sir. We can't give those details. But we are interested in Mr Stonehouse's activities, and you have some information for us, I believe?'

Charlie passed over the details about Mrs Isaac haltingly, all the time wondering why the police were already involved. 'Look,' he said, when he was finished. 'Can you tell me if this investigation of yours is connected in any way to what I've just told you?'

'It could be. In a roundabout way,' DC White said vaguely.

'Has one of his hypnotherapy clients complained? Is that it?'

White cleared his throat. 'Why are you so interested, Mr Fairhead, if you don't mind me asking?'

Charlie was about to confess that Stuart lived with him when DC White spoke again. 'Are you Mr Charles Fairhead who resides at . . .'

Charlie froze as the detective read out his home address. He could hear pages being turned in the background. When he agreed that he was, White's manner softened slightly. He said he'd been meaning to get in touch with Charlie anyway. There was nothing to worry about, but could he ask a few questions?

'Sure.'

'Tell me, Mr Fairhead. Do you also know a Mr Matthew Frazer?'

Charlie frowned. The name seemed familiar, but he couldn't place it. 'No I don't think so,' he said.

White mentioned another name, but it meant nothing to him.

'Sorry. What's all this about?'

Before the answer came, Charlie remembered that Matthew Frazer was the alias that Stuart used sometimes – the name on the front of the letters from financial institutions that had occasionally been delivered to the flat. He told White, who seemed to know already.

'Is it some kind of fraud? Is that it?' Charlie asked. 'To do with bank loans?'

'We'd appreciate it if you didn't mention this to Mr Stonehouse,' DC White said.

A few minutes later, Charlie entered the boardroom. The composition of the meeting was uncannily similar to that of the last board meeting he'd attended. The only difference was that Gavin Forbes was absent.

'Sit down Mr Fairhead,' said Mr Dalgleish. 'I'm glad you were in the building because, as you know, this meeting is directly relevant to you. We would, of course, have invited you had we known. Also this meeting was convened at extremely short notice—'

'It's all right,' Charlie said lightly. There was a stack of papers in front of Dalgleish. Fake evidence, Charlie assumed. Jill, in the far corner recording the proceedings, smiled supportively.

'You, more than anyone, have the right to know the action we have taken,' Dalgleish continued. 'The other staff will be informed tomorrow.'

He paused to look round the table. 'As you know, Mr

Fairhead, none of us liked Forbes' accusations, but they had to be taken seriously. We were obliged to conduct a proper investigation, in order to resolve this problem and put an end to the disappearance of the stock.'

'I understand,' said Charlie. 'But I also think I should be given an opportunity to speak. I don't expect you to believe me, but Forbes had it in for me right from the beginning. I'd like to express my disappointment – my formal disappointment – with the board's handling of this affair.' He looked around the table, determined to get this off his chest.

'In particular, I'm disappointed, and yes, upset, at the way I've been treated. This is maybe too personal a level for you lot to understand, but how you could believe Forbes over me, I will never know. Innocent until proved guilty? I was labelled a thief without a scrap of evidence being produced.'

'Charlie—'

'No, wait a minute,' Charlie continued, cross that they didn't even want to let him have his say. 'You have first-rate nursing staff here at Holby who have given you years of service. What are you going to do, kick them all out one by one as Gavin Forbes takes a dislike to them? It's time you got your priorities right. Down in the ward we're overworked, underpaid, and what's worse our efforts are hardly ever acknowledged. Morale is low, and this kind of threat doesn't help. Why don't you spend some time in the real world, instead of listening to a man like Forbes who came from nowhere?'

'Not nowhere,' Dalgleish told him. 'Have you heard of a company called Holby First Sales and Marketing?'

'I'm not interested,' Charlie retorted.

'Please, listen,' Dalgleish insisted. 'What I'm telling you is relevant.' He paused to glance at his papers. 'It was brought to our attention by one of your colleagues, Martin Ashford, that Mr Forbes left his last job under a cloud.'

Charlie sat up. What were they planning now?

'Quite. We thought you might be interested,' said Dalgleish. 'Now, Ashford is friendly with an individual who works at Holby First Sales, who passed on what he'd heard. None of this appeared on Forbes' testimonials, of course, or we would never have employed him. We made some tentative inquiries, but discovered that all official channels were mysteriously closed to us. So Ashford and his friend did some unofficial investigating on our behalf.'

Charlie remembered Ash mentioning something about having a friend who'd worked with Forbes. But he'd been cagey about saying anything more.

'Anyway,' Dalgleish continued. 'A number of Holby First employees were approached before Ashford found one or two who were willing to talk. To cut a long story short, Mr Fairhead, it transpires that Forbes was found to be corrupt, guilty of taking bribes from certain companies in exchange for promoting their services above others. The Holby First management of course wanted to avoid a scandal – the PR world is notoriously jumpy – so they hushed it up and got rid of Forbes, who promised to keep quiet if they did.'

'I always knew that man was a crook.' Charlie pulled a wry face. 'So where do I fit in?'

'Ashford discovered that Forbes also conducted a campaign against someone at Holby First, a colleague who was blocking his way to even greater levels of bribery. His method was to try to frame that person by accusing *them* of what *he* was doing. Does it sound familiar, Mr Fairhead?'

It certainly did, Charlie thought. So that was Forbes' game. 'Let me get this clear,' he said. 'You are saying Forbes did the same to me?'

'Precisely,' Dalgleish confirmed. 'What's more, over at Holby First, it very nearly worked. If the company auditors hadn't spotted a modest discrepancy and followed it up by contacting some of their clients, it might never have come to light.'

Charlie couldn't resist saying it: 'It worked quite well here, too.'

The trustees around the table looked uncomfortable to a man. There was much throat-clearing, adjusting of collars, shifting in seats.

'But we did find out in time,' muttered one of the men Charlie didn't know.

'And we had suspicions from the beginning,' Royston chimed in.

'Is that so?' Charlie said cynically. 'Pity you didn't think to share them with me.'

Dalgleish spoke again. 'When Ashford came to us, we made the decision not to inform you until we had concrete evidence. You were technically still under surveillance at the time. We also thought that if you knew of our activities, you might unwittingly tip Forbes off as to what was going on.'

'Was Duffy in on this too?' Charlie asked. 'And Mike?'

'We had to enlist the help of some staff from your department,' Dalgleish nodded. 'They were all eager to help prove your innocence, though it has to be said that they weren't keen on going behind your back. In the end we convinced them that it was necessary.'

Suddenly it all made sense to Charlie. The whispers, the phone calls, the sudden silences when he came into the room. 'And there was I thinking I was paranoid,' he laughed.

'We wish to apologise to you, unreservedly,' Dalgleish said sincerely. 'We all very much regret that you were placed under suspicion, if only for a short period.'

'So what's going to happen to Forbes?' Charlie asked, aware as he spoke that a weight of worry was evaporating from him, leaving him almost exhausted.

'That cleared itself up before we could take a decision,' said Dalgleish.

'Forbes was caught red-handed last night,' Royston told him. 'Or a helper of his was, taking equipment out of A and E. He was arrested, and soon led the police to Forbes. Apparently,' Royston continued enthusiastically, 'Forbes had been storing the stolen goods in a lock-up garage. The police found falsified stock records among the sixty thousand pounds' worth of materials and equipment in his possession.'

Charlie whistled. He'd had no idea the corruption had been on such a grand scale.

Dalgleish took over. 'So you see, Mr Fairhead, that's why this emergency meeting was called.'

'So Forbes has been arrested?' Charlie asked.

'Indeed he has. What's more, the police are confident of the case against him. His accomplice will testify, so there will almost certainly be a successful prosecution.'

Charlie laughed with relief. 'And I thought you were going to sack *me*!'

'You will receive a written apology in due course,' Dalgleish assured him. 'We are all very sorry for the inconvenience you have been caused.'

There was a murmur of agreement around the table. Jill, who was taking the minutes, grinned at Charlie.

Just wait till I see Duffy and Ash! he thought.

47

Duffy was surprised to see Charlie. He had never called round after work before without either asking or being invited.

'Come in,' she said. 'It's good to see you. Andrew's just got back from work. Come through and have a drink.'

He followed her into the kitchen.

'Beer?' she asked.

He looked at his watch. It was only 5.30 p.m.

'Andrew and I were just going to have a gin.'

'Beer would be great,' he said. 'But make it a small one.'

'So, what brings you round here?' she asked as she prepared the drinks.

'I've just found out that you've been doing a whole lot of snooping behind my back,' he said with a smile. 'You sound like you've been playing amateur detectives.'

Duffy laughed. 'Who told you?'

'Dalgleish. They've sacked Forbes.'

'No!'

'And restored my reputation.'

'Oh, Charlie!' she exclaimed. 'I'm so pleased.' She turned and gave him a hug.

'It was difficult, not being able to tell you what was going on,' she said. 'Especially when you were getting so upset about it all. I wanted to, many times.' She turned back to the drinks. 'We hated hiding it from you. Though sometimes it was great fun.'

'Not for me.'

'Sorry,' Duffy smiled over her shoulder. 'But other times . . . Ash nearly let it out that day in Reception, when he was telling you about his friend. I managed to stop him in time.'

'I wondered what all that was about,' Charlie remembered.

'Still. It's all OK now. What excuse did they come up with to get rid of Forbes – his falsified references?'

'They didn't need an excuse. He was caught with a garage full of stolen gear.'

Duffy's eyes widened. 'Was he indeed? Excellent! Did you hear that, Andrew?' she called as she carried their drinks through. 'They got Forbes.'

Andrew was sitting on the sofa with Peter on his knee, playing trains. 'Choo! Choo!' he said. 'I thought they'd catch him eventually. I suspected he was up to no good all along. Choo! Choo! Hello Charlie.'

'Thanks for telling me.' Charlie smiled and sank into an easy chair. 'What I don't get is, the stuff was supposed to be going walkabout before Forbes ever arrived.'

'Probably just another of Forbes' lies.' Andrew accepted his drink from Duffy. 'Thanks, darling.' He took a sip. 'I'll bet when they check the figures, they'll find they've been doctored.'

'Well, it is a hospital,' Duffy reminded them cheerfully.

Charlie and Andrew grimaced and gave her a sad look.

'Mummy made a joke,' Andrew told Peter. 'I think.'

They laughed.

'Cheers then, Charlie.' Duffy held up her drink in a toast.

Andrew followed suit. 'Yes, cheers. I bet you're relieved it's all over.'

'You could say that. I was beginning to think I'd gone barmy – seriously paranoid.'

'Choo! Choo!' said Andrew.

'I still think it's crazy we couldn't let you in on it,' Duffy reflected. 'But you must have known I'd never do anything to harm you, Charlie. It's the same with Ash.'

'The whole department was behind you from what I hear.' Andrew leaned awkwardly round Peter to take a sip from his glass. 'Mike was upset too. He wrote a letter of complaint, didn't he, Lisa?'

Duffy nodded.

Charlie was deeply touched that his colleagues should be so supportive, and a little ashamed that he'd ever doubted them. Especially Duffy. After all these years, he should have known that she'd never let him down. 'Cheers,' he said, taking a gulp of his drink to hide his emotion.

'What's going to happen to Forbes' post now?' Andrew wondered.

'The department ran a lot more smoothly before he arrived,' Duffy said. 'Even with Simon Eastman in charge.'

'I don't think Julian would have agreed with you on that one,' Charlie smiled.

'No, I suppose not.' Duffy pulled a face.

It was general knowledge that Accident and Emergency's last consultant had quit his post because of differences with Eastman.

'Julian Chapman,' Andrew sighed. 'Now there was a man of integrity. But, if it hadn't been for him, Lisa and I might never have got together again.'

'True,' Charlie nodded, as Duffy and Andrew gazed lovingly at each other. 'Julian was one of the best.'

'Let's hope the department can go back to how it used to be,' Duffy said.

'I'll drink to that,' Charlie drained his beer.

'Another?' she asked.

'Thanks. Fruit juice if you've got some.'

'Shall I get them?' Andrew half-rose.

'No, it's OK,' Duffy smiled.

As she went through to the kitchen, Charlie noticed Andrew watching her with obvious love and adoration. He was glad that she had found happiness at last.

'I understand congratulations are in order?' Andrew said. 'You're a dark horse, Charlie.'

Charlie smiled sheepishly.

'How is Joy?' Duffy asked, returning with fresh drinks.

'Well,' he shifted in his seat, feeling suddenly that he'd been brought back down to earth. 'She was upset, to say the least, at the prospect of me reporting Stuart.'

'So you reported him?'

'Yes.'

'You did the right thing. You had to.' Duffy handed him a large orange juice.

'Hmm. Joy doesn't know yet.' He felt his spirits waver as he thought about the confrontation that lay ahead.

'Surely she'll understand? You only did your duty.'

'It's more complicated than that,' he sighed. 'I didn't tell you this, Duffy, but she's been going to him. For therapy.'

'Hypnotherapy?'

'I'm afraid so. Even before we started going out together. Joy thinks Stu's great,' he explained. 'She won't hear a word against him. She thinks I should have turned a blind eye to his mistake with Mrs Isaac.'

'But the man's a menace,' Andrew said indignantly. 'Pretending to be a qualified doctor? I couldn't believe it when Lisa told me. Does he have to kill someone before she understands the dangers of something like that?'

'Andrew's right,' Duffy nodded. 'If Joy can't see that, then there's something wrong with her.'

As Charlie walked to Joy's bedsit half an hour later, he tried to decide on the best approach – how to break the news. By the time he arrived, he'd decided that it was better to tell her straight, but choose his words with care, so as not to upset her any more than necessary.

He needn't have bothered, because as soon as Joy opened the door it was clear that she already knew. And her expression left him in no doubt as to how she felt about it.

'You did it!' she cried furiously as she ushered him in. 'You told the police! How could you? I didn't believe you would actually do it.'

'Who told you?'

'No one.'

'Then how . . . ?'

'The police came round here asking for him!'

'Eh?' Charlie was bewildered. 'Why would they come here? How would they have your address?'

Joy blew out an angry sigh. Her eyes narrowed. 'Because Stuart sometimes used this as a sort of business address.'

Charlie wondered what else he didn't know about. 'Did they say what they wanted him for?'

'Of course not. But there isn't much doubt, is there?'

'Isn't there? When I rang the police, you may be interested to know, they already knew about him.'

'I don't believe you!'

'Please yourself.'

He wondered if Joy knew anything about Stuart's financial activities. 'What did you tell them?' he asked.

'I told them he was the best hypnotherapist Holby was ever likely to see, and asked them to leave.' She paused to look at Charlie in dismay. 'How could you do it, Charlie? I trusted you, but now I realise I can't. How can we have a relationship if I can't trust you?'

'I don't understand why you're always defending Stuart,' Charlie sighed.

'And I don't understand why you betrayed him!'

Charlie didn't want to go through the whole Maureen Isaac thing again with Joy. Maybe in a few days, when she was less emotional, she would be able to see the plain facts. She would probably realise that Stuart was less than the perfect being she imagined.

'It looks like Stuart's falsifying details to obtain loans,' he told her. 'Do you know anything about that?'

'Loans?' She looked blank for a moment before her anger returned. 'What he does is his business, isn't it?'

'Up to a point,' Charlie said. He was relieved that Joy didn't appear to have any knowledge of Stuart's dodgy dealings. 'Not when he uses our addresses, though.'

'What difference does that make?' she snapped. 'Letting a friend use my address isn't a major problem in my book.'

Charlie hated Joy's open hostility, and he wanted to calm the situation down. If only he could free her from this weird emotional attachment to Stuart – make her see sense – then they could get on with being together and loving each other.

'I love you, Joy,' he said sincerely. 'I don't know why you're so irrational about Stuart. Maybe it's something to do with the therapy you've been having . . .' He shrugged. 'Once you haven't seen him for a while, you'll get a perspective on what he's been up to.'

'The therapy has been important to me,' Joy muttered. 'You can't understand how important.'

Charlie took a breath. She had suddenly changed from being fiery and angry to being despondent.

'Try me,' he encouraged her. 'Explain it. I'll try to understand.'

'No. You'd think it was stupid.'

'I won't,' he assured her. 'I promise. I hear lots of stories in my work – some of them sound odd at first, but often they're not when you look at them. Tell me about it.'

'OK,' she said slowly, brushing her hair back from her face. 'It goes right back to that day at Westbourne Cove – to the pub where the four of us met.'

'I remember.'

'Stuart made me go faint with shock,' she said. 'When he walked up to us, he looked so like my father. I couldn't believe it. Not like my father is now, but as he was. As he was before he went to prison, when he was happy and jovial and proud of us all. Being with Stuart was like reliving happy childhood memories. And then when he told me about his past, about how he'd been to prison too, I knew we were linked in some way.

'Then he asked me if I wanted to be hypnotised. I jumped at the chance. We went through all sorts of stuff from my past, and because of Stuart's therapy, I began to forgive my father.'

'It was because of Stuart himself, more likely,' said Charlie. 'The physical resemblance, his personality – not through hypnotherapy.'

'I knew you'd say something like that. That you'd make it out to be nothing.'

'I didn't mean it like that,' Charlie assured her. 'I'm glad that you've managed to feel better about your father . . .'

'I really love Stuart for what he's done,' she murmured. 'Not in a sexual way, but in the way I would have loved my father if I'd had a chance – if he'd let me.'

Charlie remembered Stuart laughing about Joy, saying that he thought she was messed up.

'Joy,' he said. 'You were reliant on Stuart because he made you feel better about your father. It was just coincidence,' he shrugged. 'How he looked. Believe me, the best thing you can do is keep away from him. Don't you see? He doesn't have to ruin things between us.'

She looked miserably at the floor, as though she wanted to believe him, but couldn't.

'Look,' he tried. 'I didn't tell you because I wanted it to be a surprise, but I've booked a holiday for us. On Zakinthos!'

48

Joy turned and looked at Charlie. She weighed up her words carefully before she spoke. 'Things have changed,' she said. 'I'm sorry, but I don't feel the same way about you, and there's no going back.'

'What are you talking about?' Charlie felt a thud of panic in his chest. 'Joy?' he said incredulously. 'We can work this out.'

'It's too late.'

'What? But why? Because of this whole thing about Stuart?'

'Not just that,' she shook her head. 'Whatever happens to him, it doesn't change the fact that I've lost faith in you.'

'You don't mean that.'

Charlie ran his fingers through his hair. He paced the floor. 'Joy, let's talk about this. Can we at least have a cup of coffee or something?'

'It won't make any difference.'

He felt so helpless. Surely he couldn't be hearing this. He wanted to yell at her, tell her not to be ridiculous. As he paced, he noticed a job application form by her bedside. It was the one they'd agreed to send away for, for the position in Japan. He bent over it and saw, with a start, that Joy had filled it in. In both their names. Was that all that was left of their future together?

She saw him looking at it and half-smiled. 'That's another thing, Charlie. You weren't really interested in working overseas, were you?'

'I was.'

'We don't have very much in common after all,' she said sadly. 'Maybe you should leave now.'

'No! I'm not going to walk away from this,' he said, determined not to let this relationship go the way of the others. 'I love you, Joy. You're upset now, but this is just a . . . a hitch. We'll be all right.'

She sat staring down at the carpet. 'I thought – hoped – it might work out,' she said. 'But now I see I was only fooling myself. I was trying to break the circle.'

'What?'

'You're not my usual type, Charlie. I've told you that before.'

'So?'

'All the other men in my life have been . . . stronger.'

Charlie wasn't sure what she was trying to say. 'How do you mean, stronger?'

'My father, my fiancé, most of my old boyfriends, they've been a different type from you, Charlie.'

'You don't mean violent, do you?' he said with horror. Surely she didn't mean that.

'I don't know,' she said. 'But I don't feel right with you. You see, Stuart said I was in a circle – going from bad men to bad men – well, not bad exactly. Destructive relationships, that's what my social worker used to call it.'

Charlie frowned. What social worker?

'So with you I tried to break the circle,' she continued. 'But, although I like you, I don't really like the sort of things you do. Not really. And now, after what you've done to Stuart, I just can't trust you any more. If you can betray him, then you'll betray me, too, one day.'

Charlie massaged his temple and tried to concentrate. What was she talking about? 'Joy,' he said.

She looked up for a moment, and he noticed that her cheeks were wet.

'Oh, Joy.' He went and knelt beside her. 'Listen. I'm

going to put the kettle on and we're going to sit down and talk, and try to work this out.'

Elizabeth smiled at Charlie.

'Well,' she said, her voice tinged with a little sadness. 'This is your last session. I'd be interested to know how you feel about that?'

Charlie considered. 'I feel more confident than I have for a long time,' he said. 'But I've got used to coming here, too. Maybe even a bit dependent. It's made me understand people who get hooked on therapy.'

She laughed. 'And that's more common than you might imagine.'

'I can see why. It's so reassuring to know that there will always be someone willing to talk. To examine feelings, go over happy experiences, sad experiences; and just be there. It's comforting.'

'You can come back at any point in the future if you need to.'

'Thanks.'

He leaned back in his chair and sighed. The future. He'd been through such a lot, his crisis had passed, and now he felt almost weightless. But not unhappy. 'It's been a strange time in many ways,' he said. 'All these ups and downs. But I feel it's coming to an end now.'

'It's good to go through phases,' she told him. 'It's a natural process, it means you're developing. Changing.'

'I certainly feel changed.'

'You know what I like most about you, Charlie?' she said. 'Your trust in human nature. You always believe the best of everyone until you're proved wrong. That attitude is both admirable and rare. It leads to disappointment sometimes, but it also allows you to see life at its best.'

'And I'm beginning to see myself in a more positive way now,' he said enthusiastically. 'Which is strange considering the upheaval I've been through.'

'That's because you've got yourself – and your priorities – sorted out.'

Charlie smiled. He knew Elizabeth wouldn't say something like that unless she meant it. It felt good to be praised by someone he respected so much.

'I'm sorry it didn't work out with Joy,' she said.

'So am I,' he said. He tried to be philosophical about what had happened. He had genuinely loved her, but he knew now that they hadn't been right for each other. She needed a strong man, someone who would protect her from reality and tell her what to do. Maybe a charmer, like Stu.

'You know,' he told Elizabeth, 'I never was her type. Deep down she knew that. I think she probably only responded to me because I was the first man in her life who'd been kind to her and treated her with respect.'

'Perhaps.'

Charlie was almost sure that was the case. Respect was something Joy wasn't used to. Her needs were so complicated and so different from what he'd expected to provide for her. It saddened him, but he had to accept it.

'At least we parted friends,' he said. 'She's going to travel, you know. She was applying for all the overseas posts she could find last time I saw her.'

'And you've decided to stay on at Holby City?'

'Yes,' Charlie smiled. 'For a while I persuaded myself that I could do without the place, but actually I think I need it as much as it needs me.'

'You've done well, Charlie. You've come a long way in a short time,' Elizabeth told him. 'Your self-esteem was so low when you first came to see me, remember? And now you're able to make resolutions with confidence again. You're able to stand up for yourself and believe in your decisions.'

'Thanks to you,' he said. 'Without your help and encouragement—'

'No,' she said. 'You did it. I only pointed you in the right direction. You took all the decisions.'

'The most difficult decision of all was whether to report Stuart,' he said. 'It was tough, I admit, but it was also a kind of breakthrough for me. I knew it was the right thing to do, no matter what the consequences. At the back of my mind I was afraid Stu and Joy might never forgive me, but there was no other choice I could make. Once I'd decided, I felt that somehow I'd succeeded.'

'When you regained your confidence, you regained your faith in yourself,' Elizabeth said. 'That's the most important thing. You have always acted with integrity – that's something you never lost, all the way through your problems. You are a popular and well-respected man, Charlie. The way your colleagues backed you up is proof enough of that, if you didn't know already.'

'Yes. That was a good feeling,' Charlie nodded. 'But I still feel bad about Stuart. Despite the fact I know what I did was right. I wonder why?'

'Maybe because you lost faith in someone you trusted.'

'Maybe,' Charlie admitted.

'What's happened to Stuart, incidentally? Do you know?'

'All I know is that Joy sent the police to the wrong address and tipped him off that they were looking for him. Apparently, he left his office, taking everything that he could squeeze into a brand new top-of-the-range BMW that he'd just bought on hire purchase – typical of Stu – and drove away. No one knows where.'

'Do you have any idea?'

Charlie shook his head. 'But I wouldn't be surprised to get a postcard one of these days from the Riviera, or South America, to say he's about to make a million on some dodgy deal or other.' He laughed. 'One thing's for sure, I'll turn down my invitation to join him – even if it's on some exotic tropical island.'

Charlie smiled at the thought of Stu basking in the sun, surrounded by attractive women. 'Talking of exotic locations,' he continued, 'I'd better get home. I've still got my packing to do. Did I tell you? I'm going on holiday.'

'To the Greek island you mentioned?'

'Zakinthos? No.' Charlie felt a pang of regret, but to go to Greece without Joy would have been too painful to bear. 'No . . .' he continued, 'I managed to change the booking. I'm going to Turkey. A quiet little village just outside Istanbul.'

'Sounds wonderful.'

'It does, doesn't it?' Two lovely peaceful weeks all on my own.'

Peaceful too, he thought, because he was at peace with himself again. 'Yes,' Charlie said. 'I think I deserve a rest. A bit of sunshine and gentle sightseeing before I get back to the excitement of Holby City.'